"We need to talk," Jess said.

Sarah fell back a step, clutching her wrapper tighter against her throat. "It's late, Jess, and—"

"It's late all right, Sarah. Too late for me to come to call, too late for me to pretend any more."

She inched toward the doorway. "I—I don't understand."

"Yes you do." He followed her across the room and caught her arm. "You've been running since the day I laid eyes on you. I thought you were running from me, Sarah, but you're not. And it's not that you're worried about getting fired. It's something else."

She turned her head away. "No, you're wrong."

"Sarah, I never felt about a woman the way I feel about you. Can't you give me a chance? Can't you trust me?"

Forcing down her feelings, Sarah pulled away from him. He followed, not letting her go far, but without his touch soft and warm against her, she could think better.

"It's not a matter of trust, Jess...."

Dear Reader,

If you've never read a Harlequin Historical novel, you're in for a treat. We offer compelling, richly developed stories that let you escape to the past—written by some of the best writers in the field!

The Heart of a Hero is a darling new Western by Judith Stacy. Judith Stacy is the pseudonym for Dorothy Howell, who has written numerous historicals for Berkley and Zebra. Here, a bad boy turned rancher returns to his small Wyoming hometown and has thirty days to prove that he'll be a good father to his niece and nephew. The new schoolmarm, who believes in Jess Logan, teaches him how to win over the town's biddies, and falls in love in the process!

Rising talent Lyn Stone returns with *The Knight's Bride,* a heartwarming and humorous medieval tale of a very *true* knight who puts his honorable reputation on the line when he marries the beautiful widow of his best friend. And in *Burke's Rules* by Pat Tracy, book two of THE GUARDSMEN series, a Denver schoolmistress falls for the "protective" banker who helps fund her school. Don't miss this fun, sensuous story!

Rounding out the month is *Pride of Lions* by award-winning author Suzanne Barclay. In this continuation of her highly acclaimed SUTHERLAND SERIES, a knight and a warrioress from enemy clans join forces when they are stranded in the territory of an evil laird. It's great!

Whatever your tastes in reading, you'll be sure to find a romantic journey back to the past between the covers of a Harlequin Historical® novel.

Sincerely,
Tracy Farrell, Senior Editor

Please address questions and book requests to:
Harlequin Reader Service
U.S.: 3010 Walden Ave., P.O. Box 1325, Buffalo, NY 14269
Canadian: P.O. Box 609, Fort Erie, Ont. L2A 5X3

The Heart of a Hero

Judith Stacy

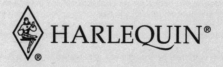

HARLEQUIN®

TORONTO • NEW YORK • LONDON
AMSTERDAM • PARIS • SYDNEY • HAMBURG
STOCKHOLM • ATHENS • TOKYO • MILAN • MADRID
PRAGUE • WARSAW • BUDAPEST • AUCKLAND

ISBN 0-373-29044-6

THE HEART OF A HERO

Copyright © 1999 by Dorothy Howell

Books by Judith Stacy

Harlequin Historicals

Outlaw Love #360
The Marriage Mishap #382
The Heart of a Hero #444

JUDITH STACY

began writing as a personal challenge and found it a perfect outlet for all those thoughts and ideas bouncing around in her head. She chose romance because of the emotional involvement with the characters, and historicals for her love of bygone days.

Judith has been married to her high school sweetheart for over two decades and has two daughters. When not writing, she haunts museums, historical homes and antique stores, gathering ideas for new adventures set in the past.

To Judy and Stacy, who are my greatest weaknesses.
And to David, who is my strength.

The author wishes to thank Nick B. Andonov, Ph.D.,
for his assistance with this story.

Chapter One

Wyoming, 1886

"I'm here to take the kids away."

Jess Logan eyed the woman blocking the doorway. Warmth radiated from the neat, well-kept parlor behind her, but her face looked as cold as the wind biting at his ears. He'd expected as much.

Alma Garrette's brows rose to a haughty arch. "I can't believe you have the nerve to show your face here in Walker after all these years."

"I'm here for my sister's kids, Mrs. Garrette. Sheriff told me you had them."

"Humph! Your sister has been by herself for nearly three years now since her husband ran off. And where have you been? You couldn't have gotten here a month ago when she was ailing and needed the help? Or three days ago when she passed on? Or yesterday for the service?" Her gaze raked him from head to toe.

Jess ran his hand over his week-old beard. "I got here quick as I could."

Her mouth curled downward as if she doubted it. "I'll tell you right now, Jess Logan, I don't like this one bit. I told the sheriff so myself. Those poor babies have never even laid eyes on you. What do you know about raising children, a man with your...past."

Beneath his poncho, Jess's hands curled into fists. "Would you just get the kids? It's nearly dark. I want to get them home."

"Your sister's home, you mean."

His jaw tightened. "*Their* home."

She gave him a final scathing look and shut the door in his face. He knew it wasn't the mud on his boots or the rain dripping from his Stetson that kept her from inviting him inside.

The door swung open quickly and a stoop-shouldered man squinted up at him. "Jess Logan? Is that you, boy? It's me—Rory Garrette."

"Mr. Garrette?" Jesus, what had happened to the man? He'd gotten so *old*.

Rory chuckled and leaned heavily on his cane. "Been a long time, boy. What? Fifteen years?"

"Yeah, about that." Jess shifted his wide shoulders. On the trail these past weeks, every bump and sway—every memory—caused his thirty-two years to weigh more heavily on him. Now, seeing Rory Garrette, the burden lifted a little. "How you been, Mr. Garrette?"

"Tolerable, I reckon." He nodded toward the muddy roadway and the misting rain. "Things in

Walker have changed, though. It's just not the same, not like when you were here.''

Jess didn't answer, the past being the last thing he wanted to discuss.

"Yes sirree, them were the days. You boys were something. Fighting, drinking—kept the saloons in business yourselves, you and the Vernon boys. And the girls…land alive, weren't no girl safe with you boys loose on the streets.'' Rory laughed aloud. "And always into mischief, too. I remember the time you boys set fire to old lady Murray's privy with her inside, she come a-running—"

"That was a long time ago, Mr. Garrette."

"Yeah, that's for dang sure." His smile faded. "Town's done gone respectable now. Got us a regular preacher over to the church, a full-time sheriff and deputy, too. Got enough ordinances and laws to choke a horse. New schoolmarm just got here, some widow woman from back East. All the ladies in town been wringing their hands since your sister took sick, wondering how we'd get us another teacher way out here. I guess you've seen some changes here in Walker already, huh, boy?''

He'd seen his sister's grave. That was enough.

Alma stepped into the doorway, sending Rory on his way with a disapproving glare. She passed a small carpetbag to Jess. "Here's their things."

Beside her stood the children. His sister's children. He'd never seen them before.

Little Maggie looked up at him with solemn eyes. Eyes older than her eight years. Jess knelt in front of her. The picture of her mother, with big brown eyes and blond curls. A lump of emotion rose in his throat.

"Mrs. Garrette says you're Mama's brother."

"That's right, Maggie. I'm your Uncle Jess."

"Mama's dead."

His chest tightened. "I know, honey." He turned to the little brown-haired boy peeking around Alma's skirt. "Hey there, cowboy."

"His name is Jimmy," Maggie told him. "He turned five last week, but we couldn't have a party or anything 'cause of Mama."

Jess held out his hand. "Come here, Jimmy. You want to go for a ride with me and your sister?"

Jimmy drew back and hid his face in the folds of Alma's skirt.

"Jimmy doesn't talk," Maggie said.

Alma glared down at Jess. "The child hasn't spoken since his mother passed on."

She made it sound as if that were his fault, too.

Jess rose. "I'm obliged to you, Mrs. Garrette, for looking after them until I got here."

She jerked her chin. "They'll be back. I don't doubt it for a minute. There's plenty of good Christian folks in this town who'd be more than glad to take these young 'uns in—you best remember that."

Jess drew in a deep breath. "Come on, kids. Let's go." Carpetbag in hand, he crossed the porch.

"Aren't you going to put his hat on for him?" Maggie asked.

"Huh?" He froze and looked back at her confused face.

"Aren't you going to help Jimmy?"

Jess felt Alma's glower and cleared his throat. "Yeah, sure."

He fished the battered hat from the boy's jacket pocket and pressed it down on his head.

"He can't button his buttons either," Maggie told him.

Jess fastened the jacket, his big fingers awkward on the buttons. He turned to Maggie. "Anything else?"

"No." She pulled the hood of her cloak over her head and took her brother's hand.

Jess stood. "All right, then, let's go."

A hand crept into his. Tiny warm fingers curled against his palm, sending a rush up his arm. He looked down at Maggie clinging to him.

"Where are we going, Uncle Jess?"

He gave her hand a little squeeze. "Home."

"Uncle Jess doesn't like people coming around the house, Mrs. Wakefield. He says they're all a bunch of nosy busybodies and ought to stay home looking after their own children."

Sarah Wakefield held tight to Maggie's hand as she picked her way around the mud puddles in the road. "This is different. I'm your teacher."

The little girl shook her head, her blond curls bouncing. "Uncle Jess isn't going to like it."

Despite the dire warnings Maggie had given her since leaving the schoolhouse, Sarah pressed on, holding up the hem of her dark skirt, dodging puddles. Like the gray clouds overhead ready to burst with rain,

Sarah had a few things she intended to say to Mr. Jess Logan, and she wouldn't wait another day.

Maggie stopped and pulled her hand from Sarah's. "This is where me and Jimmy live with Uncle Jess. We lived with Mama...before."

Breath left Sarah's lungs with a sigh of profound envy as she gazed at the cozy little house. White with green shutters and a sturdy roof, a neat picket fence bordered with shrubs and bushes, twin maples in the yard. Gray smoke billowed from the chimney, blending with the gloomy afternoon sky.

Sarah shuddered at the thought of the leaky, drafty cottage a short distance down the road near the school—her house. She told herself for the hundredth time since arriving in Walker that she should be happy with the house the school board provided. It was a place to live. And, it was a very long way from Missouri.

Maggie took her hand once more. "We always go in through the back. Mama said to keep the front clean for company."

Sarah followed the child through the front gate and around to the rear of the house. A clothesline stretched across one corner of the yard and several weather-faded outbuildings stood a short distance from the house.

"That's my Uncle Jess." Maggie bounced on her toes and pointed.

At the three-sided woodshed a man draped in a poncho slammed his axe into a log, splitting it cleanly in two. He stopped suddenly and spun around, his face shadowed by a black Stetson and a stubble of whiskers. Even from across the yard, Sarah felt the heat of his gaze upon her. She backed up a step.

"Hi, Uncle Jess." Maggie skipped across the yard to him.

Jess knelt and gave her a one-armed embrace. "Did you do all right at school today?"

She nodded, then pointed back at Sarah. "This is—"

"Go on in the house, Maggie." Stern, but not angry, he stood and gestured toward the back porch with the axe clenched in his fist. Maggie looked back at Sarah and waved before disappearing into the house.

For an instant, Sarah wanted to call the child back as she stood alone, facing Jess Logan. She'd heard the talk about him. Generally, she disregarded other people's opinions in favor of making up her own mind. Now, she questioned the wisdom of her decision.

He took a step toward her, the shroud of the poncho widening his big shoulders and increasing his height. Sarah gulped.

"What do you want, lady?"

Sarah straightened her shoulders. "Mr. Logan, I'm—"

"I don't care what your name is. What do you want?"

Not a shred of tolerance warmed his tone. She expected townspeople here to be different from the folks in Missouri, but she hadn't expected a Jess Logan so soon after her arrival. "I want to talk to you about Maggie. She—"

"Goddamn it!" Jess slammed the axe into the chopping block. "How many more of you nosy heifers is the church going to send over here?"

Her eyes widened. "Pardon me?"

"Look, lady, don't stand there pretending you don't know what I mean. I've been here less than a week, and every goddamn time I turn around one of you good-intentioned Christian busybodies is poking your nose in around here. I'm telling you for the last damn time—"

"Uncle Jess! Uncle Jess!" Maggie pushed open the back door. "Something's on fire again!"

He spat a mouthful of curses and raced across the yard. Not bothering with the steps, he leaped onto the porch and pulled Maggie from the doorway. "Stay out here."

Sarah hurried onto the porch. Surprisingly, the child looked unconcerned. She dashed into the house, Maggie on her heels.

Black smoke coiled from the cookstove as she stepped into the kitchen. Jess pulled the door of the oven open with the toe of his boot, grabbed a towel from the sideboard and fanned the billows of smoke pouring into the room. He reached into the oven and pulled out a pan full of charred remains. Coughing, he threw open the window above the sink.

"Dammit." Jess kicked the oven door closed. "Goddamn it!"

Calmly, Maggie ventured closer and peered at their burned meal. "It's all right, Uncle Jess."

"Sonofa—" Seeing Maggie he clamped his mouth

shut and held in the curses until his cheeks puffed out. He yanked off his Stetson then grabbed a handful of his poncho and ripped it over his head, wadded the garment in a knot and flung it onto the sideboard.

Sarah took a step forward, then stopped.

He had on an apron. A pink, bibbed apron with ruffles around the edges, red hearts embroidered on the pockets and green vines twining up to two blue-birds kissing on his chest.

A giggle escaped Sarah's lips and she slapped her hand across her mouth.

Jess glared at her, then looked down at the apron. Color rose in his cheeks, pink, like the apron, but he ground his lips together and drew himself up to his greatest height.

Sarah cleared her throat. "Maybe I could help you prepare something else for supper?"

"I don't need any help, lady." He snarled the words at her like a rabid dog. "I've got everything handled."

Sarah's gaze scanned the room. Crusty dishes over-ran the sink. A makeshift clothesline sagged above the table. Flour sifted across the shelf and onto the floor. Pots and pans balanced precariously on the sideboard.

She nodded. "Yes, I can see that you do indeed have everything under control."

"Are we going to have to eat eggs for supper again, Uncle Jess?" Maggie looked up at him with solemn eyes.

He blew out a big breath, visibly calming himself. "I'll figure out something, honey."

"It's okay if we do." Maggie looked at her brother peering around the table. "Isn't it, Jimmy?"

The boy scurried behind Maggie and ducked his head.

Sarah's heart ached at the sight of the two children and she even felt a pang of compassion for their uncle. The red flannel shirt beneath his apron outlined his muscular arms and wide shoulders. His brown hair grew a trifle too long, and that gave it an unruly wave across the back. Dark trousers and boots emphasized his height. He should have been riding the range, not cooking a roast for two small children.

Jess plowed his fingers through his hair and turned to Sarah again. "Look, lady, if you don't mind, I've got things to do."

His invitation to leave stirred her conscience again. "There's a very nice restaurant on Main Street where you could eat tonight."

He cringed and waved away her suggestion with both hands. "I don't need your help and I don't need your suggestions. I told you, I can handle anything. Anything."

"Uncle Jess? Jimmy wet his pants."

Jess groaned softly and his shoulders sagged.

Sarah tried again. "I could—"

"Just leave, lady. Okay?" Wearily, he held up one hand. "I'm sure you're anxious to tell everybody in town what you saw here, anyway."

"Mr. Logan, I have no intention of telling anyone in town anything. I'm Maggie's teacher."

He froze, then his gaze impaled her. "You're the schoolmarm? *You?*"

Heat flushed her cheeks and ran the length of her as his bold gaze covered her. At once she was conscious of the mud on the hem of her skirt, the mend in her cloak, the press of her blouse against her throat, the wisps of her light brown hair loosened by the breeze. She felt her cheeks pinken and heard her heart pound in her ears.

Determinedly, she squared her shoulders and inched her chin higher, reminding herself that at age twenty-five and with several years' experience, she was well qualified for the job; surely, that was the reason behind the look he gave her.

"Yes, Mr. Logan, I'm the schoolmarm. And I am here because today, for the third time this week, Maggie has come to school without a proper meal."

His brows furrowed. "I sent her lunch pail today."

"It was empty."

His shoulders sagged farther. "I forgot to put food in it?"

"If you're unable to send her with adequate nourishment, I will talk to the school board and see what can be arranged."

His back stiffened again. "Now just a damn minute. Don't you go talking to—"

"That's all I came to say. Good day, Mr. Logan." Nose in the air, Sarah glided out of the kitchen.

The cool, damp wind hit her square in the face as she rounded the house and went through the gate. What had gotten into her? What had she been thinking? First, offering to help with supper, then threatening to go to the school board? She'd broken her own rules—something she'd sworn wouldn't happen.

Keep to herself. That's the promise she'd made when she'd taken this job. She'd been lucky enough to find this position out here so far from everyone she knew—everyone who knew her—that she wouldn't risk losing it. If that happened, where would she go next?

Sarah lifted her skirt and hurried down the road less concerned about the puddles than putting some distance between herself and Mr. Jess Logan. A man with a past. That was the rumor she'd heard. She shouldn't provoke him. She was a woman with a past and she had far more to lose than Jess Logan if the good people of Walker found out what she'd done.

After all, who would want her for a schoolmarm once they found out how she'd killed her own husband?

Chapter Two

Golden rays of sunlight sifted through the pristine priscillas, rousing him gently. Jess groaned and rolled over, punched his fist into the pillow and snuggled deeper into its softness. He closed his eyes, ready to drift off again, then shot straight up in bed.

"Good God! What time is it?"

Tangled in the quilt, he scrambled out of bed, reaching for his trousers with one hand and his pocket watch with the other. Nearly nine o'clock. Damn.

"Maggie! Maggie, get up!"

Jess hopped into his trousers, fastening them as he hurried down the hall. At the door to the bedroom the children shared, he stopped. Both Maggie and Jimmy were gone.

"Dammit. Maggie!"

"I'm here, Uncle Jess."

He ducked into his own bedroom again, grabbed his shirt and boots and followed his niece's voice to the kitchen. Maggie and Jimmy sat at the table.

"I slept too late, Maggie. We've got to hurry or

you'll be tardy for school." He shoved his arms into his pale blue shirt and rummaged through the sideboard. "You'll have to eat quick, then get dressed."

"We already ate."

Jess looked back at the bread and jam on the table. "Oh, yeah. Okay, then, get dressed and—"

"I am dressed." Maggie slid from the chair. "See? So is Jimmy."

"Okay. Yeah, that's good." Jess raked his fingers through his hair. "Get your books, then."

Maggie disappeared down the hallway as Jess balanced beside the table, pulling on his socks and boots. Outside, the school bell began to clang. He mumbled a curse and looked at Jimmy. "Let's go, partner."

The boy bit into a slab of bread; strawberry jam squished out and dripped onto his shirt. He chewed slowly, making no move to leave.

"Maggie! Hurry!" Jess grabbed a towel from the sideboard and wiped at Jimmy's shirt. The child grunted, pulled away and shoved the rest of the bread into his mouth.

Jimmy still hadn't spoken and only occasionally tolerated Jess's touch. Jess tried to wipe the child's sticky hands, but Jimmy grunted again and slid them both down the front of Jess's shirt, smearing jam all the way down.

"Jesus...." Jess jumped back and looked down at the mess. He ran the towel across his shirt, but only managed to make it worse. Outside, the school bell clanged again. Resolutely, he lifted Jimmy out of the chair. "Come on, we've got to go."

Jimmy ran down the hallway ahead of him.

"Maggie!" Jess tossed the sticky towel aside. The last thing he needed was to be tardy for school and have the schoolmarm poking her nose into his business again. He headed down the hallway. "Come on, Maggie, let's get going."

She came out of her room, books in one hand and two red ribbons in the other. "Braid my hair."

Jess stopped dead in his tracks. "What?"

She shook the ribbons at him impatiently. "Yesterday, Mary Beth Myers had her hair all braided and she said her hair was prettier than mine and it's not. I want my hair braided today."

His jaw slackened. They were already going to be late for school. There was no time to braid hair, even if he knew how.

Jess pulled the ribbons from her hand and tossed them aside. "It doesn't matter what Mary Beth Myers says. Come on, now, we've got to hurry."

He shepherded her out the back door, then nearly stepped on her when she stopped suddenly.

"Where's Jimmy?"

Jess slapped his hand over his face. Jesus, he'd nearly forgotten the other kid. He yanked open the back door again. "Jimmy! Come on!"

Seconds ticked by and finally Jimmy appeared, licking his fingers. Jess led the way around the house. At the gate he stopped, remembering to shorten his strides so the children could keep up.

In the house across the road the curtain in the parlor window parted ever so slightly and Jess saw Mrs.

McDougal peek out. He cringed at the sight of her. Not once since he'd moved into his sister's house had the woman come outside and spoken to him, but she kept constant vigil at her window, spying on his every movement. He fought back the urge for an obscene gesture, then strode off with both the children at his side.

The schoolyard was empty when they got there, the small, one-room school building quiet. Red with white trim, it sat sedately among tall oaks and elms, an even lawn surrounding it, and several wooden tables and benches at the side. Jess's stomach tightened and he pushed the image of his sister from his thoughts.

"Mrs. Wakefield must have started class already." Maggie looked up at Jess. "I've never been late for school before. Am I going to be in trouble?"

"No, honey. You're with me. It's okay." He gave her hand a little squeeze. The day he couldn't handle a schoolmarm was the day he'd call it quits for good.

Jess pushed open the door and strode inside. The students, seated in neat rows of desks, turned and stared. Mrs. Wakefield stood at the head of the class. She looked up at Jess, folded her hands in front of her, and gave him a look that froze him to the floor.

"Mr. Logan."

It was not a question or a greeting, but a reprimand, plain and simple.

Jess fidgeted, suddenly feeling as if he were a student in the little schoolhouse again. "Sorry we're late," he mumbled.

Her frosty glare warmed not one iota. "Maggie, you may take your seat."

Maggie gave Jess a little smile and went to her desk; Jess winked at her.

In the back of the room, an older boy laughed. "Hey, it's not like he robbed the bank or anything."

The students giggled.

"That's enough, Luke," Sarah said.

Jess glanced at the boy in the desk near him, a scrawny-looking kid, maybe fifteen; he was grateful that icy stare of Sarah Wakefield's was focused on someone else.

Warming to the attention of the students, Luke laughed again. "Maybe we should get the sheriff over here, have them locked up."

Sarah's gaze turned sterner. "Luke, I said that will do."

The boy threw his head back and laughed. "Or maybe—"

Jess reached down and grabbed the boy by the shirt-front. He hauled him out of his seat and leaned down until they were nose to nose. "The teacher told you to shut your mouth."

The boy's eyes rounded and he pulled back.

Jess gave him a shake. "Understand?"

Luke gulped. "Y-yes, sir."

"Good." Jess released him and he clattered into his desk. He hadn't yelled at anyone in a long time; it felt good.

A startled hush fell over the classroom and all the students shrank back, their eyes wide, mouths gaping.

Jess suddenly felt like a brute, towering over the children. He shifted uncomfortably, gave a curt nod to Sarah and strode out of the school.

"Feel that chill?" Jess mumbled to Jimmy as they walked down the steps. "That woman can lay down a blanket of ice quicker than Jack Frost."

The child remained silent, so Jess was startled when someone called his name. He spun around and saw Sarah on the steps of the schoolhouse, glaring down at him.

"Mr. Logan, in the future, I will thank you to keep to yourself when in my classroom."

She was all drawn up like a banjo string ready to pop, glaring at him as if he were one of her disobedient students. He'd expected a kind word for shutting up that kid, or at least a thank-you, but not this.

"Is that so?"

Her chin crept up a little. "I will not have you undermining my authority, Mr. Logan. Is that clear?"

Lordy, she was a pretty thing, all puffed up and full of vinegar. She stood straight and tall, her ample bosom rounded against the hundred little buttons up the front of her dress. Her light brown hair was pulled back in a bun, but stray wisps curled around her face. Her dark eyes sparked with fire.

Jess shook his head. What was he thinking? She was the schoolmarm, for God's sake.

"The boy was shooting off his mouth. I wasn't going to stand there and put up with it."

She folded her arms under her breasts. "I will handle situations like that, Mr. Logan."

"I didn't see you handling anything, Mrs. Wakefield."

"Perhaps if you hadn't interfered, you would have."

He rolled his eyes. "Well, pardon me all to hell."

Color rose in her cheeks and he saw the quick intake of her breath as she clamped her mouth closed. But instead of feeling pleased that he'd shut her up, he was embarrassed by his foul language.

"Look, Mrs. Wakefield, I—"

She turned on her heels but stopped at the door and looked back at him. "You have jam on your face."

Jess felt his cheeks pinken as she disappeared into the school. He dragged his hand over his chin and looked down at Jimmy. "Thanks a lot, partner."

The boy just stared up at him.

"Come on." They headed home.

After getting cleaned up and having breakfast, Jess headed for town, Jimmy at his side. He'd put it off as long as he could, but now his shelves were too bare to delay another day.

The late morning sun shone brightly on the hills in the distance, turning them greener than expected, thanks to the spring rains. Jess tried to look at them, tried looking at the sky too, but eventually had to turn his attention to the houses they passed.

His heart rose in his throat. God, it had been a long time since he'd walked down this road.

Cassie came into his mind, and recollections of the two of them running, playing with friends filled his head. Growing up here—the early years, at least—had been magical. He'd done most of his mourning on the trail getting here, but still it hurt, being here, thinking of her. Cassie, gone. His only relative in the world.

Except now for these two kids. Jess looked down at Jimmy skipping along beside him and he forced down the swell of emotion. He'd gotten over the other deaths. He'd get over this one, too.

They passed the schoolhouse as the road curved slowly toward the west. Across from the school squatted a tumble-down shack and Jess wondered why somebody didn't just tear the thing down; it didn't look inhabitable. On the other side of the road stood the church and a nice house, both with tended lawns.

"They're new," Jess said to Jimmy. "In fact, all of this is new. It was all farmland back when I lived here."

Jimmy looked up at him for a second, then gazed off at the house.

"That was a long time ago. Before you were born. Me and your mama used to play here."

Jimmy stopped suddenly and his bottom lip poked out. Jess knelt and pushed his Stetson back on his head.

"It's okay if we talk about her. I know you miss her."

Jimmy jerked away and ran ahead of him. Slowly, Jess got to his feet. His heart ached, sharing the pain the boy felt. He just wished he knew how to help him.

Jess pulled his Stetson lower on his forehead and followed the boy into town.

The place had grown, Jess realized as he stepped up onto the boardwalk. Lots of new businesses had cropped up. The streets were full of horses, wagons and people, all looking prosperous. He gazed around until he finally spotted something familiar. Jess crossed the street to the Walker Mercantile.

The bell jingled over the door as he stepped inside. Jimmy ran in ahead of him. All sorts of merchandise filled the shelves, the pickle barrel stood by the door, and cane-bottom chairs that had seen better days surrounded the potbellied stove in the corner. Behind the counter was an array of teas, coffees and tins.

Cautiously, Jess surveyed the store. The merchant was tallying an order for another customer, and Jess's tension eased a bit when he recognized the customer as Rory Garrette. At least he knew one friendly face in Walker.

"Morning, Mr. Garrette."

The older man leaned on his cane and squinted up at him. "Jess, where you been, boy? I thought you'd left town again already."

Before he could answer, the merchant looked up.

"Jess Logan?"

A moment ticked by before Jess recognized the man in the apron. Years had creased his face and peppered his dark hair with gray, but there was no mistaking that distinctive voice, deep and strong.

"Leo Turner." Jess said, and nodded, unsure of the welcome he'd get here—or anywhere in Walker. "Good to see you again." He offered his hand and they shook.

"Last I heard, you'd died in a Mexican prison. Good to see you, too. Sorry to hear about your sister."

"Thank you."

"Jimmy?" Leo took a licorice from the glass jar beside him and held it up. "Want one?"

The boy scampered over and Jess lifted him onto the counter. He took the candy and bit into it.

Leo chuckled. "That boy loves sweets."

Rory offered a gap-tooth smile. "Who don't?"

"Cassie used to bring him in with her every Saturday, you know, give him licorice if he was quiet while she shopped."

"He's not talking much these days," Jess said. "Maybe this will do the trick."

"Bribing the child into talking? I should hope not." A woman breezed in through the curtain from the back room and stared disapprovingly at the men. "Leo, I think you'd know better."

"Now, Emma, honey," Leo said, "we're not hurting anything."

Efficiently she straightened the counter beside Leo and gave Jess a glance. "You've certainly got your work cut out for you, young man."

Memories stabbed him like a knife, Leo's wife looking at him in that way, using that tone of voice, those exact words so many years ago. Years had changed her looks, but that was all.

Jess nodded. "Yes, ma'am."

"Your sister was a treasure in this town. We'll miss her." Emma brushed the countertop with a linen cloth.

Rory coughed and sagged against his cane. "What

about you coming over to the house and sit a spell, boy? Have supper with us?''

He could imagine the look on Alma Garrette's face, seeing him walk into her parlor and sit down at her dining-room table. ''Can't today. Some other time.''

''I'm gonna hold you to that, boy.''

The bell jingled as the door opened again. Leo waved. ''Morning, Sheriff.''

Rory's lip curled down. ''Horse's ass,'' he muttered.

''Morning Leo, Emma.'' The sheriff sauntered to the counter, hung his thumbs in his gun belt and reared back, giving Jess the once-over. His lips curled down. ''I know who you are, Logan.''

Jess's back stiffened. He hadn't especially liked Sheriff Buck Neville when he'd first arrived in town and asked about his sister's children. Now, looking at the stocky, muscular man with the tin badge pinned to his vest, he liked him even less. ''Is that so?''

''Yeah, that's so.'' Sheriff Neville leaned forward, crowding Jess. ''I know about you. I know about what you did over in Kingston.''

Jess felt every gaze in the room bore into him; apparently everybody knew about Kingston. Jess's gut tightened but he didn't flinch.

''I run a clean town here. I don't like your kind hanging around. You so much as spit wrong, Logan, and I'll throw your ass in jail so fast you won't know what hit you.'' Sheriff Neville jabbed a finger at him. ''Don't you forget it.''

He left the store and slammed the door behind him.

A long awkward moment dragged by before Leo spoke. "Don't pay him no mind, Jess."

Rory squirted a wad into the spittoon. "Mighty uppity for a lawman in a sleepy little town like Walker."

"Well, I think Sheriff Neville is doing a fine job," Emma declared. "I don't know where you could find a better lawman."

Rory waved away her comment. "He thinks he's some big-time sheriff, stopping train robberies and rounding up gangs. Just like—what's his name? That lawman in them dime novels. Who is it, Leo?"

Leo laughed. "Oh, yeah, I know who you mean. He thinks he's Leyton Lawrence."

"Show him." Rory pointed at the display of dime novels behind the counter. "Show ol' Jess."

"Just got these new ones in yesterday." Leo took the slender book off the shelf and held it up. "See? *Leyton Lawrence, The Legendary Lawman.*"

"Yeah, that's him." Rory laughed, then fell into a coughing fit.

"Honestly, you men." Emma breezed past them. "You'll all be singing a different tune if the Toliver gang heads this way. You'll be glad Sheriff Neville is on the job."

Leo shook his head. "Oh, Emma, the Toliver gang hasn't been to these parts in months."

Rory squinted up at him. "I'll bet ol' Neville wishes they'd come this way. Maybe he could have got a book writ about him, too."

"Don't be silly," Emma said. "That Leyton Lawrence isn't real."

Leo shrugged. "You wouldn't know it by the way these books sell. I can't keep them on the shelves. Everybody wants to read about the next adventure of the Legendary Lawman. You ever read these things, Jess?"

Jess eyed the book, then blew out a heavy breath. "Read them? No."

"Ol' Sheriff Neville does—I'll guarantee it." Rory laughed again.

"I need some supplies, Leo." Jess passed the dime novel back to him.

"Sure thing. Your sister ran an account with me. You want me to add it to hers?"

Jess caught Emma's disapproving glare. He shook his head. "No, I'll pay cash. Did Cassie owe you anything?"

Leo waved him away. "Nothing worth mentioning."

"I want to make it right."

Jess ordered his supplies and paid for them, including Cassie's tab, and made arrangements to pick them up later on the way out of town.

"See you later, boy," Rory called. "And watch out for that Legendary Lawman."

Jess chuckled as he guided Jimmy out of the mercantile ahead of him. That laugh caught in his throat, though, as Alma Garrette stepped up onto the boardwalk in front of him.

"Morning, Mrs. Garrette." Jess tipped his hat.

She bristled. "I didn't see you at services on Sunday. Everybody wanted to know why. Your sister always brought the children to services, you know.''

He hadn't felt like praying lately, and certainly not in this town where he knew everyone would stare a hole through him if he walked into the church.

Alma bent and pulled Jimmy closer. ''Now, let's have a look at you.'' She tugged at his clothes and peered behind his ears. ''Thin, mighty thin. And in need of a good scrubbing, too. Did you let him bathe himself?''

Jess frowned. Was he supposed to wash the boy? He'd set out soap and a pan of water for him in the kitchen, wasn't that enough?

''Humph! I thought so.'' Alma's lips drew together in a tight pucker. ''The good people of Walker aren't going to stand by and let your sister's children fall to ruin, Jess Logan. You best remember that.''

She pushed past him and into the mercantile. Through the window, Jess saw her huddled together with Emma Turner. He knew they were talking about him.

Well, damned if he cared. Jess strode off down the street, a knot hardening in his belly.

''Those two old biddies can talk all they want,'' Jess said to Jimmy. ''They made up their minds about me, anyway. A long time ago.''

As they passed the Green Garter Saloon a hand reached out. Jess spun around and grabbed his Colt Peacemaker on his thigh.

''Whoa, there!'' The saloon keeper threw up both

hands and laughed heartily. "Pretty fast on the draw. I guess what they said about you is true, Jess."

He relaxed marginally and glared at the barrel-chested man with the bushy mustache.

"Don't tell me you don't remember me, after all that liquor I slipped you and Nate when you were kids."

"Saul?"

He laughed again and patted his round belly. "That's right. Come on inside and have a drink."

Jess holstered his gun and nodded toward Jimmy. "I got the boy here."

"Won't take a minute. Sit over here, son." Saul pointed to the wooden bench alongside the saloon and urged Jess inside. "We've got some catching up to do."

Jess looked back over his shoulder at Jimmy swinging his feet, still eating licorice. "You stay put."

A couple of men sat in the corner, but Jess didn't recognize them. More new faces in the town he used to call home. He edged up to the bar.

"Bring back some memories?" Saul slid him a beer.

Jess looked at the faded picture over Saul's head, the dusty shelves and the scarred floor. "Nothing much has changed."

"Seen the Vernon brothers since you've been back?"

"Are they still around?"

"Shoot, yeah. And you'll be glad to know they ain't changed a whit." Saul leaned his elbows on the bar.

"Remember the time you and the Tompkins boy got drunk—well, hell, I guess you weren't ever in the place that you weren't drunk—and you climbed up on the bar here and shot out the lights in the store across the street. Then the two of you took off out of here when the sheriff came in, and ran smack into Mrs. Murray and knocked her right into the horse trough. Lordy, I thought I'd bust a gut laughing."

Jess leaned on the bar and chuckled at the memory. "How is old Mrs. Murray, anyway?"

Saul's face grew solemn. "She passed away a couple of years back."

Jess averted his eyes and sipped his beer.

"Sorry to hear about your sister. She was a good woman, teaching at the school, fending for herself and those kids all alone. Everybody in town thought the world of her." Saul laughed again and chucked Jess on the arm. "Fact is, couldn't nobody figure how she ended up with a no-account fellow like you for a brother."

Jess shifted uncomfortably and drained his glass. "I got to be on my way, Saul. Thanks for the beer." He tossed coins on the bar.

"Keep your money." Saul pushed the coins back at him. "Having you in town again is going to send my profits right through the roof!"

Jess pulled his Stetson lower on his forehead and left the bar, sucking in a big gulp of fresh air. Somehow, being in the Green Garter again seemed stifling.

The crowd on the street had picked up some. It was nearly noon and his belly reminded him of the meager breakfast he'd had; he'd lost most of his appetite cleaning strawberry jam off the table, chair, floor, Jimmy and himself.

He motioned to the child still seated on the bench. "Let's go eat."

With no desire to run into anyone else who remembered him, Jess chose the Blue Jay Café. It looked crowded and that was a good sign, so he went in and took a seat in the corner.

"Nice place," he said to Jimmy as the boy climbed into the chair across from him. Jess looked around at the clean, orderly restaurant. "Don't recall the last time I ate on a tablecloth."

Jimmy squirmed onto his knees and said nothing.

Jess laid his Stetson on the chair beside him as the serving girl headed his way. A pretty woman, he decided, though he wasn't usually partial to blondes. He preferred dark-haired women, with equally dark eyes. Round, soft women. Women like Sarah Wakefield. Now, there was a woman who could—

Jess plowed both hands through his hair. What was he doing, having such thoughts? About a teacher, no less. A prim and proper teacher.

His belly warmed suddenly, reminding him of the weeks he'd spent on the trail getting to Walker. Weeks of hard riding, with no stops for taking care of life's necessary pleasures. He wondered if Miss Flora still had her parlor house at the edge of town. He needed to pay her a call soon. Real soon.

"What are you two gents wanting today?"

The soft, feminine voice caused Jess to jump and

he looked up at the blond woman standing over his table; for a moment he imagined she could look straight through him and see what he really wanted. She was shapely, maybe twenty-three, and had a pretty smile.

"Jimmy likes the chicken." She smiled down at him and tickled the boy's chin. "You must be Cassie's brother. I'm Kirby Sullivan. Welcome to Walker."

She was the first person to utter those three words to him, and they sounded good. Jess got to his feet and introduced himself; he accepted her condolences when she offered her sorrow over his sister's death.

"Jimmy used to stay with us while Cassie taught school. I live just down the road from the schoolhouse with my folks. We miss having Jimmy around." Kirby fluffed the boy's hair and he pulled away. "Nate told me you two used to be friends."

"You know Nate Tompkins?"

"Sure. You ought to stop by and see him while you're in town. He's at the jail."

Jess chuckled. "Jail, huh? That figures."

Kirby smiled gently. "Nate's the deputy sheriff."

"Nate? The deputy? Well, damn...." Jess shook his head. "I guess a lot of things really have changed in Walker."

"Yes, and no one more than my Nate." An easy smile crossed her face. "So, what do you say? How about the chicken plate?"

"Sounds good." Jess eased into his chair and watched as Kirby disappeared into the kitchen. How could a worthless bastard like Nate Tompkins have gotten a fine-looking woman like her? His belly heated up again.

Trying to distract his thoughts, Jess turned back to Jimmy. "So, you like chicken, huh?"

Jimmy ignored him and fiddled with the silverware.

"I'll bet your mama used to make the best chicken in the state. Even when we were kids, she was a good cook."

Jimmy folded his hands on the table and laid his head down.

Jess sighed. "Come on, Jimmy. Talk to me."

The boy looked up suddenly and stuck out his tongue.

Stunned, he felt a laugh slip out. "Well, I guess that's a start," Jess said.

A few minutes later when the food was served, Jess ate hungrily, satisfying at least one of his suddenly pressing needs. The food tasted delicious, a far sight better than his own cooking. He finished off his own plate and the remains of Jimmy's, plus a thick wedge of apple pie and two cups of coffee.

"You might want to bring Jimmy over to the church. My papa preaches there. We always have children's Bible study on Thursday nights." Kirby took away their plates. "Bring Maggie, too."

Jess rocked back in his chair and patted his belly. "I'll see—Holy Jesus!"

He surged from the chair, nearly knocking the dishes from Kirby's tray. Maggie. He'd forgotten Maggie's lunch pail this morning. He'd been in such a rush it had completely slipped his mind. And surely this time that Mrs. Wakefield would go straight to the school board.

Kirby gasped. "What's wrong?"

"Nothing, nothing." Jess pulled at his neck. "I just thought of something else I need. Could you box up some food? Chicken, bread, maybe?"

"Of course. Anything else?"

"No—yes."

Jess drew in a deep breath. Yes, he needed something else, something that would appease a certain schoolmarm. And he knew exactly what it would be.

Chapter Three

Damn. He was too late.

A few children still sat at the benches, but most played in the schoolyard. Girls jumped rope while several boys shot marbles in the dirt. Other children ran squealing around the schoolhouse while a few older ones huddled under the shade of the elms. Jess clutched the box lunch as he crossed the schoolyard looking for Maggie. Finally he spotted her standing beside Mrs. Wakefield. Of course.

Jess pulled his Stetson lower and sucked in a deep breath. "Hi, honey. I brought you something special."

"Uncle Jess!"

He gave her a hug and passed her the box. "I wanted to surprise you. Sorry I'm a little late. I didn't think your teacher would have you eating so early." He felt Sarah glare at him but he refused to look at her.

"Thanks, Uncle Jess."

"I brought something for your teacher, too." He pulled out a big, red apple and presented it to Sarah.

"Come on, Jimmy. You can eat with me."

"There's cookies in there. Enough for the both of you," he called as Maggie headed for the tables at the side of the schoolhouse.

He watched the two children, determined not to acknowledge Sarah Wakefield standing three feet from him. She could stare at him until her eyes crossed, if that's what she wanted to do.

The breeze shifted and a delicate scent tantalized his nose, winding its way inside him. His gaze came up quickly and settled on Sarah. Good God, was it her that smelled so sweet?

But that expression of hers wasn't sweet at all. She didn't buy the special meal excuse, not for a minute. And the apple hadn't helped at all.

"Mr. Logan, Maggie was quite upset that she had nothing to eat."

"I know, I know."

"It's extremely important that she have continuity in her life. Especially now with all the changes that have taken place."

"I know that, too."

"She's at a very vulnerable point that could—"

"Would it make you feel better if you just got out your ruler and busted my knuckles?"

Sarah stiffened. "As appealing as that sounds, Mr. Logan, I sincerely doubt it would be effective."

"Is that right?"

"That's exactly right." Sarah softened her voice. "You needn't take this personally. I'm only thinking of what's best for Maggie."

He hated it when other people were right. It seemed like a good time to change the subject.

Jess gestured at the children in the schoolyard. The boy he'd had the confrontation with in class this morning lounged beneath an oak. "That kid still shooting off his mouth?"

Sarah followed his gaze across the schoolyard. "Luke Trenton? He's not so bad, really. But he lacks self-discipline. He's the youngest of twelve, I understand, and apparently his folks grew weary of parental responsibility several children ago."

"Twelve kids, huh?" Jess whistled low. He couldn't keep up with two. "Looks like he's got himself a girlfriend."

Seated on the ground beside him was a young girl about his age, with soft brown hair.

"That's Megan Neville. Her father is the sheriff. Have you met him?"

Jess's stomach tightened. "Yeah. We've met."

"Megan and Luke are nearly inseparable."

"Pretty sweet on each other, huh?"

Sarah shook her head. "I don't think they're more than good friends. They don't display any of the usual signs, so far."

"Signs?"

Sarah's cheeks flushed. "Yes. Signs. Passing notes, holding hands when they think no one's looking, making eyes at each other."

"You pay attention to those things?"

"I make it a point to pay attention to everything about my students."

Jess looked at her and some of her frostiness evaporated. He'd never in his life had a teacher pay any attention to him, until it was time to swing a hickory stick, of course.

"Megan's lucky to still be in school at her age," Sarah said. "Some girls are married by fifteen, with children of their own."

"Were you?" Urgency clenched his gut. Suddenly, he had to know.

Well, there it was. The first question about her past. Sarah steeled her feelings. "No." The word barely slipped through her tight, dry throat.

"No, what? No, not married young? Or no, no children?"

Sarah cleared her throat and forced herself to face him. "No, I did not marry young, and no, I do not have children. If you'll excuse me, Mr. Logan, I have lessons to prepare."

Jess watched her climb the steps to the schoolhouse, her back rigid, her shoulders square. That conversation had turned her deathly white. Somebody had said she was a widow. Was it the fact that she had no children that upset her? Maybe. Every woman wanted kids. But if she hadn't married young, that meant she'd married more recently. Very recently, perhaps. And recently widowed, too. That would account for her reaction to his question.

She wasn't wearing a mourning dress, so at least a year had passed. Time meant nothing, though, when it came to losing your loved ones. He'd learned that the hard way when he was only twelve years old. For an instant Jess was tempted to follow her inside the schoolhouse, but didn't. The farther he kept from everybody in Walker, the better off he'd be. And that sure as hell included Sarah Wakefield.

"Thank you for inviting me, Reverend Sullivan."

Sarah stepped into the warm parlor of the preacher's home next door to the church, more grateful for the invitation to supper at the Sullivans' than anyone could know. She smiled at Emory Sullivan as he took her cloak. How wonderful not to eat another meal alone, in that horrible house she called home.

Emory nodded, lamplight reflecting off his balding head. "We're just so pleased to have you in our town, Sarah, just so pleased. Thank God for bringing you to us. Isn't that so, Fiona?"

His wife clasped her hands together. "We were all worried silly about getting another teacher out here. We ran newspaper advertisements everywhere. Walker isn't exactly St. Louis."

Thank God for that, too, Sarah thought. "Good evening, Kirby, Nate."

She'd met the Sullivans' daughter and Nate Tompkins, the deputy sheriff, at church on Sunday and they'd seemed close, displaying some of the same signs she'd seen in her students, on occasion, so she wasn't surprised to find Nate here for supper. Tall, broad-shouldered with a head full of black wavy hair, Nate looked comfortable, as if he'd spent many an evening in the Sullivans' parlor. But the other man rising from the settee was a stranger, and a feeling of foreboding crept up her spine.

Fiona smiled brightly. "Sarah, I'd like to present Dwight Rutledge. Dwight is one of our most prominent businessmen. He owns Walker Feed and Grain on the other side of town."

A tall, older man with a round chest and thinning hair, Dwight took her hand delicately in his. "Glad to make your acquaintance."

A flash of light glinted in his eye. She'd seen that look before. She offered a silent prayer, hoping it would carry more weight emanating from the preacher's home, but Dwight's hand clung to hers a trifle longer than necessary.

"Shall we all go in for supper?" Dwight looped his arm through hers, then followed Fiona into the dining room. Sarah ended up seated at Dwight's elbow; she was certain it was by design and not chance.

"How are things going at the school?" Kirby asked from across the table where she sat beside Nate. The dining room was cozy, like the rest of the house, the table set with nice dishes and a lace cloth. Apparently, the congregation in Walker was a generous one.

"Quite well, actually." Sarah passed a bowl of potatoes on to Emory. "The students and I are adjusting to each other, getting to know one another. It's all gone very well, actually."

"At least you don't have any of the Gibb boys in class." Fiona shook her head. "A more disreputable family I've never known."

"You've got Zack Gibb working for you, don't you,

Dwight?'' Nate asked as he spooned peas onto his plate.

''I was reluctant to take him on. Bad blood in that family.'' Dwight leaned closer to Sarah. ''Inbreeders. Keep marrying their cousins, the lot of them.''

Sticky heat rolled off him; Sarah blushed.

Fiona gasped. ''Mr. Rutledge, really.''

''It's the truth. And the Lord knows it.'' He glanced at Emory at the head of the table. ''Zack's not so bad. He's the youngest, twenty years old now. Seems to have a good head on his shoulders, despite his up-bringing. Of course, you never know.''

''Got word at the jail the other day that Zack's brother, Gil, was in a gunfight down in Laramie. Heard Gil's quite the shot. And not too particular about who he shoots at. Wouldn't be surprised if I saw a Wanted poster come in on him.''

Sarah felt her stomach flip over. She'd known Walker would be different from St. Louis, but this different?

''There, there, now. Don't be frightened.'' Dwight covered her hand with his. ''You've nothing to fear.''

Kirby smiled proudly at Nate. ''We have very competent lawmen here in Walker.''

Dwight laughed suddenly. ''Yeah, with Leyton Lawrence on the job.''

Everyone laughed but Sarah.

''The Legendary Lawman,'' Dwight explained. ''In the dime novels.''

Sarah nodded. ''Oh, yes, I've heard of him. Those

books are quite the rage. I recall reading in the newspaper that sales have set records.''

''Surely you read that before you got to Walker,'' Kirby said. ''Our little newspaper hardly carries any news from back East.''

Fiona smiled. ''That's why it's so good to have new people in town.''

''I don't think many people are saying that about our other newcomer.'' Dwight reared back in his chair and sucked his gums. ''That Logan fella is causing a stir, the way I hear it.''

The name sent a tingle racing up Sarah's spine. She'd heard a few comments here and there about Jess, but didn't allow herself to be drawn into gossiping.

Fiona dipped her head wisely. ''I understand he was quite the troublemaker here in Walker.''

''Now, Fiona, that was years ago when he was just a boy, and we didn't even live here then.'' Emory waved away her comments. ''It's not our place to be spreading rumors and gossip.''

''I've heard the talk,'' Dwight said. ''And it doesn't sound like rumors to me.''

Kirby turned to Nate. ''You know what really happened. You grew up here. Jess was a good friend of yours, wasn't he?''

Despite herself, Sarah's ears perked up.

Nate put down his fork and chuckled. ''I can't say it was all Jess's doing. We were both pretty wild back then. But we were just kids.''

"So it's true?" Sarah asked. "The stories about the shooting and drinking and…other things."

"Yeah, they were all true." Nate laughed again.

"I say it's disgraceful," Fiona said.

Dwight thumped his fist on the table. "For all the joking we do about Buck Neville, at least we don't have those problems in town now. It's safe for decent, law-abiding people." He cast a sidelong glance at Sarah. "Of course, a man would still want to protect his woman himself."

Sarah turned away, avoiding his eyes.

"Alma Garrette told me Jess Logan was into all kinds of trouble even after he left Walker." Fiona pursed her lips. "And to think, someone like him is raising Cassie Hayden's children."

"Fiona," Emory cautioned. "The Lord stands in judgement, not we ourselves."

"Of course." She dipped her eyes contritely. "But, look at how well Cassie did for herself after her husband ran off. Teaching, caring for those children, always helping out any neighbor who needed it. She even bought that nice house and kept it up herself. And don't you think it would have been easier for her if Jess Logan had been here to help? Where was he when his sister needed him?"

Dwight nodded. "You do have to wonder about a man like him raising those two children all alone. A man with his past."

"I heard he turned his back on Walker and everybody in it years ago," Fiona said. "Took off. And hadn't been heard from until Cassie passed on. Now, I ask you. Is that the right thing to do?''

"There's something you should know about Jess." Nate wiped his mouth and laid his napkin aside. "Back when we were kids, Jess lost almost his whole family in a fire. His ma and pa, his two sisters and little brother. He was only twelve years old. Just he and Cassie got out of the house alive. His pa picked him up, threw him out the window. He's got a scar on his arm where the glass cut him. Must be pretty hard, looking at a thing like that every day of your life, remembering the screaming and the flames."

Everyone at the table fell silent. Sarah's heart pounded.

"Cassie settled in with the Newton sisters here in town but they wouldn't take Jess. He got passed around from one family to another. He got worse every time, too, and that just got him handed around more and more. He never had a home or a family. Never had anything he could call his own. Not after the fire."

Sarah's heart squeezed nearly to a stop. At that moment she wanted to take Jess in her arms and hold him close, take away all the pain and misery he'd suffered. The feeling nearly overwhelmed her.

"So that's why he's here," Kirby said softly. "He doesn't want the same thing to happen to Maggie and Jimmy."

"Good intentions don't make good actions. What's best for those children is what's important." Dwight nodded curtly.

"But all of that happened so long ago," Sarah said. "He certainly could have changed."

A hush fell over the table. Fiona's brows arched. "Talk like that will do you no good, Sarah. After all, you have a position in the community to maintain. I'm sure you wouldn't want anyone to get the wrong idea."

Sarah felt her cheeks flush. "No. Of course not."

A schoolteacher's job hung by the slender thread of her reputation, her reputation as perceived by the school board and the townspeople. They wouldn't entrust the minds of their children to just anyone. Sarah knew she had to be careful, particularly where Jess Logan was concerned.

Dwight thumped his fist on the table. "That Logan fella may have good intentions, but I doubt he'll be around for long. Probably will take off again, just like he did before."

Sarah squirmed in her chair. She'd had enough of this conversation.

"Make plans now to come to the school a week from this Saturday," she said. "I'm planning a pie social that afternoon and everyone's invited."

"Pie, huh?" Nate smiled broadly. "Count on me. I'll be there."

Sarah smiled. "Good. I'll put you down for an apple cobbler."

Everyone chuckled as Nate blushed. "I can't bake anything. But I know a certain restaurant in town where I can get something good to bring."

Kirby swatted him on the arm. "Mighty sure of yourself, Nate Tompkins."

"I just know good pie when I eat it."

A special look passed between Nate and Kirby that touched Sarah's heart and left her with a profound feeling of happiness…and envy.

After supper Dwight helped her with her cloak, then latched onto her arm. "I'll see you home."

"No, thank you. It's just a short walk."

He leaned closer. "I insist."

Behind him, Fiona smiled and bobbed her brows. Sarah felt everyone staring at her. She didn't want to make a scene. "Well, all right. Thank you."

Dwight patted her hand. "And, I'm going to show you the sights of Walker, such as they are. We'll have supper, too. Tomorrow evening."

"Really, Dwight, I don't think—"

"I insist." He wagged his finger at her and led her out the front door.

Dwight talked about his feed and grain business as the cool night air swirled about them, but Sarah hardly listened. Dwight was nice enough—and certainly respectable—but she didn't want to become involved with him. She'd vowed to keep to herself, not draw attention to herself. Fiona had been right. Talk circulating about her in town so soon after her arrival would do her no good.

Lights shone in the window of Jess's house a short distance down the road and Sarah found her gaze drawn to it like a beacon on a stormy night. A figure moved across the window. It had to be Jess—big, sturdy, nearly blocking out the light. The place seemed inviting, with the children inside and, of course, Jess.

Sarah's stomach tightened as she stopped in front of her own home. A single dim lantern burned in the window, illuminating the sagging porch, chipped paint and broken steps.

"I'll see you inside." Dwight's voice spoke directly into her ear; she felt his hot breath against her skin.

Sarah pulled away. "No, Mr. Rutledge. That would hardly be proper."

"You're not in St. Louis anymore. Things are different out here. People in Walker don't stand on all that formality."

"Perhaps the people of Walker don't, Mr. Rutledge. But I do. Good evening."

Sarah hurried up the rickety steps, Dwight's soft chuckle resting on the evening breeze. She went into the house and turned the lock.

A more unappealing meal she'd never seen, and it took all the control Sarah could muster to sit by and not offer some of her own food to Maggie.

The midday sun shone through the white, billowing clouds as most of the children closed their lunch pails and hurried off to play. Seated next to Maggie at the benches beside the school, Sarah looked down at the food the child picked at.

Chicken, probably. It was hard to tell under all that charred crust. And that black, hard lump might have been a biscuit.

"I see your uncle packed your lunch today." Sarah smiled down at her as she ate her own meal.

Maggie nodded. "Uncle Jess cooks all the time. He lets me help. I read Mama's recipes to him. But they don't taste the same."

Sarah's stomach rolled. "No, I don't expect they do."

"That's 'cause I don't know all the words."

"Then maybe your uncle should read." Anything would be an improvement.

"He says for me to read 'cause it's good to be able to read."

Mildly surprised, Sarah nodded. "Does your uncle ever read to you?"

"No. Mama had lots of books. She used to read to me and Jimmy sometimes at night. But Uncle Jess doesn't read them." Maggie pulled off a crust of chicken. "He makes up stories. He says they're better than book stories."

"And are they?"

Maggie laughed. "They're funny. Uncle Jess makes up funny stories. He tells us one every single night."

Sarah laughed, too, unable not to. "Still, wouldn't you like to hear the stories in the books and look at the pictures?"

"Uncle Jess says he can paint the pictures in our heads with the words. He says you don't have to be able to read to make good stories."

Sarah's stomach knotted. Was that the reason for the unpalatable meals? Jess couldn't read?

"Can I go play now?" Maggie licked her fingers.

"Certainly, dear." Sarah's thoughts ran wild, imagining Jess's childhood, the horrible death of his family right before his eyes, then bouncing from home to home having little guidance. He'd been such a behavior problem, maybe no one had taken the time to teach him. Maybe Jess Logan couldn't read.

Sarah pushed herself to her feet and stalked across the schoolyard. No. No, she wouldn't get involved. She couldn't. She had to keep to herself. She needed this job and she needed this town. She needed a home. And she would be a part of Walker—albeit a distant, detached part—no matter how much her heart ached to help.

With a deep, cleansing sigh, Sarah climbed the steps to the schoolhouse. Absolutely, positively, without a shadow of a doubt, she would not get involved with Jess and the children. She would not.

"It's just a simple stew. I thought you and the children might like some."

Sarah held out the black kettle, bearing up under Jess's harsh gaze from the back porch.

"I made too much for myself."

His eyes narrowed.

"It's beef and vegetables."

His brows furrowed.

"It's good."

The line of his mouth hardened.

"It's heavy." Sarah winced and braced her outstretched arm with the other one.

He came down the steps and took the kettle from her, but still just stared at her.

"Besides, I owe you." Sarah rubbed her forearm.

"For what?"

"Luke Trenton." She waved him toward the door. "Put that on the stove before it gets cold."

Jess looked at the kettle, then at her, at the house, then back to Sarah again. "You want to eat with us?"

A lump rose in Sarah's throat. She shouldn't even be here, let alone go inside. But it was doubtful anyone had seen her come to Jess's house; the only close neighbor was Mrs. McDougal across the road and Sarah knew she was having supper with the Sullivans tonight.

She glanced around. "Well, all right."

Jess held the door open for her and Sarah walked inside. He seemed bigger, growing taller and wider each time she saw him. And somehow it made her feel smaller, weaker, until her knees trembled, and made it harder to breathe.

Maggie and Jimmy were both in the kitchen, oblivious to the dirty dishes, the pile of dust under the broom in the corner, the disarray. They sat at the table, drawing with nubby pencils on sheafs of white paper.

"Hi, Miss Sarah." Maggie smiled broadly. "We're making pictures, aren't we, Jimmy."

The boy spared her a glance and turned back to his drawing.

Sarah stood in the corner, feeling uncomfortable. "I brought stew for supper. Anybody hungry?"

"Uncle Jess said we could make oatmeal cookies for supper. I told Mary Beth Myers we were."

Sarah looked at Jess. "You giving the children cookies for supper?"

"After supper." He pushed aside a greasy frying pan and sat the kettle on the stove. "Anything wrong with that?"

"No, of course not." Sarah took off her cloak and unpinned her hat. "Let me help you."

He glared at her. "I can do it."

"I'm only offering to help with supper, Mr. Logan, not bear your child."

The kettle lid slipped from Jess's fingers and clattered onto the stove, then flipped onto the floor. His gaze riveted her in place.

Sarah turned away, her cheeks flaming. What on earth had she said? Why had she blurted out such a suggestive remark?

"See my picture, Miss Sarah?"

Grateful, Sarah peered over Maggie's shoulder, admiring her drawing of a house with trees and flowers in the yard. Her own home, obviously.

"That's lovely, Maggie. Let's have a look at your brother's work."

Sarah pursed her lips as she gazed at Jimmy's picture, crude sketches of bared teeth, narrow eyes on angry faces. She walked to the stove.

"I thought drawing might help him," Jess said as he stirred the stew. "Since he won't talk, maybe he'll say what's on his mind with the pictures."

Sarah glanced over her shoulder at the table. "He's very troubled."

"With good reason."

"What has the doctor said about him?"

Jess shuddered. "I'm not taking that boy to any doctor."

"I understand Dr. Burns is very capable—"

"No."

His reasoning was only too obvious. Sarah pursed her lips. "Really, Mr. Logan, just because you're afraid of the doctor, doesn't mean—"

"Afraid?" His gaze riveted her. "Who said anything about being afraid?"

She gave him an indulgent look.

Jess shifted uncomfortably. "I'm not taking Jimmy to any doctor, and that's all there is to it."

"What's best for you, Mr. Logan, isn't necessarily what's best for Jimmy."

Dammit. There she went, being right again. Jess clamped his mouth shut.

"At least consider it. Won't you?"

"Yeah, I guess I will." Jess looked down at her standing at his elbow. "Since I've got these two children already and don't need anymore borne for me tonight, would you mind setting the table instead?"

Sarah's cheeks pinkened, but she laughed, and to her surprise, Jess laughed with her, a deep, masculine laugh that rippled through her.

Together they got the meal on the table, Sarah's stew, old coffee that was too strong, milk for the children, and warmed-over lumps of what were probably intended to be biscuits. Next time, she'd bring bread, Sarah thought, before she could stop herself.

The children ate two bowls full and Jess had three, scraping the last of the stew from the kettle and licking the spoon standing at the stove.

"Can Miss Sarah stay and bake cookies with us, Uncle Jess?" Maggie gathered dishes from the table.

Sarah's gaze met Jess's. She couldn't tell what he wanted, but knew she should go.

"I have lessons to plan for tomorrow."

"Please stay." Maggie took her hand. "Please. Make her stay, Uncle Jess."

"Stay if you want." Jess pushed dirty dishes around on the sideboard. "Besides, since I owe this meal to that Trenton boy I'd like to know what exactly I have to thank him for."

"Oh yes, Luke." Sarah carried a stack of bowls to the sink. "After your little talk with him in class the other morning, he's behaved much better. I guess he doesn't get much discipline at home. So, I wanted to thank you."

Jess gave the spoon a final lick. "For stew this good I'll rough up every kid in the class. You just say the word."

His eyes crinkled at the corners and danced with flecks of blue. Sarah laughed with him.

A knock sounded on the back door. Jess pointed with the spoon. "Get that, will you, Maggie?"

Sarah's heart skipped a beat as the door opened and Nate Tompkins walked into the room. He raised an eyebrow at seeing her there, but didn't say anything.

Jess shook his hand. "Sit down. Have some coffee, Nate."

"I can't." The deputy looked uncomfortable.

Jess stopped in the center of the kitchen and braced himself. "What's wrong?"

"Sheriff Neville sent me over here, Jess. They're having a hearing in town tomorrow. You've got to be there." He looked at Sarah. "You, too."

She touched her throat. "Me? What for?"

"Yeah, Nate. What's going on? What sort of hearing?"

"Circuit judge will be here." Nate pulled at his neck. "Sorry, Jess. They want to take the kids away from you."

Chapter Four

Jess paced the boardwalk across the street from the Walker courthouse as townspeople streamed inside. He punched his fist into his open palm. Damn them. Damn them all. Bunch of busybodies who ought to be taking care of their own problems, not nosing into his.

He shook his head, anger tightening his chest. He ought to go into that courtroom and tell them off—every one of them.

"Jess?" Nate Tompkins rounded the corner and stopped in front of him. "I want you to know, Jess, I had nothing to do with this hearing."

Jess jerked his jaw toward the courthouse across the street. "I know who's behind it. The same people who're always causing problems in Walker."

"It's Sheriff Neville who started it."

"The sheriff?" Jess's brows pulled together in a tight scowl. "What does he care about Cassie's kids?"

"It's not that, Jess." Nate drew in a deep breath. "What you did over in Kingston, you know, with the sheriff there? Well, that sheriff was Neville's cousin."

Jess blanched and fell back a step. "Damn...."

"The other folks in town, well, I guess they're really concerned about the kids. Everybody loved your sister, Jess. They want to see Maggie and Jimmy taken care of proper."

"I don't believe that, not for a minute." Jess shook his head.

"Truth is, a couple of families already spoke up for them."

Jess's stomach tightened. Some other family raising Cassie's children? No, he wouldn't allow it. He wouldn't let Maggie and Jimmy be handed over to strangers.

"You watch yourself in court today," Nate said. "Judge Flinn would like nothing better than to throw you in jail. And Sheriff Neville would like nothing better than to be the one locking you inside."

Jess nodded. They crossed the street and went inside the courtroom.

"All right, all right. Come to order." Judge Percy Flinn rapped his gavel, silencing the murmur that rippled through the crowd. He shuffled papers and peered over the rim of his spectacles. "Jess Logan? You here, Logan?"

He and everyone else in town. Jess fought his way through the crowded aisle, feeling every hot gaze in the room on him. Damn bunch of nosy bastards, gawking at him like a circus sideshow. He wanted to slam his fist into each and every face, curse at them all until the knot in his gut unwound. Instead, he kept his eyes forward and stepped in front of the judge.

Judge Flinn gave the papers another cursory glance. "Logan, your past has brought into question your fitness to raise the children of your deceased sister. And judging from these reports, your actions of late only confirm it. What have you got to say for yourself?"

Jess squared his shoulders, blocking out the people leering at him. They were all here, Alma Garrette, the preacher, Emma Turner from the mercantile. Even Mrs. McDougal peeked in through the window. All here, all waiting to see him fail.

"Cassie was my only sister. When I found out she'd passed on I knew it was up to me to take care of her kids. I didn't want them raised by strangers."

The judge peered over his spectacles. "But you'd never seen them before. You're a stranger to them, aren't you?"

Jess shifted. "I'm their family."

"I don't like your past, Logan. I don't like what happened down in Kingston." Judge Flinn jerked his thumb toward an empty chair. "Sit down."

Buck Neville rose and hung his fingers in his vest pockets. "I've got people willing to testify, Your Honor."

"All right. Get them up here."

Jess mumbled under his breath as Alma Garrette threw him a smug look and eased her wide frame into the chair at the corner of the judge's desk.

"Well, Your Honor, we were all shocked that Jess Logan showed his face in town after all the trouble he'd caused here before. Wanting to raise those children—why, he never lifted one finger to help his sister

and he never even laid eyes on the children before."
Alma jerked her chin indignantly. "I saw him in town
with little Jimmy, and the boy looked like he hadn't
bathed in a week. His clothes were wrinkled and
soiled. Jess Logan was wearing his gun, like some sort
of gunslinger. I'd heard that's what he was."

A murmur rippled through the courtroom.

Alma pursed her lips. "I heard he'd been paid to
shoot the governor of Texas a few years back."

The crowd rumbled and Judge Flinn rapped his
gavel again. "Order!"

"Well, then—*then*—I saw him leave little Jimmy
sitting all by himself outside the Green Garter Saloon
so he could go in and drink."

Jess winced as the crowd grumbled, and Alma Garrette sailed back to her seat, her nose in the air.

Buck Neville glared at Jess. "Mrs. Turner, you want
to come on up here?"

Emma, from the Walker Mercantile, took the chair.
"I don't know much about Jess since he left Walker
years ago, except what I heard around town. And that
story of how he disgraced that young woman down in
Galveston, then refused to marry her really upset me."

"Tell the judge about Jimmy," Buck instructed.

"Oh, yes, that." Emma cleared her throat uncomfortably. "The child refuses to speak, Your Honor. But
Jess had him in my store bribing him with licorice to
get him to talk. I just didn't think that was right."

The judge grunted and jotted a note on the papers
in front of him. "Anybody else?"

Lottie Myers took the stand next. "Little Maggie

goes to school with my Mary Beth. They're good friends. Well, it seems Mr. Logan lets the children eat whatever they want for supper. One night all they had was cookies. And that poor child's hair is a snarl of tangles. Cassie used to keep it so pretty. But it looks like no one is tending to her now.''

Jess's chest tightened as Lottie stepped down. Nosy busybodies. They didn't know what the hell they were talking about—any of them. His anger and hatred for the people of Walker grew.

Reverend Sullivan spoke next. He, at least, had the decency to offer Jess an apologetic look.

"No, Mr. Logan hasn't brought the children to church or to Bible study. But I figured it was just a matter of him getting settled here in town.''

"Thank you, Reverend.'' Sheriff Neville turned to the crowd again. "Mrs. Wakefield?''

Sarah's heart rose in her throat as she made her way to the front of the room. Settling into the chair she chanced a look at Jess. He appeared composed, maybe even at ease. But Sarah saw the tic in his cheek, the tightness in his jaw, the blue of his eyes harden to cold, steely gray. The people of Walker were going to take the children away from him. She knew it. And it was obvious to her that Jess knew it, too.

Judge Flinn consulted his papers. "You're the schoolmarm here in Walker. Just moved here. Is that right, Mrs. Wakefield?''

"Yes, Your Honor.'' Her voice was a tight whisper.

"Speak up, ma'am.'' The judge whipped off his

spectacles. "What have you observed about Mr. Logan, the children, and their living conditions?"

She glanced at Jess, then cleared her throat. "Admittedly, Mr. Logan isn't the best housekeeper I've ever met. And, too, there've been times when Maggie's lunch could have been better. But Maggie is very happy, Your Honor. She speaks highly of her uncle. He helps her with her reading, and tells the children stories every night at bedtime. He's very affectionate with them."

The judge peered down his long nose at her. "Is that so?"

"Yes, Your Honor. And it's true that Jimmy won't talk, but that problem existed before Mr. Logan even got to town. I don't know why he would have come here in the first place if he wasn't interested in their well-being. He seems to genuinely care for the children. They care for him, too. And isn't love just as important as proper meals and clean clothes?"

The courtroom fell silent. Sarah felt every gaze in the room boring into her as she took her seat again.

Jess heard his heart pounding in his ears as Judge Flinn settled his spectacles on his nose once more and looked down at him. He rose to his feet.

"Seeing as how you're the children's only blood kin, the court will give you time to prove you can take proper care of them. But you see here, Logan, I don't like you and I sure as hell don't like what happened in Kingston. I'll be back next month, and if I hear that you've as much as spit downwind in this town, I'll give those children to somebody else. Understand?"

Jess gave him a curt nod. "I got it."

The judge pounded his gavel. "Next case!"

The crowd grumbled and headed for the door. Sarah pushed her way outside, anxious for some fresh air. On the boardwalk, Alma Garrette caught her arm.

"I hope you're pleased with yourself. The judge would have given those children a proper home if it hadn't been for you."

Sarah's breath caught. "I told the truth, Mrs. Garrette. That's all."

"The truth? You don't know the truth." Alma leaned closer, her eyes narrowed. "The truth is that Jess Logan gunned down the sheriff over in Kingston. Shot him in cold blood. And went to prison for it, too. Now, do you still think he's the kind of man who ought to raise two small children? Do you?"

Breath left Sarah's lungs in a single huff. Passersby on the boardwalk glared at her. She heard someone mumble her name.

Alma tossed her head. "The judge will be back in a month. You'd better think long and hard about what you say next time."

Sarah stumbled away, her mind racing. Prison? Jess had been in prison? He'd shot a lawman—in cold blood?

She wrung her hands as she hurried down the boardwalk. Why had she gotten involved? She should have refused to testify. She should have kept to herself. She'd broken the vow she'd made and now look at what had happened. The town was turning against her. She could lose her job. And all because of Jess Logan.

He should have told her about his past. He should have known what she'd say in front of the judge. But he hadn't opened his mouth. He'd let her stick out her neck, all for his own good.

Anger rose in her throat, pulling her heart with it.

Jess stepped out in front of her at the corner of the bank. He was mad, too.

"Bastards." He flung his hand toward the crowd of people still filing out of the courthouse. "Nosy hypocrites. I'm not living my life to suit them—any of them. And if they think I'm going to kiss their butts just to keep those kids, they can all think again."

Sarah rounded on him, fury roiling in her. "Oh, is that right? You listen to me, Mr. Jess Logan. They'll take those children away from you in a heartbeat—and enjoy doing it. Don't think they won't. So if you really care about your sister's memory, if you really want what's best for Maggie and Jimmy, then I suggest you pucker up."

Sarah whipped around and stalked away.

While she'd have preferred to bury her head under her pillow and never show her face in town again, Sarah met Dwight Rutledge at the Blue Jay Café for supper, as she'd promised. Dwight, at least, was respectable company. Being seen with him couldn't hurt.

"Quite the doings in court today." Dwight settled back in his chair across from her.

"Were you there? I didn't see you." Maybe now

he wouldn't want to be seen with her. Sarah's stomach soured. Goodness, what had she gotten herself into?

"I think it was a good thing you did, speaking out like that." Dwight nodded emphatically, then grinned slowly. "I didn't realize you had such strong feelings about children and…love."

She wished he'd stop looking at her that way. "I told the truth. That's all. Of course, I'm not sure everyone else in town feels the same way as you."

Dwight reached across the table and laid his big hand over hers. "You did the right thing. It shows integrity. I like that in a woman."

"Thank you." She eased her hand away, wondering if the rest of the town would see her single-handed influence on the judge in such a favorable light.

Kirby Sullivan stopped by their table to take their supper order. "I heard what happened at the courthouse this afternoon. I'm glad Jess got another chance."

Relieved that not everyone had turned on her, Sarah sighed. "I hope it works out for him." But in her heart, she didn't see how it could. Not with the way Jess felt about the townspeople.

Dwight ordered steaks for them both and talked about his business straight through to dessert. The sun was slipping toward the horizon, painting the sky a gorgeous blue as they stepped out onto the boardwalk.

"Let me show you my store while we're in town." Dwight tugged proudly on his vest. "Doing quite well, if I say so myself."

A look at Walker Feed and Grain was only marginally more appealing than spending another evening alone at her house, so Sarah agreed. They walked, Dwight pointing out places he considered interesting. Shops and businesses had closed and the boardwalk at this end of town was nearly empty. Seeing Megan Neville was a surprise.

"Oh! Hello, Mrs. Wakefield." Megan touched her brown hair and smoothed her skirt, seeming as surprised as anyone at the chance meeting.

"Hello, Megan."

"What brings you down here at this hour?" Dwight frowned at her. "Mighty late to be out and about. Does your pa know you're here?"

She glanced nervously at him, then back at Sarah. "Actually, I—I'm looking for Papa. Have you seen him?"

"Is something wrong?" Sarah asked.

"No. No, nothing. Nothing at all. I'd better go." Megan hurried away.

Dwight watched her leave, then looked down at Sarah. "Such a delightful child. Turned out real good, what with her ma dying and all. Been hard on Buck Neville, too, handling his sheriff duties, raising a child. A man needs a wife. Don't you think?"

Sarah turned toward his store, deliberately ignoring his question. "Is that a light on inside? I thought you'd closed up."

"I did." He pulled the big brass key from his pocket and opened the door. "Who's there?"

"It's me, Mr. Rutledge. It's Zack."

Peering around Dwight, Sarah saw a tall, lanky

young man step in from the back room. He looked to be about twenty, with even looks and black, curly hair.

He pushed both hands through his hair, smoothing it in place, and shoved his shirttail deeper into his trousers. "I stayed late to get a jump on tomorrow's work, Mr. Rutledge. That's all."

"All right. Lock up when you're done." Dwight closed the door. Finding someone already inside, Dwight seemed to have little desire to show Sarah around. She wondered why.

He linked his arm through hers as they walked back down the boardwalk. "That's Zack Gibb. You remember, I told you about his family."

The inbreeders who married their cousins. How could she forget?

"Working late, without being asked." Dwight nodded slowly. "Family ties are tight with those Gibbs. Zack and Gil, especially, even though Gil is a real hothead. Remember, I told you he was the gunfighter. But it looks like I picked the right Gibb to work for me. That Zack. A dedicated worker."

Sarah glimpsed Megan Neville disappearing around the corner ahead of her. "Yes, I suppose so."

Twilight settled as Sarah reached her little house across from the school, Dwight beside her. After hearing him talk all evening, she felt sure she could open her *own* feed and grain store.

Dwight suddenly stopped short and squared his shoulders. Sarah's breath caught as she saw Jess sitting on her front steps, Maggie and Jimmy playing in the side yard. A myriad of emotions surged through Sarah, causing her heart to beat harder.

Jess rose slowly, put away his pocket knife and tossed aside the stick he'd been whittling.

"Logan."

"Rutledge."

The men glared at each other.

Sarah stepped away from Dwight. "Thank you for supper."

He tore his gaze from Jess, a scowl drawing his features together. "I'll come to call after services on Sunday."

Sarah glanced at Jess and saw his shoulders stiffen. "No, I won't be here. I'm having supper with the Sullivans."

His expression soured. "Another time, then."

Dwight stared at Jess again. Jess braced his arm against the porch roof support column, making it clear he didn't intend to leave. Finally, Dwight touched the brim of his hat. "Good evening."

Sarah watched him until he faded into the gray shadows stretching across the road. She turned to Jess and his bravado dissolved.

"I, ah, I brought back your kettle." He gestured to the black pot sitting on the porch.

"You didn't have to wait."

"I didn't wait. I just got here."

The heaping mound of wood chips he'd whittled told a different story.

Jess ignored her unspoken challenge and walked down the steps. He waved his hand at the house. "Do you really live in this place? It looks like it's ready to fall down.''

''It could use some work.''

''What about the school board? Did you talk to them about fixing it up?''

''There seems to be a shortage of money.'' Sarah nodded toward Jess's house down the road. ''I wish I knew how your sister managed such a nice place. I can't seem to get my twenty-dollar-a-month salary to go very far.''

Jess shrugged and gazed off at the church across the road.

Sarah watched him, her thoughts running wild. So this was what a criminal looked like. Sarah studied his features in the fading light. He'd shot a lawman. In cold blood. And done prison time, too. She glanced at Maggie and Jimmy chasing each other in the yard, heard their laughter riding on the breeze. Somehow, the ideas didn't mesh.

''Well, thank you for returning the kettle.'' Sarah climbed the steps to the porch.

He looked up at her and pulled on his neck. ''I, ah…''

''Yes?'' She walked down a step, bringing her gaze level with his.

''Nothing.'' He paced a few steps across the yard, turned back and stared at her.

Sarah came down the stairs. She'd seen a similar look on her students' faces at times, hovering around her desk, getting up nerve to ask a question or confess

to something. Jess Logan was certainly no schoolboy.
She let another moment drag by.

"Did you want something?" she finally asked.

"No."

She shrugged. "Well, good night, then."

"Wait." Jess took a step forward.

"Yes?"

He drew in a deep breath, then pressed his palm
against his chest. "You're right."

The words were so soft she barely heard them.
"About what?"

"Everything." His shoulders slumped and he
plopped down on the steps. "They're going to take
Maggie and Jimmy away from me. And, hell, maybe
they should. I can't get the house clean. As soon as I
get the floor swept, one of the kids or I spill something. I hardly get the dishes washed from one meal
and it's time to cook again. I burn nearly everything
I stick in the oven, or else it doesn't get cooked all
the way. Every time I turn around, something else
needs tending to. Jimmy wets his pants quicker than I
can get the clothes scrubbed. Maggie's hair is a mess,
but she won't let me touch it anymore. She sees me
with the brush and takes off. I can't do it all."

Jess scrubbed his hands over his face and looked up
at her. "I need help, Sarah. I want to make a home
for these kids. Everybody in town is waiting for me
to fail—hoping I will. You're the only one who had
anything good to say today. Will you help me, Sarah?
Please?"

A knot twisted in her stomach, pulling her heart into

it like a giant sinkhole. She wanted to run to him. She wanted to make everything better for him and the children. She tasted the words on the tip of her tongue.

But she couldn't say them. She didn't dare.

"I can't." Sarah hurried up the steps and into the house.

Chapter Five

The children filed past, barely seeing her, clutching books and lunch pails, glad the day had ended. Sarah stood at the schoolhouse door, a little bit of herself leaving with each of them. Megan murmured goodbye and hurried down the steps to where Luke waited. Maggie gave her a big smile as she passed, piercing Sarah's heart like a dull arrow.

She'd lain awake most of the night, seeing Jess's face in front of her, his pleas for help echoing in her thoughts. Visions of Maggie and Jimmy being carted off to live with strangers haunted her. But still, Sarah clung to the belief that she'd done right. Jess had stirred all sorts of odd feelings in her, making the possibility of getting involved with him even more dangerous. She just couldn't.

"Need any help with the pie social?"

Kirby's voice jarred Sarah from her own thoughts. She managed a smile as she descended the stairs. "Yes, I do. I hoped the church could spare some tables and chairs for the social."

Kirby smoothed a lock of her blond hair into place. "Certainly. I'll ask Nate to bring them over on Saturday morning. Dwight will offer to help, too, I'm sure."

"No, really. That's all right."

Kirby smiled. "He's got his eye on you."

Her stomach soured. "Yes, I'm afraid so."

"Blame it on my mother. She's the biggest matchmaker in the state, maybe the whole country. She thinks everyone should be married."

"Even you and Nate?"

"Especially me and Nate." Kirby grinned. "And I don't disagree. But Nate is reluctant."

From all she knew of Kirby, she was a wonderful person. "Nate is being foolish. Isn't he afraid someone else will come along for you?"

Kirby sighed wistfully. "I'm willing to wait on him. When you've found the right man, you know it. But of course, you understand. You were married."

"Yes," she murmured.

"Then you know the feeling."

Sarah nodded but didn't say anything, her marriage being the last thing she wanted to discuss.

Lottie Myers joined them, holding her daughter's books and lunch pail while the children played in the schoolyard. "I've decided to bake a peach pie for the social. It's my specialty."

"We haven't had a social at the school in years." Kirby nodded quickly. "It was just too much for Cassie, with the children and her house to look after."

Lottie turned up her nose. "That husband of hers

ran off when Jimmy was just a little thing. Nobody knew why, not even Cassie. At least if she knew, she wasn't saying.''

Kirby nodded. "Some men are hard to figure."

"And there's another one just like that." Lottie nodded and they all turned to see Jess at the edge of the schoolyard waiting for Maggie. "He seems like a nice enough man, coming to raise Cassie's children the way he has. But all those stories about him. I heard he was a hired gun, only taking on big important people to kill."

Kirby waved away the idea. "I find that hard to believe."

Lottie leaned closer. "Just this morning he got a mysterious package delivered at the express office— all the way from New York City."

Sarah and Kirby both gasped. "New York City?"

"Yes. For as long as my husband has been the senior agent here in Walker, nobody has ever got a package from New York City."

Kirby nodded in agreement. "Sherman would know."

"Did he see what was inside?" Sarah asked.

"No," she admitted. "But Sherman said Mr. Logan got a funny look on his face and left without saying anything. Sherman says there's probably some secret instructions inside telling him who to kill next."

The three women peered at Jess again. He stood at the well, hauled up a bucket of water and held the ladle for Jimmy, then took a drink for himself. He looked as though he'd been working. Sweat glistened on his face and dampened his shirt. He rolled up his sleeves and pushed back his long johns, dipped his hands into the water and splashed it on his face. Sunlight glistened off the water droplets that hung in the dark hair of his forearms.

"I wonder," Lottie said softly, "if he's plotting his next killing right now."

Maggie ran up and Jess knelt to hug her. Sarah saw the child's head bobbing, talking a mile a minute.

And then Sarah saw the scar. Razor thin, running from his wrist to his elbow. A constant reminder of the night his parents had died, the night his brother and sisters were lost, the night his life had changed. She wanted to turn away but couldn't.

Sarah's heart sank into the pit of her stomach and she knew she could never turn away. And she couldn't abide any more gossip, either.

"I'll appreciate all the help you can give me on the pie social. If you'll excuse me, I have lessons to plan for tomorrow."

Sarah hurried inside the schoolhouse and shoved her books into her satchel. By the time she'd closed the windows and locked up, Jess was gone, the schoolyard empty. She went straight to his house and banged on the back door.

He opened it slowly, then seeing it was her, widened his stance and glared at her.

"Vinegar." She spat the word at him.

He frowned. "What?"

"Vinegar. Rinse Maggie's hair with vinegar and the tangles will come out."

He looked as though she'd taken leave of her senses. "You want me to pour a bottle of vinegar over her head?"

"No, just— Never mind. Where's Maggie?" Sarah leaned past him. "Maggie! Come here, dear!"

"What are you doing?"

"You're going to have to bake a pie."

"Bake a what?"

"Any kind. It doesn't matter."

"I don't know how to—"

"Well, you're going to learn." Sarah took Maggie's hand as she scampered out the back door. "And get the children's good clothes ready. You're going to church on Sunday."

He waved his hands. "Hold on here—"

"You're keeping these children. And you're going to do whatever it takes. There's a lot of backsides in this town and you're going to have to kiss them all." She pulled Maggie down the stairs with her. "We're going to my house. You can come get her later."

"But—"

"If I were you, Mr. Logan, I'd start practicing my pucker."

"It's just not right that Sarah Wakefield is as ornery as a mule and still smells so sweet." Jess looked down at Jimmy walking beside him on the road. "You know what I mean?"

The boy just looked at him.

"You'll see for yourself one day."

The little house Sarah lived in looked worse each

time he saw it and in the late afternoon sun it fared no better. The porch roof sagged, some of the shutters hung askew, the steps were loose, and it could use a fresh coat of paint. Jess felt inexplicably guilty that his own house was so nice.

"Do you know how long it takes women to wash their hair?"

Jimmy ran into the yard to play.

"Me neither," Jess muttered.

Ignoring the precarious steps, Jess leaped onto the porch and knocked on the door. It rattled beneath his fist but brought no answer. Mumbling, he walked around to the back. The outbuildings were in no better shape than the house itself and he started to take a closer look. But he heard laughter. Soft, delicate laughter that drew him to the back porch.

What a sweet sound. He loved to hear Maggie giggling like this. It made him chuckle, too. Through the shutter that dangled from one hinge over the kitchen window, he caught sight of Maggie in her white cotton chemise and pantalettes standing on a chair.

He heard Sarah laugh.

Then he saw her.

Standing behind Maggie, gliding a comb through the child's wet blond curls, was Sarah in her chemise and pantalettes. Thick brown hair—wet, like Maggie's—lay down her back, curling at the ends at her waist. Jess's mouth went dry.

The sweet, innocent figure of the child blossomed to all woman on Sarah. She looked soft and round, her full breasts filling the chemise. Her hips swelled the pantalettes, then tapered to supple legs. Her throat looked long and graceful, her shoulders and arms delicate. And those eyes, alive with laughter that lifted her full lips into a smile. She was beautiful.

Jess stared, unable not to. Before, he'd thought she was pretty, for a schoolmarm. But now, seeing her like this, he was stunned. His heart slammed against his ribs, and only as an afterthought did the rest of him react.

"Look, Miss Sarah! Jimmy and Uncle Jess are here!"

Maggie's tiny finger suddenly loomed large, pointing through the window at him. In a heartbeat, Sarah whirled away and disappeared. Jess gulped.

Jimmy appeared beside him and suddenly he felt more guilty than ever before in his life.

"It's not like you think. I wasn't looking." Jess dragged his sleeve over his brow. "Okay, I looked, but I didn't see anything. Well, yeah, I did see something, but— Hell, a schoolmarm isn't supposed to be all soft and round. It's not natural. How could I help myself?"

Jimmy shrugged his slim shoulders and scurried away.

"Uncle Jess! Uncle Jess! Look!" Maggie raced through the back door and bounced on her toes. "Miss Sarah fixed my hair all pretty. She said she'd braid it and put ribbons in it, too. Just like Mary Beth."

Jess scooped her up and whirled her in a circle, her hair blowing around her shoulders. "Well, aren't you just the prettiest thing?"

Maggie laughed wildly and locked her arms around Jess's neck. "Miss Sarah says she'll teach you, too."

He stopped suddenly. "Teach me what?"

She giggled again, pressing her tiny fingers to her mouth. "To braid my hair. Like Mary Beth's."

"You need to learn."

Jess swung around and saw Sarah standing in the doorway. His stomach bottomed out. She was done up all proper now, wet hair coiled at her nape, her armor of corset and petticoats, skirt and blouse shielding her. But he knew what was beneath it all, every curve, every soft, pliant mound of feminine flesh. His gut reacted, swift and urgent.

"Isn't this what you want?" Sarah stepped onto the porch.

"Oh God, yes."

"Then come inside."

Maggie wiggled from his arms. "Hurray! Uncle Jess is going to braid my hair!"

"What?" Jess shook his head. What had he just agreed to?

"Jimmy!" Sarah waved the boy over. "Come inside. I have cookies."

All four of them squeezed inside Sarah's tiny kitchen, crowded with a table and chairs, cookstove, and cupboards. She poured milk and laid out a plate of cookies for Jimmy.

Jess reached for one and she swatted his wrist. "After your lesson."

"Hey, that hurt." He rubbed his hand.

She grinned. "Just be glad I don't have my ruler. Come along, Maggie. Up on the chair."

At Sarah's instruction, Jess stood beside her while she demonstrated hair braiding, parting Maggie's hair down the center, then dividing one of the halves into three smaller sections.

She glanced at Jess standing over her shoulder. "Pay attention, now. There'll be a test later."

"Yes, ma'am."

"It's not as hard as it looks. Just cross the outside section over the middle one, alternating each side. See?"

Standing only inches away, the woman was a magnet. Jess was nearly overwhelmed with the need to press himself against her, feel her softness give way to his hardness, bury his nose against the sweet scent at her throat. He shoved his hands into his hip pockets, fighting the demands of his body.

"There. Now you do the other side."

He glanced at Sarah, hoping to glean some confidence but all he saw were her lush dark lashes fluttering against her porcelain skin. He blew out a heavy breath. "All right. I'll try."

Sarah's long fingers had looked graceful, working the strands of hair into a neat braid, but Jess had never felt so uncoordinated in his life. Finally, with Sarah's quiet coaching, he got through it.

Jess stepped back, comparing the two braids. "Looks like I'll be wearing the dunce cap."

"You'll get better with practice." Sarah nodded her head. "I'll give you a gold star for effort."

"Can I have a cookie, too?"

She grinned. "I'd say you've earned it."

Maggie jumped down from the chair tugging at the braids. "Wait till Mary Beth sees me."

"Run along and get dressed, honey." Sarah poured milk for everyone. They ate together, then the children went out to play, wiping off milk mustaches.

Seated across the table, Jess and Sarah gazed at each other over the last of the cookie crumbs. For lack of anything else to say, Jess gestured to the empty plate.

"Good cookies."

"I'll give you my recipe." Sarah sat forward and cleared her throat. "There's a pie social at the school a week from Saturday. You'll have to bake."

Jess sat back. "Bake?"

"Yes, and you'll have to take the children to church on Sundays and to Bible study, too. The saloons are out of the question."

Jess bristled. "Look, I'm not—"

"The whole town is watching you. You were right when you said they're waiting for you to fail. You want to keep the children, don't you?"

"Of course, but—"

"Then you're going to have to make a lot of drastic changes. All in full view of everyone in town."

Jess's jaw tightened. "Nobody in this town ever gave a damn about me. I was just some good-for-nothing kid for everybody to point at and whisper about. Not one of these so-called fine Christians ever lifted a finger to help me."

Sarah's expression softened. ''I heard about what happened to your family.''

He pulled back, the memory etching lines in his face. ''Yeah. Figures. They're still talking about me.''

Sarah reached across the table and covered his hand with her own. ''I don't blame you for feeling the way you do. And believe me, I know how hurtful gossip can be. But you have to put it behind you, for the sake of Maggie and Jimmy.''

Her warm hand atop his sent tingles up his arm, reminding him of what it was like to be alone. And how good the press of another body felt.

''Yeah. You're right.'' Jess pulled his hand away and blew out a heavy breath. ''Okay, you've got me baking a pie, going to church, staying out of the saloons. Anything else?''

''If you're going to kiss backsides in this town, you may as well start with the biggest.''

He chuckled. ''Alma Garrette.''

''Women love to talk about their children. Ask Alma for her advice on what to do about Jimmy when he—''

''I don't give a damn what that woman thinks about anything.''

Sarah held up her hand. ''I know. But believe me, it will go a long way with her, and all the other women in town. And I didn't say you had to follow her advice. Just ask for it.''

''I've got them all sticking their noses into my business, that's for sure,'' Jess grumbled. ''Even Mrs.

McDougal across the road. I can't make a move without her peering out her front window, spying on me."

"Then the next time you see her, smile and wave."

His expression soured.

"You have to show everyone what a good father you'll be to the children. But you'll have to make them all like you first."

"Damn...." Jess muttered. "All right. Pies, church, no saloon, kissing backsides. Anything else?"

"You'll have to keep the children with you at all times. No leaving them off for Fiona Sullivan or anyone else to watch, not even for a short while."

"I only asked her to watch them that one time at the hearing. I didn't want them there. I don't want them knowing there's a problem."

Sarah nodded. "Yes, and you were right to leave them that time. But not again."

"Okay."

"And, one more thing." Sarah sat straighter. "You shouldn't wear your gun anymore."

"Like hell!"

Sarah cringed. "Make that two more things. Your language."

"What the hell is wrong with my—" Jess clamped his mouth shut, fuming silently. He shifted in the chair. "All right. I'll be more careful what I say."

"Good. Now, back to your gun." She laced her fingers together. "There's a rumor going around town, and I think it would demonstrate to everyone—"

"What sort of rumor?" He glared across the table at her.

Sarah waved her hands, dismissing the whole idea as idiotic. "Well, it seems that since you got that package from New York City—"

"You know about that package?"

"The whole town knows. And, now everyone thinks you're some sort of hired assassin."

Jess grunted.

"Isn't that silly?" She tried to laugh. "Everyone thinks instructions for your next kill were in that express package."

The lines of his face went rigid. Sarah thought he'd deny it outright. Or at least chuckle and wave away the idea. But he did neither.

Suddenly uncomfortable, Sarah rose and got matches from the cupboard. She lit the lantern in the center of the table against the fading sunlight.

"Anyway, I feel that if you stopped wearing your gun in town, everyone would forget the whole idea." She sat down again. "Besides, a lot of men don't wear guns. Walker is a very safe place."

"That doesn't mean it will stay safe. The Toliver gang isn't that far away, and you never know when Zack Gibb's brother might decide to pay a visit."

Sarah rose from the table. "It's your decision to make, Jess, but I've heard the talk. I really believe that if you want the town to forget your past, you should leave your gun at home."

He gazed up at her for a long moment, then ran his hand over his mouth and got to his feet. "I'll think about it."

"Good. But the other things aren't optional. You have to do them."

Jess followed her across the kitchen. "So which of those fine ladies in town should I ask for a pie recipe?"

"All of them. But just ask for baking tips. They'll never give away their recipes." Sarah stopped at the back door. "I thought I'd come down to your house and help you with some cooking and cleaning, if that's all right with you."

He eased close. Closer than he should. "I'd like that."

She leaned her head back to look up at him. She didn't remember him being this tall. "I'll come by after school tomorrow and help with supper."

He grinned. "I'd like to see something edible come out of my kitchen."

She laughed too and stepped out onto the porch. The last rays of the sun slipped behind the horizon as the children played together in the back yard.

"Looks like Jimmy wet his pants again."

Jess pulled on his hat and followed her outside. "I'd better get him home."

"Uncle Jess, we saw somebody over behind the church." Maggie pointed toward the road.

"Probably just Reverend Sullivan."

Maggie shook her head, her braids swinging. "Uh-uh. Nobody is home. See? Look at the windows. They're all dark."

Jess walked to the corner of the house and gazed

across the road. As Maggie had said, the Sullivan place and the church were both dark.

"Maybe I'd better go have a look."

The sound of breaking glass echoed in the cool, still evening. Jess pulled out his gun and turned to Sarah. "Take the children and go inside."

Chapter Six

Footsteps silent in the thick grass, Jess edged his way down the side of the church. His gaze darted from shrub to bush to tree, ears straining, nerves taut. At the back of the building he tightened his grip on his Colt when he heard scuffling feet and a dull thud. Jess leaned around the corner.

Beneath the limbs of two apple trees stood a young man. In the fading light Jess recognized him immediately. Luke Trenton.

Jess holstered his gun, ready to head back home when the boy hurled an apple at the back window of the church. It missed and splattered against the side of the building.

"Hey! What the hell do you think you're doing!"

Luke froze just long enough to make eye contact with Jess, then took off running. Jess went after him.

The boy was quick, but didn't stand a chance against Jess's longer legs. He caught him at the storage shed on the other side of the apple trees, grabbed the back of his shirt and shoved him against the building.

Luke hit the shed hard, but tried to run again. This time Jess whirled him around and swatted him on the seat of his pants, then pushed him against the building, holding him in place with a fist curled in the front of his shirt.

"Let go!" Luke doubled up his fist and took a swing at Jess.

Anger shot through Jess. He jerked his chin back, dodging the fist, then bent the boy over and spanked him on the backside, hard, until he yelped. Jess pushed him against the building again.

Luke's jaw shot out defiantly. "Who do you think you are? The sheriff?"

Jess grabbed his arm again and showed him the palm of his hand. "You want more of this? Suits me fine."

"No!" Luke pulled back, holding his hands against the seat of his pants.

They glared at each other for a long moment. Finally, Luke spoke.

"Go ahead! Tell my folks! I don't care."

"Is that right?"

"Yeah! Tell them. Tell them all you want. They won't do nothing."

"It's pretty obvious that if they cared anything about you, you wouldn't be here doing this in the first place." Jess drew himself up to his greatest height, towering over the boy. He rested his thumbs in his gunbelt. "I think I'll just haul your scrawny butt over to the sheriff and have you thrown in jail."

Luke shrank back against the building, fear showing

in his eyes for the first time. "Sheriff Neville...you can't do that."

Jess leaned closer, his eyes narrow. "I can't?"

Luke shook his head frantically. "No. No, don't do that. If he thinks I'm a troublemaker, he won't let Megan—" Luke clamped his mouth shut and swallowed hard.

So, the boy was sweet on the sheriff's daughter, just as he'd suspected. Even all of Sarah's talk about her schoolmarm observations of her students had been wrong. Jess relaxed his stance.

"What are you doing throwing apples at the church window?"

Luke shrugged. "I don't know. Nothing else to do."

Lord, did he remember that feeling. Bored, restless, looking for something to get into. And more often than not, he'd ended up in trouble. Like Luke had. And neither of them with anyone who cared enough to make them stop.

"You can't go around busting up other people's things."

"I didn't hurt anything." Luke gestured to the back of the storage shed. "That window was already half busted anyway. Just forget it, okay?"

Jess shook his head. Better than anyone in town, he knew what an episode like this could lead to. "You're paying for that window."

"Hell...."

Jess poked him in the shoulder. "Watch your mouth."

Luke straightened. "I'll get money from my pa and—"

"Money is not the kind of payment I had in mind."

The boy's eyes narrowed. "What are you talking about?"

"A day of hard work ought to make you think twice about tearing up what doesn't belong to you." Jess saw the boy's mouth open, ready to protest. "Unless you'd rather head on over to the sheriff right now."

Luke ground his lips together, angry, but was left with no choice. "All right."

"Be at my place first thing Saturday."

Luke grumbled something under his breath. Jess grabbed a handful of his shirt and hauled him up on his toes.

"You got something you want to say?"

Luke's eyes rounded. "No."

"Good." Jess let him go. "Now get on home and stay there."

He watched Luke run across the churchyard and disappear around the corner.

Jess shook his head. What the hell was he doing getting involved with that boy? He had two kids of his own to take care of. But Luke reminded him so much of himself at this age it scared him. He understood the boy, knew what he needed. And he didn't need his hair braided, wet pants changed, stories read or supper cooked. Luke needed what Jess had needed, and that, he knew how to give.

Somehow, Sarah's tumbledown little house looked warm and inviting as he left the churchyard and crossed the road. Warm lamplight shone in the windows and the faint scent of the oatmeal cookies she'd baked earlier hung in the air. A curtain pulled back and two little faces appeared at the window.

Jess's heart soared. Bless them. Smiles from Maggie and Jimmy always lifted every burden from his shoulders.

At the back porch, the children clamored to meet him.

"What happened, Uncle Jess? Who was it?" Maggie held up her arms to him. "You were gone so long."

"Just somebody helping themselves to the apples off the tree behind the church." Jess knelt and gave her a hug, then reached out for Jimmy. The boy stood still long enough to let Jess squeeze his shoulder, then ran past them into the yard to play.

"I was worried."

Jess's gaze traveled the length of Sarah as she stepped into the doorway. He rose and patted Maggie's back. "Catch up with your brother, honey, I'll be right there."

Sarah closed the door behind her, her gaze steady on his face. "The children were worried, too. I told them you were a big, strong man and you'd be fine, but…"

She looked pretty in the fading light, pretty even with the fine lines of worry etched around her mouth. Jess moved closer, bracing his hand against the door casing beside her head. God, she smelled sweet.

"Why are you doing this?" he asked softly.

His height, his warmth overwhelmed her, forcing her back against the door even as she felt the tug to lean closer. Her senses came alive, sending tremors racing through her limbs, scattering her thoughts, robbing her breath.

"I just wanted to assure the children you'd be all right."

He shook his head. "No. The other stuff. Why are you helping me? Why are you the only one in town who wants me to keep these children?"

"Because…" Because he had the biggest shoulders she'd ever seen on a man? Because he had the bluest eyes she'd ever imagined? Because he'd touched something in her that had never been tapped before?

Sarah's lungs burned from the breath she held as she stood rooted in place by nothing more than Jess's gaze, reaching for some modicum of her sanity. No, she couldn't let this happen. If he'd tapped something inside her, then she had to bury it. Deep. The consequences were too dire.

Sarah stepped away, breaking the spell between them. She turned her back to him and gazed out at the children chasing fireflies in the yard. "Because Maggie is my student. I want what's best for her."

"And that's all?" He spoke the words to the back of her head. God, he wanted to touch her.

Her chin went up but she didn't turn around. "Yes. I told you, I'm always concerned about my students. Remember?"

Jess slid his fingers into his hip pockets. She was all stiff and proper now, and his hands itched to make her melt against him. He backed away, putting some cool air between them, and went down the steps, his footsteps heavy on the wooden planks.

"Thanks for helping Maggie with her hair." He silently cursed himself as the memory of seeing Sarah in her delicate, feminine underthings through the kitchen window sprang to life in his mind. He turned away, as another part of him sprang to life as well.

"Good night," Sarah called.

"'Night." Jess gave her a wave over his shoulder and hurried away.

Naked. That's how he felt. Just plain naked.

Jess stepped up onto the boardwalk in town, drumming his fingers against his thigh where his Colt Peacemaker should have been.

Would have been, too, if it weren't for Sarah Wakefield's big idea. Now, instead of feeling confident and secure, he felt naked.

His belly coiled into a tight knot, sending a hot rush through his veins that slammed hard into his gut. Sarah Wakefield and nakedness in the same thought. Jess winced. What the hell was happening to him?

Just ahead, the door to the Blue Jay Café opened and Nate Tompkins stepped outside. His gaze took in the street and landed on Jess. He stopped short.

Grateful for some place different to direct his thoughts, Jess offered his hand. "Nate, how's it going?"

Nate smiled and took his hand. "Let's go over to the jailhouse and talk."

Jess pulled back. Inside a jail was the last place he ever wanted to be. "I've got some errands to see to."

"Come on. We've got some catching up to do."

Jess gestured back over his shoulder. "The boy here is with me."

"He'll like it." Nate leaned down to Jimmy. "Hey, fella, want to see the inside of a real jail?"

Jimmy looked back and forth between the men, then nodded.

"Great. Let's go."

Jess sucked in a big gulp of air and followed them down the street to the jailhouse.

"Where's Neville?" he asked as he stepped inside.

Nate hung his hat on the peg beside the door and eased into the chair behind the scarred desk. "Gone out to the Blue Sky Ranch this morning. Some trouble out there he needed to check on. Sit down, Jess."

He lowered himself into the cane-bottom chair across the desk and gazed uneasily at the rifle racks and Wanted posters cluttering the walls. "I guess I can tell you, jailhouses don't sit too well with me."

The chair creaked as Nate leaned back. "Yeah, I guess not."

Jess glanced at Jimmy staring wide-eyed at everything in the room, and tried to relax. He wasn't a prisoner any more. He'd done his time. And he'd do it again, given the same circumstances.

"Sorry the court hearing didn't turn out better for you," Nate said.

Jess uttered a bitter grunt. "I didn't expect any different."

"Sheriff's got it in for you, Jess. I tried to talk to him, but he just won't listen."

"Figures…"

"Sheriff Neville might not be your only problem." Nate folded his arms on the desk. "Jed Hayden might show up again."

Jess sat straighter in his chair. "Cassie's husband? I thought he was long gone."

"That's what the town thought, too. I only knew because Cassie came to me, asking me what to do. Seems Hayden showed up from time to time wanting money."

"That bastard…"

"Yeah, he was that, all right." Nate nodded. "She was afraid of him, Jess. Afraid for herself and the children. She'd pay him just to get rid of him."

Jess pulled at his neck. His sister had been tormented by her husband all these years and he'd never known?

"Why didn't she tell me? We stayed in touch. She knew where to find me after I got out of prison." Jess looked up at Nate. "I'd have come home, if I'd known. I'd have killed that bastard."

"That's exactly why Cassie didn't tell you."

"Damn.…"

"Anyway, don't be surprised if Hayden shows up in Walker again."

Jess's gaze came up sharply. "He's not getting his hands on Cassie's kids."

"Don't worry about that. He doesn't want them. All the times before when he showed up, Cassie kept the kids away from him, and that was okay with Hayden. Money was all he was after.'' Nate looked hard at him. ''But, Jess, promise me that if Hayden shows up you won't do anything crazy.''

Much as he'd like to see Hayden pay for all the heartache he'd caused Cassie, Jess knew he couldn't do anything. That was exactly what Sheriff Neville wanted. And besides, Hayden really was Maggie and Jimmy's father.

''Anyway, I just wanted to give you fair warning,'' Nate said.

''I appreciate it,'' Jess said. ''And don't worry about me doing anything crazy.''

Nate rocked back in his chair and drew in a deep breath. ''So, what are you going to do about keeping those kids?''

Jess grinned. ''Got me a plan.''

Nate chuckled. ''I seem to remember you having a lot of plans when we were growing up. And likely as not, I ended up in a well of trouble because of it.''

Jess laughed, too. He and Nate had been best friends, nearly inseparable. The only difference had been Nate's father holding a tight rein, and Jess having no father at all.

''So what's your plan?''

''I'm not letting anybody take Cassie's kids—including any of these good folks in Walker.'' Jess grew serious. ''So, I'm reforming myself into the perfect citizen. Going to church, taking in socials, cleaning up my language and making up to every old biddy in town.''

Nate whistled low. "That's a tall order. But, it just might work."

"I've even quit wearing my gun." Jess slapped his palm against his bare thigh.

"I heard the rumor that you're a hired gunman."

Jess shifted uncomfortably and looked away. "Yeah, I heard that one, too."

"Pretty smart plan." Nate reared back in his chair. "Did you think it up on your own?"

"I had help. Maggie's teacher."

"Sarah Wakefield?" Nate smiled appreciatively. "That's a good-looking woman."

"She's the schoolmarm."

"How come there weren't any teachers like her when we were in school?" Nate sucked his gums. "So, are you and her…?"

"Hell, no." Jess sat forward. His quick answer didn't sound convincing, even to himself.

"Dwight Rutledge is courting her."

"That old bastard over at the feed and grain?"

Nate nodded, then pulled on his chin. "Thought I might ask her out myself."

Some deep-set, possessive urge clawed up Jess's chest. "I don't think that's a good idea."

"Why not?"

Jess didn't know exactly. He just didn't like the notion of anyone—even Nate—spending time with Sarah. "You've already got you a woman."

"Kirby." A genuine smile pulled at Nate's mouth. "She's something special, all right. But we're not serious, or anything. We're just seeing each other."

"Huh." Jess pulled on his jaw. "Well, she's a fine-looking woman. You ought to keep a hold on her."

"Kirby's ma has got wedding bells ringing in her ears."

Jess winced, but after a second the thought didn't seem so frightening. "What's wrong with that? You could do worse."

"Not interested." Nate rose from his desk. "I've got rounds to make. Want to walk along?"

Jess got to his feet. "I've got to buy some supplies, find a couple of big backsides to kiss, and get back home before Maggie gets out of school."

Nate chuckled, then grew serious. "It's a good thing you're doing, Jess, looking after Cassie's kids. If you need anything, you let me know."

The warmth of Nate's friendship seeped inside him, finding the place it had occupied when they were boys. "Thanks, Nate. I appreciate it."

He laid a hand on Jess's shoulder. "Watch yourself around Sheriff Neville. And you let me know if Jed Hayden shows up."

Jess nodded and left the jail, Jimmy following behind. When they reached the corner, Jess reached for Jimmy's hand, then groaned softly and knelt in front of him. He eyed the dark, wet circle in the front of the little boy's pants.

"Hey, cowboy, why didn't you tell me you had to go?"

Jimmy rolled his eyes, looking skyward.

"If you don't want to talk, just pull on my arm and point. Understand?" Jess cupped his little chin and turned Jimmy's face to meet his. "I won't be mad, if that's what you're thinking. I've never said one cross word to you. But I know it can't feel so good, walking around with wet pants. So tell me, okay?"

Jess rose, holding Jimmy's hand, and caught sight of Lottie Myers heading his way. Great. He'd come into town prepared to make up to as many of these old busybodies as he could, and here he stood with a kid in soggy pants.

"Morning, Mrs. Myers." Jess tipped his hat.

She dipped her gaze to Jimmy's pants as she walked by. "Good morning, Mr. Logan."

Jess almost grinned as an idea blossomed in his head. Maybe some of the women really could help him. "Mrs. Myers, could you spare a minute?"

Surprised, Lottie turned back to him. She eyed him warily. "What is it?"

"I've been having a heck of a time with Jimmy here. He keeps wetting his pants and, well, I just don't know what to do about it."

Her expression softened. "Yes, I see the problem."

"You've got children of your own, and it's plain as day what a good mama you are. What should I do?"

Right before his eyes the woman transformed from cold and aloof to warm and caring. "I know exactly what you mean, Mr. Logan."

"Call me Jess."

She smiled. "Of course, Jess. My Derrick was the same way, very difficult. But that's not unusual for boys."

"So you're saying it's nothing to worry about?"

"I wouldn't worry," she assured him. "He'll outgrow it. Just give him a little time."

"Well, thank you, ma'am." Jess tipped his hat. "You've sure taken a load off my mind."

"You're welcome." She ruffled Jimmy's hair and walked away.

As soon as she was out of earshot, Jess looked down at the boy. "I think you're smarter than Mrs. Myers gives you credit for, so you tell me when you need to go."

He took Jimmy's hand and headed out of town.

"You're having supper with us? Really, Miss Sarah? You're eating at our house?"

"No, not exactly, Maggie. I'm helping out, that's all." Sarah took the child's hand as they walked down the road away from the school. Everything she'd done so far could be construed as helping her student, something she could easily defend, if she had to. But having supper at Jess Logan's house was a different matter.

Maggie smiled up at her. "Uncle Jess will let you stay and eat with us. He likes you."

Her heart tumbled. "Why do you think that? What did he say?"

"He's got to like you." Maggie flung out both hands. "'Cause you're the nicest teacher in the whole world."

Sarah smiled. "Why, thank you, Maggie."

They circled the house to the back yard and found Jimmy climbing on the logs in the woodshed and Jess hanging out wash. Holding wooden clothespins between his lips, he waved as he fastened a wet shirt on the line. Maggie ran to him and he scooped her up.

"Can Miss Sarah eat supper with us tonight? Can she, Uncle Jess?"

He took the clothespins from his mouth and looked at Sarah coming across the yard. A comfort settled over him, having Maggie home, seeing Sarah.

"Sure, if she wants." He lowered the child to the ground.

Maggie jumped up and down. "Goody! You can eat with us!"

Jess grinned sheepishly at Sarah. "Of course, you might want to change your mind, with me doing the cooking."

"I'm only here to help."

It would have been easy to lose herself in his smile, to give in to whatever it was that kept pulling at her innards, but Sarah fought it off, remembering her purpose.

She straightened her shoulders and pointed at the drippy shirt waving in the breeze. "If you pin that at the bottom instead of at the shoulders, it will be easier to iron."

"I don't think much is going to help my ironing. See?" He reached under his vest and pulled out his shirttail, showing her the scorch mark on the fabric, then turned up his elbow and showed her another.

She glimpsed his long johns snug against his tight waist and felt her heart racing into her throat.

"And that's not even the half of it." He shoved his

shirt into his trousers again, his long fingers sliding into the waistband. "Got any ideas?"

Mesmerized, Sarah dragged her gaze up to his face again. "Yes. More than you can imagine."

His belly tightened. What was that look on her face? Was she—

"Uncle Jess? Jimmy wet his pants."

Jess plowed his fingers through his hair. "Take him inside, will you Maggie, while I finish out here? He's got clean clothes in the drawer."

"Sure, Uncle Jess."

Maggie took Jimmy's hand but he pulled away, then hit at her. She grabbed for his arm and he screamed angrily, striking out at her with his open hand.

"Hold on there. Don't hit your sister." Jess hurried to them and pulled the children apart. Jimmy stomped his feet.

Sarah joined them. "Why don't you take him inside? Maggie and I will finish the laundry."

Jess looked at Jimmy poised on the verge of an all-out tantrum, and nodded. "I guess I'd better. Come on, cowboy." He swept the boy into his arms, holding him away from his own clothing, and carried him into the house.

"Can you give me a hand with the wash?" Sarah asked.

Maggie smiled. "I know how. I used to help Mama."

Her heart quickened looking down at the golden-haired child, afraid she'd made a mistake by reminding her of her mother.

"Mama's in heaven. She's an angel. That's what Reverend Sullivan says. She watches us all the time." Maggie turned her face to the brilliant sky and waved both hands. "Hi, Mama!"

Sarah thought her heart would break.

Maggie bounced up and down. "See me, Mama? I'm helping, just like you said."

Struggling to hold back tears, Sarah bent down and took the child into her arms. She hugged Maggie hard. "Your mama would be very proud of you."

"That's what Uncle Jess says."

Sarah pressed the child's head against her shoulder, getting more comfort than she was giving. The wondrous thing about children was their ability to adapt to new situations. Maggie seemed to be handling things better than anyone. Including Sarah, at the moment.

How could she walk away? How could she turn her back on this struggling little family, just because the townspeople might frown on her involvement?

Sarah rose and sniffed. "Well, let's get this wash done."

They worked together until all the laundry hung from the line, then carried the basket into the kitchen. Jess was there hooking up Jimmy's suspenders.

"I cleaned up today." Jess gazed around the kitchen. "Some."

It looked better than it had before, but not much. "Why don't we get started on supper? Then we'll go over a few other things."

"Okay, sure." Jess opened a drawer and passed a plain white apron to Sarah, then took one for himself.

She grinned up at him. "I liked the other one better. The pink one with the hearts and birds. It was a good color on you."

Jess snorted in distaste and tied the apron around him. "It's gone."

Maggie climbed up onto the sideboard. "It caught on fire."

"I hope you weren't wearing it at the time."

"Only for a second." Jess took down a recipe book from the shelf. "Read for us, Maggie."

Behind them, Jimmy hurled two building blocks across the room, barely missing the window.

"No throwing things in the house, cowboy," Jess said.

Jimmy drew back another block, ready to let it fly.

"Jimmy, I said—"

"I need some help with this corn, Jimmy." Sarah exchanged an ear of corn for the block in his hand and led him to the sideboard. "Come help us."

"Yeah, Jimmy. Sit by me." Maggie scooted over.

Sarah ignored the scowl on Jess's face as she helped Jimmy up beside his sister and demonstrated how to shuck corn.

They got supper on the table with a minimum of fuss and no open fires, Sarah calmly giving Jess cooking tips, suggestions on cleaning and getting the children involved. She sat down and ate with them because it seemed silly not to, despite what the town might say, if they knew.

"That was a good meal." When he finished, Jess sat back and wiped his mouth with a napkin.

Sarah smiled. "You're becoming a good cook."

"Thanks to you." Jess rose from the table and gathered the plates. "Maggie, why don't you and Jimmy play outside a while before it gets too dark."

Sarah remained quiet until the children clamored out the kitchen door. "Jimmy is still wetting his pants, I see."

Jess shook his head as he moved about the kitchen, cleaning. "Yeah, and I wish I could get him to stop."

"Does he tell you when he needs to go?"

Jess shook his head. "He's not saying anything."

Sarah worked alongside him. "Then you'll just have to take him anyway."

He paused, dirty dishes in both hands. "And how am I supposed to know when he has to go if he won't talk?"

"Use your judgement," she suggested. "Take him whenever you go."

Jess turned away, feeling heat rising in his cheeks. What was it about having kids that took away every bit of your dignity?

Sarah took the dishpan from the cupboard. "I have an idea about why he keeps doing it."

"Yeah, what's that?" At this point, he'd try anything.

"He's telling you."

Jess pumped water into the kettle. "In case you hadn't noticed, the boy hasn't spoken one word."

"He's telling you. You're just not listening."

His brows drew together. "There's nothing to listen *to*."

"Children—and people—don't always speak with words. But that doesn't mean they're not trying to tell you something."

"You want to solve this little mystery for me, or just keep teasing me?"

Sarah stacked the last of the dishes on the sideboard. "Have you noticed how he wets his pants whenever someone else is around? I think he's doing it as a way to get your attention."

"I pay attention to him."

Sarah shrugged. "Maybe you should do more for him."

Jess blew out a heavy breath. "You know, Sarah, this is a lot harder than I thought it would be. The kids, the cooking, the cleaning, the washing and ironing, trying to keep up on all the chores."

A cool breeze floated in through the open window above the sink, bringing the laughter of the children into the kitchen. Jess gazed outside and laughed softly.

"But you know what? I'm not sorry I'm here. Not sorry at all."

Sarah smiled. At the moment, she wasn't the least bit sorry she was here either.

"I'm glad," she said. "The children seem quite taken with you. I didn't know your sister, but I think this would have made her happy."

Jess nodded. "Yeah. I believe so, too."

By the time they'd done the dishes, swept, wiped down the table and the sideboard, and put everything away, Sarah had recited every bit of information on housecleaning and cooking she knew.

"And remember," she said as she took off her apron, "cold water in the biscuit dough, very hot oven."

"Cold water, hot water, cold oven, hot oven. Hell, I'm getting a headache. Let's go outside." Jess tossed his apron aside and led the way out the back door.

They sat on the back steps together as darkness closed in. Sarah scooted all the way to one side, leaving plenty of room for Jess beside her.

"Oh, one more thing before I forget. I'll write down my recipe for apple pie and give it to Maggie in school tomorrow. That way you'll have time to get the ingredients before the social next week. Just give the list to Emma at the mercantile in town. She'll get everything for you." Since she'd seen Jess instruct Maggie to read from the recipe book tonight, Sarah felt certain Jess didn't read well, if at all.

He raked both hands through his hair and dragged them down the sides of his face. "Do I *have* to bake a pie?"

"Yes. The whole town is talking about you. We want to give them something good to say, for a change."

Jess leaned back, resting his elbow on the step above him. "I'm not the only one they're talking about, you know."

Suspicion zipped down her spine. Sarah turned to look at him. "Do you mean—me?"

"I hate to be the one to tell you, but your secret is out."

Chapter Seven

Sarah stiffened. "What are they saying?"

"Things about where you came from. Wondering why a nice lady like you from a big city would want to live here in Walker." Jess nodded slowly. "Mostly talk about the reason you left St. Louis."

Sarah's stomach rolled. No, they couldn't know. They couldn't have found out. She'd told no one in St. Louis where she was going. She'd handled all the correspondence and references personally when she'd secured the job here.

She gulped down a lump of emotion and pulled together her courage. "What, exactly, have you heard?"

Jess shifted on the step. "For one thing, people are wondering about you and that Dwight Rutledge."

"Is that all?" Could she be that lucky?

Jess slid his hand over his mouth. "Now, I'm not one to spread gossip, but somebody said that back in St. Louis you'd had an illegitimate baby by a high government official."

She gasped. "That's a lie!"

He shrugged. "That's what I heard. Then, somebody else told me you'd been run out of town for flirting with everybody's husbands."

Her mouth flew open.

"And I heard you were a—lady of the evening, shall we say—looking to turn over a new leaf."

"Lies! Outrageous lies!" Sarah surged to her feet and charged into the yard.

He sprang off the porch after her. "Hold on, now."

"How could anyone in this town have the audacity to say such ridiculous things!" She paced to the edge of the house. "Complete, unmitigated falsehoods!"

Jess stopped in front of her, holding her in place. "Calm down."

"Calm down? I've never been so—"

A little grin tugged at his lips, so faint no one would recognize it if they didn't know him well, as she did. Sarah's anger vanished, to be replaced by another version of the same emotion.

"You made that up."

A full smile bloomed on his face and he did everything he could to suck it back in. And looked guilty as sin in the process.

She inched closer, chin up, eyes bulging. "You made that up! Every word of it! Didn't you."

Jess ducked his head sheepishly. "Well... All except the part about Dwight Rutledge."

"Oh!" Sarah waved her clenched fists in the air, then clapped them to her sides. She'd never been so angry in her life. Or so relieved.

The fight drained away. Despite herself, Sarah laughed.

"Maggie was right when she said you made up good stories. You certainly had me going."

Jess chuckled. "You're saying none of that is true?"

She rolled her eyes. "Of course not."

"What about Dwight Rutledge?"

A note of seriousness tinged his voice. Sarah shrugged. "Mr. Rutledge and I had supper together a couple of times. That's all."

A moment passed while she studied him in the faint light from the kitchen window. It was easy to see why he'd been a handful for anybody—at any age.

"So, why did you leave St. Louis?"

The question hit her like a cold blast of wind. She'd rehearsed some answers, knowing sooner or later someone would ask, but still, it wasn't easy.

"My husband…died."

"What happened to him?"

A ribbon of panic threaded through her. She hadn't expected any detailed questions.

Sarah cleared her throat. "I don't know, exactly."

"You don't know how your husband died?" Jess raised a brow. "Did he get sick, run over by a wagon, fall off the roof? What?"

"Howard fell ill. It was very sudden." Humiliatingly sudden.

"Were you married long?"

She wasn't sure their brief union even counted as a marriage. "Not long. Not long at all."

"So you didn't know him well?"

Sarah pulled at the collar of her blouse. "He was a friend of the family. I'd known him for years."

Jess grunted. "Must have been tough."

Sarah waved away the conversation. "It was some time ago. I'd rather not think about it. I've got to go home."

When she started to leave, Jess planted both hands on the side of the house, caging her in.

"Don't go yet. I've got something I want to show you."

Thoughts of her dear departed suddenly evaporated as Jess pressed closer. She leaned her head back. "What?"

He lowered his head, ever so slightly. "I've been doing like you said, cooking, cleaning, being friendly to the ladies in town. I even waved at Mrs. McDougal today."

"Did she wave back?"

"Hell no."

"It's good that you made the effort." The words were mere whispers forced through her suddenly tight throat. She swallowed hard.

"I've been practicing, too, like you told me."

She looked up at him, caught in his gaze like a helpless butterfly in a sticky web. "Practicing what?"

"My pucker."

The rush of blood roared in her ears. "No...."

His mouth covered her in a lazy kiss, moving slowly, languishing in the feel of her lips against his. Then he groaned and pressed deeper, plying her determinedly until she leaned back her head and parted her lips for him.

He explored her carefully, thoroughly, with a reverence that wound a knot tight in her stomach. She was lost in the spinning sensations he cast over her.

God, she tasted sweet. Hot, wet, pure. Primal urges begged to be unleashed. He wanted to push himself against her, show her what she'd done to him with only one kiss, plunder her with more than his tongue.

But Jess held back. Somehow, he held back. In the depths of his mind, the tiny portion of his brain that hadn't melted into a bubbling puddle told him that with Sarah Wakefield, he had to take it slow.

Jess broke off the kiss, easing his lips away from hers. He felt her breath, hot against his face. Sweet. He drew in a ragged gulp of air and stepped back. Cooler air swirled between them. It felt foreign.

His thumb skimmed the hair at her temple. "Well? Do I need more practice?"

His pucker was the closest thing to perfect she'd ever imagined. Sarah felt her cheeks burn, her skin tingle, her insides surge.

"I'd better go." She ducked around him and ran all the way home.

What was he doing in the schoolyard so early?

Sarah turned away and quickened her pace. She'd deliberately gotten up early this morning to safely ensconce herself in the classroom before Jess arrived with Maggie. And here he was, arriving as early as she.

Children played around her, laughing, calling to friends as they arrived. Sarah's whole body tingled from head to toe. She could feel Jess's gaze bathing the back of her, and thought about bolting into the schoolhouse. But it was his fault she looked so bad this morning. If he hadn't kissed her last night she'd have gotten some sleep and wouldn't have these bags under her eyes.

"Sarah?"

Her name spoken from his lips caused her stomach to quiver. She couldn't pretend she hadn't heard.

"Good morning." Sarah pulled her courage together and turned to face him. Only then did she realize what was different about him this morning.

He led his horse. A coat was strapped over the bulging saddlebags; a canteen hung from the pommel. Jess looked different, too. Withdrawn, aloof. None of the humor she'd seen dancing in his eyes last night showed there now.

Sarah took a step toward him. "Are you going somewhere?"

Jess knelt and hugged Maggie. "You remember what I told you, honey. I'll see you soon as I can."

Maggie planted a wet kiss on his cheek. "Bye, Uncle Jess."

Maggie skipped away to join the other little girls gathered at the foot of the stairs. Jess watched her for a long moment, then rose.

"Jimmy is over at the Sullivans' today. Fiona said she'd watch him for me. I'd appreciate it if you could get him after school and take him to your place along with Maggie."

"I don't understand."

He turned the reins over in his hands. "I'm riding over to Fairmont today. I probably won't be back by the time school's out."

"I don't think it's a good idea for you to leave the children. We agreed—"

"I've got business."

A sickly feeling crept up her spine. "The stage-coach runs to Fairmont. You can take Jimmy with you and be back in plenty of time—"

"No." Jess swung into the saddle. The stallion pranced and tossed its head. "Will you take care of my kids for me?"

His eyes looked cold beneath the brim of his black Stetson. Sarah felt the chill. "Of course."

Jess nodded and trotted his horse away from the school.

Sarah watched him go, her gaze glued to the pistol on his hip and the rifle in his scabbard.

She'd just lit the lanterns in the kitchen when she heard hooves pounding against the ground and the creak of leather outside her window. Sarah peeked out the crooked shutter. "Your uncle is home."

Both children hurried out the back door. Sarah followed, envious of Maggie and Jimmy's unabashed affection for Jess.

"Come here, you two." Jess threw an arm around

each of the children and hugged them hard against him. This time, Jimmy didn't pull away.

"We missed you, Uncle Jess."

He kissed them both on the cheek. "Have you two been minding Miss Sarah?"

"Course we have," Maggie giggled.

"Okay, then, I got something for you." Jess reached into his shirt pocket and gave them each a small bag filled with an assortment of candies. The children thanked him with a hug and turned their attention to the sweets.

Jess rose, watching them dig through their bags. He'd missed them like hell today. After spending so much time together, he'd felt empty without them. All day long he'd caught himself reaching for a hand that wasn't there, looking back to keep a protective eye on nothing.

"How was your trip?"

He looked up at Sarah standing on the porch. Damn, she was a welcome sight.

"Took longer than I thought. Sorry to be so late." He pulled off his hat and wiped his sleeve across his forehead. "Kids give you any trouble?"

"Of course not," Sarah said. She didn't mention the questioning look Fiona Sullivan had given her when she'd picked up Jimmy after school.

"Are you hungry?" Sarah asked.

Starved. But he'd asked enough of her for one day. "I'd better get the kids home. It's getting late."

She gestured toward the kitchen. "I saved some supper for you. Roast with potatoes."

His stomach growled, making the decision for him. "Just let me wash up."

Inside, Sarah took out the plate of food she'd left warming in the oven, poured a steaming cup of coffee and placed them on her rickety little table. When she stepped outside again to let him know his meal was ready, Sarah froze in her tracks.

Jess stood at the rain barrel scooping handfuls of water onto his face and neck. His shirt was off, the sleeves of his long johns dangling.

Breath caught in Sarah's throat. Hard muscles rippled up his arms and flexed across the wide expanse of his back. He turned away from the rain barrel, scrubbing water over his face. Dark, crispy hair curled across his chest and arrowed straight down the center of his belly, disappearing into his trousers. His tight, washboard muscles tensed as water trickled down.

A tiny mewl escaped from Sarah's lips and she rushed back into the kitchen.

When he stepped inside a few minutes later, Sarah kept her back to him, busying herself at the stove. She'd blush to high heaven if she looked at him—she knew she would.

"Smells good."

She heard the chair squeak and chanced a look across the room at him, oddly disappointed to see him fully dressed now.

What was the matter with her? The sight of her own husband hadn't affected her this way, not that she'd gotten a good look at him, that is.

Sarah poured herself a cup of coffee and sat down across from him. "How was Fairmont?"

"Pretty quiet," he said around a mouth full of food. He jabbed his fork at his plate. "This is good."

He ate as if he hadn't had a bite all day and it pleased her to see him eat. "Did you do anything special while you were there?"

His chewing slowed. If special meant standing in front of a whorehouse for half an hour and not going inside, then yes, he'd done that.

"Like I said, it was pretty quiet." Jess took another bite.

"It's a long trip. You must be anxious to get into bed."

Their gazes collided across the table. Both their cheeks flushed. Sarah grabbed for her coffee cup. Jess shoved a potato into his mouth.

A long, awkward silence crept by until Sarah couldn't stand it any longer.

"Why did you go to Fairmont today?" She'd spent the whole day imagining every possible reason, but kept ending up with the town gossip echoing in her thoughts: Jess completing his mission as a hired assassin.

He looked up at her. "Just business."

"What sort of business?"

"You got something on your mind?"

Sarah stirred in her chair. "I know how hard you're trying to improve your reputation in Walker. Disappearing for a day only makes people speculate about what you're doing, especially after you got that package from New York City.''

Jess grunted and kept eating.

"And, of course, there's that incident in Kingston.''

He pushed his plate away and leveled his gaze at her. "You want to know about Kingston?''

"No, I—'' Sarah cleared her throat. "I heard.''

"Did you hear the story everybody gossips about? Or the truth?''

Her gaze came up quickly to meet his. "I heard you'd shot a lawman and gone to prison.''

"That's right.'' Jess sat back in the chair. "And I'd do it again, too.''

The edge on his voice gave Sarah a chill. She thought she knew Jess Logan, but now...

"I came across the sheriff forcing himself on a young girl. Forcing himself. Do you know what that means?''

Sarah felt the color drain from her face. "Yes.''

"I told him to quit. He wouldn't. He pulled his gun on me. I shot him. Simple as that.''

"But—he was wrong. He shouldn't have been—'' Sarah touched her hand to her throat. "Weren't there any witnesses?''

"The deputy sheriff witnessed the whole thing. Problem was, he was there waiting his turn.''

Sarah's stomach pitched. "What about the girl? Didn't she testify for you?''

Jess shrugged. "I didn't know who she was. She didn't come forward at the trial, but who can blame her? It's not the kind of thing a woman would want the whole town knowing about.''

"You did this—all of this—for a girl you didn't even know?''

His expression hardened. "I had a mama. I had three sisters. I wasn't going to stand by and let that happen to any woman, sheriff or not. All I can say is, too bad the bastard didn't die.''

A long moment dragged by while Sarah took it all in. "He was certainly no Leyton Lawrence, was he?''

Jess jumped, startled by the name.

"You know, the Legendary Lawman in those popular dime novels.''

"Yeah, I know who he is.'' Jess pulled on his neck. "Just my luck the bastard I shot was related to Sheriff Neville.''

"So that's why he's being so hard on you.''

"Yep.'' Jess got to his feet. "I'd better get the kids home.''

Sarah rose and laid a hand on his arm. "It was a brave thing you did, helping that girl. You're a good man.''

An ache, deep and painful, bore down on his chest. Nobody had ever said that to him. And hearing it from Sarah's lips made the words sweeter. The light touch of her hand on his arm, the look of sincerity on her face swirled inside him, warming him.

Suddenly uncomfortable, he moved away. "I'll help you clean up.''

They fell into the routine they'd practiced a few times before, then went outside, leaving the kitchen spotless. From the back yard, Jess glimpsed the interior of the kitchen through the broken shutter and recalled with clarity the time he'd seen Sarah in her delicate, lacy underthings.

The memory sent a fresh surge of desire through him, melding with his already tender feelings for her. He'd fought it all day, but the long ride with nothing to do but think had left him little choice. He'd never had one single kiss affect him so. But last night, Sarah's lips on his had burned straight through to his brain and left a mark there that wouldn't disappear. Hell, he couldn't even go to the whorehouse in Fairmont today for thinking about her. And he needed—*needed*—to go.

"Well, thanks for keeping the kids."

"They were no trouble." Sarah hovered by the steps, cautious of venturing too far into the yard as she had last night when he'd kissed her. Maybe if she stayed close to the light from the kitchen window, he wouldn't be tempted to do the same again.

Jess walked closer. "Did Jimmy wet his pants?"

"No, he didn't." Sarah backed up into the porch railing. She'd seen that look in his eye last night. She knew where it would lead. And she absolutely could not allow Jess to kiss her again.

"I guess you were right. He's only doing it for attention." Jess braced one arm on the railing. "You know a lot about kids, for somebody who doesn't have any of your own."

Her breath came in short puffs. Heat rolled off him

as he leaned closer, seeping into her pores. Fighting it, then losing hopelessly, she looked up at him.

"Students," she whispered. "My students—"

His mouth settled over hers, closing off her words and robbing her of thought. Warm and delicious, his lips moved over hers, and for a long moment she was hopelessly lost.

Then reality struck with the vision of the school board condemning her, running her out of town for associating with Jess Logan.

Sarah pulled her mouth from his, but he followed, plying her persistently. She pressed her palms to his chest, intending to push him away, but the feel of his hard muscles tantalized her fingers, burned them until she ached to explore him further.

He moaned and shifted closer, looping his arms around her, teasing the tips of her breasts with his chest. Sarah squealed and pulled away, wrenching her lips from his, turning her head.

"No...you musn't."

Suddenly she looked like a frightened doe, not the warm supple woman who had heated his blood so easily only a second ago. What had happened?

"Sarah, I—"

"Please leave." She whirled away, clinging to the porch railing.

"If I hurt you..."

"You didn't."

Then what the hell was wrong with her?

"You should go." She chanced a glance over her shoulder. "Please."

"All right." He'd go, but he sure as hell wasn't happy about it.

From the shadows of the house, Sarah watched Jess swing both children into the saddle and lead the horse toward home. Her heart ached at the sight. But what else could she do?

Glumly, Sarah went up the steps and into the house. And with all the feelings and emotions churning inside—the lovely time with the children today, Jess at her supper table, the thrill and fear of his kiss—she didn't realize until she'd settled into her bed that Jess had never really told her the reason for his business in Fairmont today.

Chapter Eight

What in the world?

Sarah pushed the quilt back and sat up in bed, squinting her eyes against the morning sun that slanted across her room. What was all that racket?

Slipping from bed, she pulled on her wrapper and went to the parlor. Peering out the window, she saw Maggie and Jimmy in her front yard and heard a commotion on her porch. She pulled open the door.

"Jess?"

He stood in the yard amid an array of hammers, saws, nails and other tools she didn't recognize, supervising the unloading of wood from the Walker Lumber Company wagon.

"Morning." Jess walked to the edge of the porch and touched his finger to the brim of his hat.

The morning air was crisp and cool, the sun brilliant. Sarah crossed her hands over her wrapper and leaned farther out the door. "What's going on?"

He gestured to the supplies behind him. "Your house needed some sprucing up."

"The school board did this?"

"No." He shrugged. "I'm taking care of it."

"You?" Forgetting herself, Sarah stepped into the doorway. "But why? I mean, I don't understand."

Unable to stop himself, his gaze swept her fully, taking in her hair swinging around her shoulders, her pink wrapper and her tiny bare feet. His belly clenched.

"It needed doing, so I'm doing it."

She waved her arms at the materials mounting up in her yard. "But, Jess, all this money. I can't accept this. It's too much."

His expression darkened. "You're helping me keep my kids, Sarah. What kind of price can you put on that?"

The intensity of his words startled her, and brought reality back. She stepped behind the door, shielding herself from view.

"I don't know what to say, except, how about some coffee?"

Jess grinned. "Sounds good."

Sarah dashed to the kitchen, stoked the fire and slid a few oat muffins she'd baked the day before into the oven. She put on a fresh pot of coffee. By the time she'd washed and dressed, the kitchen smelled delightful. She arranged the muffins on a tray with butter and honey, stacked cups, glasses, and a pitcher of milk, then made her way to the front porch carrying the coffeepot.

Sarah paused for a moment as the disapproving vision of the townspeople flashed in her mind. What would they say when they realized Jess was here working on her house? Surely it would be the topic of gossip in Walker, and as a result, so would she.

A little knot formed in Sarah's stomach, pushing her spine straighter. Her house desperately needed fixing and only Jess had offered to help. How could anyone find fault with that?

The lumber wagon had gone, the children were amusing themselves and Jess was in a deep conference with Luke Trenton. Sarah blinked twice just to be certain she recognized him. What was Luke doing here?

"Anybody hungry?" She pushed aside the tins of struggling flowers and placed the tray on the small table in the corner of the porch. The children hurried over, followed by Jess, pulling off his gloves.

"Good morning, Luke," Sarah called. He stayed in the yard, eyeing them. "Come have something to eat."

He didn't move.

"Get over here, boy." Jess barked at him. Luke threw him a sour look, but joined them on the porch.

"This is a nice surprise, Luke." Sarah poured milk for the children and passed them muffins. "I wasn't expecting any of this."

Luke glared at Jess.

"Luke had an urge to help out in the community." Jess slapped him on the back, a little harder than necessary. "Isn't that right?"

Luke grunted and fell forward a step. "Yes, sir."

"Well, thank you very much, Luke. I certainly

wasn't expecting such a delightful Saturday.'' She passed him a glass of milk and a muffin.

Jess helped himself to coffee. ''We'll start out here, fix up this porch, then do the roof. I'm guessing you've got a leak or two.''

''A leak or two in each room, actually.'' Sarah served him a muffin. ''I didn't realize you knew so much about building things.''

''Didn't you hear that rumor in town? The one where I built the capitol building down in Texas, single-handed?''

Sarah laughed. ''No, I guess that's one I missed.''

Jess sipped his coffee. ''Don't let us being here stop you from doing whatever it is you do on Saturdays. You just go on, pretend we're not here. I don't want to interfere with your plans.''

Saturday, the longest day of the week for her always dragged by with no one to talk to in the small, empty house, and only a few chores to fill her time. Sarah was thrilled to have the company.

''I'm glad you're here, really. Will you be here all day?'' She hoped he would be.

Jess gazed around at the porch. ''Probably take a couple of days to get everything done like I want it.''

Luke grunted, but didn't say anything.

''I'll keep an eye on the children while you work.''

Jess nodded and finished off his coffee. ''Let's get at it.''

Luke eyed him with disdain, dragged his sleeve across his mouth and followed him into the yard.

"Come along, children, let's give these men some room to work." Sarah lifted the tray.

Jimmy ran out into the yard and folded his hands over his chest in a pout.

Jess looked up at Sarah. "I think I understand what you mean by the boy talking without using words."

"I believe he's telling you he'd rather stay out here."

"Yeah, I'd say you're right. Come on, Jimmy. I've got some work for you, too." Jess fished the smallest hammer from the toolbox, gave the boy some nails and a plank of wood and let him go.

Sarah gave Jess a nod of approval and disappeared inside with Maggie.

At the lumber pile, Luke looked back at the house. "This place is a mess. You ought to just plow the whole thing under and forget about it."

"Is that how your pa fixes things?" Jess pulled on his gloves.

Luke shrugged. "I don't know. My brothers do most of the work around our place."

"That's right. You're the baby of the family."

Luke bristled. "I can do just as much work as they can."

"Yeah?" Jess tossed him a hammer. "Show me."

They set to work prying up the old, rotted boards from the front porch and steps. Luke demonstrated little carpentry skill, and even less desire to be there. He hit himself on the hand with the hammer right away.

"Yeowww!" Luke stuck his injured thumb in his mouth.

At the other end of the porch, Jess chuckled.

"It's not funny!" Luke shoved out his hand. "Look! I busted it!"

Jess ambled over and gave Luke's thumb a cursory glance. "You'll live."

Luke threw the hammer to the ground. "I hate this!"

"You want to go in the house with the women and let Jimmy and me finish this job?"

Luke glared at him, grabbed up the hammer and went back to work.

Jess watched him for a minute. "There's your problem. Do it like this."

He took the hammer and demonstrated the correct way to drive a nail. Luke grumbled and went back to work, but didn't hit his thumb again.

Inside, Sarah straightened up the kitchen with Maggie at her side, talking nonstop. The child always overflowed with words, ideas and questions. She had a very bright mind and was a delight to be around.

"Would you like to give me a hand with the wash, Maggie?" Sarah asked as she put the broom away.

"Sure." She jumped down from the table. "Uncle Jess does our wash. Like Mama used to. But Uncle Jess gets all wet. All over. And makes big puddles everywhere."

Sarah grinned. "Doing the laundry is quite a chore, especially for so many people."

Hers was a much quicker task, with only herself to do for. Maggie helped fill the tubs in the back yard, wash, rinse and hang the laundry on the line. Of course the chore took twice as long, but Sarah didn't mind. Her patience was nearly limitless; it was one of the reasons she enjoyed teaching.

Sarah breathed a heavy sigh as she stood back and looked at her week's worth of clothing waving in the breeze. "I'll bet the men are thirsty. Let's take them some water."

"Okay." Maggie skipped across the yard.

Sarah pulled up a cold bucket of water from the well and they carried it between them around the house, Maggie holding the ladle that hung by the crank. Sarah stopped abruptly at the corner, water sloshing over the sides and onto her skirt.

The steps and floor of her front porch were gone. A new support column stood at one end. Luke was on his knees hammering new boards into place. Jess braced a plank against a sawhorse, the metal teeth of the saw cutting through it.

He looked competent and strong, his face set in deep lines of concentration, his muscles flexing. An odd sensation of contentment overcame her as she watched him, and for an instant, she wished she could take back what she'd done last night and let him kiss her again. Surely, after her rebuke he'd never try again.

"We got water!" Maggie hopped across the yard, her blond braids bouncing.

Jess and Luke laid their tools aside, the noise fading into the distance, and headed for Sarah.

"You've certainly made a lot of progress." Sarah passed the ladle of cool, clear water to Jess.

He pushed his hat back on his forehead and drank it down. "We're making better time than I thought."

Sarah gazed out toward the road as she passed the ladle to Luke. "Look, here comes Megan."

He turned quickly, spilling water down the front of his shirt.

"Good morning, Mrs. Wakefield, Mr. Logan." Megan approached them slowly, but kept her distance.

"Are you feeling better today, Megan?" Sarah asked.

She pushed a stray lock of her brown hair behind her ear. "Yes, ma'am. Can I talk to Luke for a minute?"

He didn't wait for permission, just gulped down the water, dropped the ladle in the bucket and hurried to her side. They walked toward the road.

"Megan missed school yesterday and the day before," Sarah said. "And three days last week. She must have been very sick. She got a certificate the last two school terms for perfect attendance."

"Was Luke absent those days, too?"

She looked up at him. "No. Why?"

Jess dipped his handkerchief in the bucket and wiped it across his forehead. "Those two seem pretty taken with each other."

"I don't think so."

But the actions of the two young people did little to confirm Sarah's opinion. They stood close together, Luke's head bent slightly to listen to Megan. She spoke quickly; she looked upset.

"Maybe I should talk to her," Sarah said.

Jess took another drink of water. "Having Sheriff Neville for a father is her only problem. Nothing you can do about that."

"You're probably right. He's very protective of her, I understand."

"Good. He ought to be."

Sarah raised her brows. "You're agreeing with Sheriff Neville?"

"I was that boy's age once. I know exactly what's on his mind." Not that he was any different now. Only now, he could control it better. Usually. Jess glanced at Sarah. Yeah, he knew exactly what Luke was thinking, all right.

"Well, I still say you're wrong. Luke and Megan are just friends." Sarah moved the bucket to the shade of the porch. "Hungry? I'm fixing chicken."

"Sounds good." He watched her hips sway as she headed around the house.

With Luke still talking to Megan, Jess ambled around to the back yard. He wanted to see what repairs needed to be made here, but instead got an eyeful of ruffled, lacy, white things hanging on the clothesline.

Jess groaned and rubbed his eyes. He should turn away. It wasn't proper to ogle a woman's underthings. Especially the schoolmarm's underthings.

He looked anyway. Pantalettes with pink ruffles. A chemise with yellow bows. Were these the delicate things she'd worn the afternoon he'd glimpsed her through the broken shutter?

Jess's heart slammed in his chest sending tremors reverberating lower and lower until they blossomed against his fly. Damn, how did this woman have such an effect on him? And it was only her underclothes, for God's sake.

What the hell was happening to him?

Near sundown, Jess started packing up the tools. Luke had been quiet all afternoon, speaking only when spoken to. Jess wondered if he was still annoyed over having to do the work, or if it was something more.

"You can go home now," Jess told him when everything was put away.

Instead of bolting across the yard as he had expected, Luke lingered for a minute looking over the work they'd done. "There's still a lot to do. I guess you'll make me come back on Monday."

"No, you're free to go. You put in your time." Jess pulled off his gloves. "You fooled me though, Luke. You're a hard worker and a quick learner. A good man to have on the job."

A hint of a smile tugged at Luke's lips. "Yeah?"

"Yep. Anytime you feel like coming by, you're welcome." Jess glanced at the house. "I can sure use the help."

Luke shrugged noncommittally. "Well, good night."

He watched Luke head toward town, knowing full well where he'd be come Monday afternoon.

This is probably what they would all look like at the second coming, Jess decided, as he took in the faces staring up at him from the church pews, eyes bulging, mouths sagging, heads turning to whisper.

Drawing in a deep breath, he took Maggie and Jimmy by the hand and led them down the aisle looking for a empty seat, hoping for a friendly face.

Nate Tompkins was there, but he sat with Kirby on the front pew. A little too close to suit Jess. Rory Garrette waved then ducked his head when Alma threw him a hot glare. Mrs. McDougal peeked at him from across the room, but didn't speak.

"Can we sit with Miss Sarah?" Maggie asked.

"Sure." This was Sarah's big idea, anyway.

The three of them piled into the pew beside her.

"You made it," she whispered. "I was beginning to worry."

"Had a little problem this morning," Jess whispered over top of the children's heads.

Sarah leaned closer. "Nothing caught fire, I hope."

"No." Jess jerked his chin toward Reverend Sullivan, who was taking the pulpit. "I figure I'm due for some fire and brimstone here, though."

"He's not bad."

"The kind of preacher that makes you glad twice?" Jess grinned. "Glad when he stands up, and glad when he sits down?"

Sarah pressed her fingers to her lips to keep from laughing aloud. "Watch yourself. The Lord's listening."

Along with everyone in the pews around them. Jess could feel their nosy gazes all over him and the children. Well, let them look. He'd been up late last night getting the children their baths, ironing their clothes, reminding them to use their proper manners this morning. He'd done the best he could. And the kids looked pretty darned good, too.

Reverend Sullivan delivered his sermon without making Jess squirm too much in his seat, but Jimmy was another matter. Jess took a small pad of paper and a pencil nub from his shirt pocket and let him draw. Sarah whispered to Maggie, keeping her from fidgeting too much. When Deacon Foley sent the collection plate down their aisle Jess dropped in a double eagle, hoping everyone would gossip about his twenty-dollar offering instead of the scorch marks he'd ironed into the leg of Jimmy's pants.

Miss Marshall pounded the keyboard, closing the service with "Onward, Christian Soldiers." Jess knew the woman had been at least a hundred when he'd left Walker and here she was, still playing. But her notes still rang true despite her age. It gave him an odd feeling being in church again. He thought of Cassie and how they used to whisper to each other through the services, being brother and sister until one of the Newton sisters silenced him with a whack across the back of his head.

At the door, Reverend Sullivan spoke to each member of the congregation as they departed.

"Glad you could join us." He shook Jess's hand as he passed by.

"I plan to bring the children over for Bible study this week."

At her husband's side, Fiona's eyes brightened. "Please do. Thursday night, right after supper."

"Yes ma'am. Thank you." Jess herded Maggie and Jimmy outside.

In the churchyard the congregation clustered together in groups, the men talking about business, weather, the crops, the women discussing children, recipes and homemaking. Maggie and Jimmy raced off to join their friends, leaving Jess alone and more than a little uncomfortable. Where the hell was Sarah? This was all her idea.

Nate Tompkins suddenly appeared at his side. "Good to see you, Jess. How's things going?"

Relieved to see his old friend, Jess smiled. "Doing all right."

Rory Garrette hobbled over on his cane. "Heard the bank over in Fairmont got robbed a few days ago."

Nate nodded. "I was pretty surprised to hear it myself. Fairmont is a quiet town."

"You reckon it was the Toliver gang? They headed this way next?"

"It wasn't the Tolivers," Nate said.

"How about that Gibb boy? You know, Zack's brother."

"Don't think so."

Rory squinted up at him. "Then who was it?"

"The sheriff over in Fairmont didn't know. Nobody recognized the robber." Nate gave him a confident nod. "Me and Sheriff Neville are keeping a sharp eye out."

"Horse's ass," Rory muttered. "If something big ever happened in Walker, Buck Neville would have to read up on it in them dime novels—see what ol' Leyton Lawrence would do—before he stuck his nose out of the jailhouse.''

''Morning, Deputy.'' Dwight Rutledge eased into their circle, looking dapper in a black coat, brocade vest and string tie. ''Couldn't help overhearing what you said about the Toliver gang and I just want you to know, Nate, that if you need help you can count on me.''

''Another horse's ass,'' Rory grumbled under his breath.

''I'll pass that along to the sheriff.'' Nate nodded across the churchyard to the group of young people standing under the elms. ''Has Zack said anything about his brother Gil coming back to town?''

''Not a word.'' Dwight hung his thumbs in his vest pockets. ''That boy's done a fine job for me. Works like a dog. Only missed one day of work this past year, and that was just last week. Yes sirree, I got me the pick of the Gibb family, all right.''

Nate lowered his voice. ''You tell Zack to watch himself around Sheriff Neville. He's got no use for any of them Gibbs. He'd have run Zack out of town a long time ago if he weren't working for you.''

''It's no secret to Zack how Neville feels. One thing about the sheriff. You know where you stand with him.'' Dwight shot a look at Jess. ''Isn't that right, Logan.''

Jess's temper heated up a notch. Something about Rutledge rankled him to no end. ''I know Neville doesn't like any man who's got guts enough to stand up to him.''

Dwight's jaw tightened. "Meaning I don't?"

"Meaning—"

"Jess, come on over here a minute." Nate pushed between the two men. Jess glared at him, then shot Dwight a contemptuous look and went with Nate.

"Thought we'd get us a fight right here in the churchyard. Damn…" Rory hobbled away.

"What the hell do you think you're doing?" Nate demanded when they reached a quiet corner of the churchyard.

"That bastard—"

"That bastard isn't worth Cassie's kids. Is he?"

Jess glared at him, then exhaled slowly. "You're right."

"I know I'm right." Nate slapped him on the back. "You've got to stick to that plan you and Sarah came up with. Sheriff Neville is eyeing you like a hawk."

"All right. I'll watch it." Jess nodded slowly. "And Nate? Thanks."

Nate grinned. "I'm watching you like a hawk, too, old friend."

At the corner of the church, Sarah held her breath as she saw the group of men break up. Whatever had been said to Jess had made him plenty mad. She hoped no one else recognized the jut of his jaw, the stiffening of his spine, the shrug of his shoulders and knew what they meant, as she did. Thank goodness Nate had intervened.

Alma Garrette sidled up beside Sarah. She looked down her long nose. "I couldn't help notice who you chose to sit with in services this morning."

A knot wound tight in Sarah's stomach. "Maggie is one of my students. That's all."

Alma's brows rose nearly to her hairline and her lips drew into a tight pucker. "Oh. I see."

Sarah forced herself not to look across the churchyard at Jess. She knew this was a difficult day for him and wanted to go to him. But she dared not. At least, though, Alma was speaking to her, her debacle at Jess's trial put aside temporarily. Sarah dared not speculate how long that would last.

Lottie Myers joined them, pushing between Sarah and Alma. "I changed my mind. I'm making cherry pie for the social."

Alma nodded. "It's good you're having the social, Sarah. The school needs it. The whole town needs it. Cassie never did anything like that. She couldn't, with no husband around to help."

Lottie leaned closer. "To tell you the truth, I never liked that husband of hers."

"Jed Hayden always struck me as shifty." Alma nodded wisely. "Couldn't hold a job. Why, if he hadn't made Cassie sell off her parents' property, I don't know how they would have made ends meet. She didn't want to sell it, though she couldn't bear to do anything with the land, after the fire and all."

"Seemed mighty suspicious to me that after that money was gone, Jed Hayden was, too," Lottie said.

"And Cassie was left with those two children, living in that tumbledown little house, and no money. I'd say she was well rid of him." Alma gazed across the churchyard. "And now that Jess Logan shows up taking everything Cassie worked so hard for. Seems mighty suspicious, if you ask me. He's not shown his face in Walker in years, and when that nice house of Cassie's is vacant, here he comes.''

''I wonder where he gets his money.'' Lottie pressed her lips together. ''He doesn't have a job, and there's not enough land to farm. How does he live?''

''Did you hear the bank over in Fairmont was robbed?''

Dwight joined their circle, positioning himself at Sarah's elbow.

''Fairmont?'' Lottie's eyebrows rose. ''It's such a quiet town. Cassie used to go over there from time to time. She never had a bit of problem.''

''I heard Logan had been there, too. And now the bank got robbed?'' Dwight nodded knowingly. ''Coincidence?''

Sarah's back stiffened. ''Are you making an accusation, Mr. Rutledge?''

''I keep my ear out for trouble.'' He puffed his chest out. ''A man's got to. It's his duty to look out for his woman.''

Sarah's stomach rolled.

''There you are, Sarah.'' Fiona Sullivan floated into their group, her perpetual smile glowing. ''Please, come have supper with us. I can't bear the thought of you sitting alone on this glorious afternoon.''

She couldn't bear it either, though she'd hoped for company of a different sort, all the while knowing it was unlikely. Yesterday had seemed so full, with Maggie and Jimmy at her house, Luke, Megan coming by, and of course, Jess. But he'd only been there to work on the house, in repayment of the debt he felt he owed her. She could hardly expect him to stop by today for a social call. And even if he tried, she'd have to refuse him.

"Thank you, Fiona. I'd like that."

"Good." She folded her hands together. "Mr. Rutledge is joining us, too."

"I'll walk you over. Good day, ladies." Dwight tipped his hat to Alma and Lottie and slid his arm possessively through Sarah's.

He patted her hand. "Don't you worry your pretty little head, Sarah. I'll see you safely home, too."

Grinding her teeth together, it took all her willpower not to pull away from him. Glancing back over her shoulder she saw Jess under the oaks, Maggie and Jimmy at his side. And suddenly the thought of spending the afternoon with the Sullivans seemed very lonely.

Chapter Nine

Jess brought the hammer down hard, driving the nail into the board with one stroke. He did it again, and again, pounding the planks into place on Sarah's porch with single-minded determination.

"Something wrong, Mr. Logan?"

Jess stopped and looked up at Luke. Hell, yes. Something was wrong all right. Only he wasn't exactly sure what it was.

"You look kind of mad." Luke ventured closer to the porch and waved his hand back toward the schoolhouse across the road. "I got here quick as I could. I just stopped for a minute."

Sitting back on his haunches, Jess wiped the sweat from his brow with his shirtsleeve. School had let out a little while ago and Sarah had come straight home, pausing only long enough to offer him a quick hello, then disappeared inside her house, taking both Maggie and Jimmy with her. And for the life of him, he didn't know why that bothered him.

"Nothing's wrong, I guess."

"So it's okay if I help?"

Jess snorted. "I can use the company. Grab a hammer."

Luke tossed his books aside and fished a handful of nails from the bucket by the porch. "You're sure you don't mind?"

"I'm sure." He leaned forward on his hands and knees again and drove in another nail. From the corner of his eyes, he saw that Luke hadn't moved.

He sat back again. "Something eating at you?"

"No, sir," Luke said quickly. He glanced back toward the road. "It's just that— Never mind."

Jess didn't need to look down the road to know it was Megan who held the boy's attention. "All right, then. Let's get going while we've still got light."

Luke crept onto the porch on his hands and knees. "My pa never let me help much at home, 'cause I have so many brothers."

"His loss." Jess pounded in another nail.

Luke hammered nails alongside Jess, but stopped after a minute and sat back.

"Is it all right if I ask you something?"

Jess's knees were hurting and it was a good time for a break. He rolled to the edge of the porch and sat up. "Shoot."

"It's about…" Luke frowned and sat cross-legged on the porch. "It's about…ladies."

Oh boy. Jess's first thought was to run, send the boy home to his father, or hit himself in the head with the hammer. But he stopped his racing thoughts. He'd gotten to know Luke pretty well after spending all day

Saturday with him, and knew his father had little time for him. And, somehow, it made him feel good that the boy now trusted him enough to bring up such a delicate subject.

Jess sucked in a quick breath. "Ask away."

"Well, how do they know when they've got a baby inside them?"

Jess folded his arms across his chest, relieved that at least he hadn't asked how the baby got there. "You have sisters, right? So you know about their monthly."

"Yeah…I think so."

Thank God he didn't have to explain that. Jess pulled off his hat. "All that stops when the baby is growing."

Luke nodded as understanding dawned on him. "Do they get a baby every time you…you know?"

"No. Not every time."

"Then, which times?"

Jess shrugged. "It's got something to do with their monthly. But I don't know what, exactly."

A long moment dragged by before Luke spoke again. "Can you make it stop?"

"Their monthly?"

"No. The baby."

The words were nothing more than a whisper. Luke dropped his gaze to the hammer clutched in his hand, sending a lightning bolt up Jess's spine. A long moment crept by while Luke seemed to sink farther and farther into himself.

"There's a way. Women know what to do. I don't."

Jess touched his slim shoulder. "It's a big decision, Luke."

After a long, tense silence, Luke looked up at him. "Well, thanks."

"Anything else you want to talk about?"

He worked his lips together, then shook his head. "No. Nothing."

Jess knew there was more. Luke wouldn't be looking scared and half sick right now if there weren't. And if what Jess suspected were true, he couldn't blame the boy.

"You know, Luke, carrying a problem around all by yourself makes for a heavy load," Jess said. "Spreading it out some can lighten your burden."

Luke gazed out into the yard for a moment, then looked at his lap again. He didn't say anything.

Jess's gut ached seeing Luke. It made him remember all the times growing up when he'd had no one to turn to. He tried again.

"Are you sure you don't want to tell me something?" Jess asked.

A minute passed before Luke shook his head. "No, sir. We'd better get this porch done."

Jess could do nothing more but hope Luke would come to him sometime in the future.

"If you change your mind, let me know." Jess picked up his hammer again.

Inside the house, Sarah kept up the valiant effort not to peep out the window, not to sneak a look at the front yard. She swept, dusted, worked on her teaching plan, read to the children, did everything she could think of to remain in the house.

But she was fighting a losing battle. Over and over she was drawn to the parlor, if only to hear the sound of Jess's voice talking to Luke, catch a glimpse of him hammering or sawing something. She couldn't stay away.

Now, forcing herself into the kitchen to cook, she kept herself busy talking with Maggie and Jimmy. Jess came through the back door. She tried not to look, but couldn't stop herself. He was so handsome.

"Is Luke staying for supper?"

"No. He left already." Jess hung his hat on the peg beside the door. "Maggie, why don't you and Jimmy play outside for a while."

"Okay." Maggie got up from the table, pulling her brother along with her.

Jess closed the door behind them and turned to Sarah. The room seemed to shrink, the heat from the cookstove suddenly more intense as he looked at her. Her whole body quivered.

"I need to talk to you about something," he said.

Sarah took potatoes from the cupboard and placed them on the sideboard. "Is something wrong?"

Jess stepped closer. "I think you're wrong about Luke and Megan being friends. He was just asking me about babies and…things. Seemed pretty upset."

"It's normal for young people his age to be curious."

"I think this is more than curiosity." Jess leaned his hip against the sideboard.

"I can't believe I was wrong about them." Sarah shook her head. "But anyway, do you think they're serious about each other?"

"Babies, Sarah. He was asking about babies."

"Oh, dear." Her hands stilled on the potatoes she was peeling. "Maybe I should talk to Megan."

"Do whatever you think. You know more about this sort of thing than I do. Luckily, I've got a lot more years before I have to worry about it." Jess picked up his hat again. "I've got a few things to finish up outside before it gets dark."

Sarah watched as he went out the back door again, fighting the temptation to follow. He kept himself away from her now, never venturing too close. And while she should be thankful for his restraint, somehow she missed his nearness. The scent of him, the feel of his muscles, even his lips against hers.

With a silent rebuke, Sarah turned back to the potatoes. It was thoughts like that which could cause her a mountain of trouble. She had to stop them. But it would have been so much easier to accept the distance Jess had put between them if only she could make herself stop caring about him.

"Both of you settle down. Right now."

Jess caught Maggie and Jimmy by the hand and guided them out of Walker Mercantile holding down his temper. Jimmy had been a handful all day long, dumping a sack of flour out on the kitchen floor and tracking it all over the house, refusing to eat anything Jess fixed, climbing onto the sideboard and smearing a jar of preserves all over everything. Maggie had behaved only marginally better since getting home from school, demanding to know why they couldn't go to Sarah's, complaining about the supper he planned to fix, asking question after question on everything under the sun until Jess thought he'd explode.

So, he'd brought them both to town, thinking a change of scenery would do them all good. It hadn't.

Walking along with the children, who held small bags of sweets he'd bought them at the mercantile, Jess wondered if they weren't simply reacting to his own foul mood. He hadn't been the easiest person to live with in the last couple of days, he knew that.

And he knew the reason for it, too. Sarah. She'd been on his mind day and night, smelling sweet, sashaying around with her bustle swaying, then giving him dreams that left him aching. Doing the repairs on her house every afternoon only made it worse, being that close, but not able to touch her.

She was friendly all right, kind and caring with the children, making him supper. But she kept her distance, almost like she was afraid of him.

And how could that be? He'd done nothing more than kiss her. She'd been married. She knew what it was like to have a man.

But still, he had to respect her wishes. He couldn't force himself on her. He'd promised himself he wouldn't try and kiss her again. He didn't like it and it was nearly killing him, but so far, he was managing.

Jess tightened his grip on the children's small hands as they waited for a freight wagon to pass, then crossed the street. From the corner of his eye he caught sight of Walker Feed and Grain. Dwight Rutledge was on the boardwalk talking to Zack Gibb.

Suddenly the thought that Rutledge might have kissed Sarah too curled his stomach into a knot. His bad mood would be relieved considerably if he could put his fist through that bastard's face right now.

"I'm hungry, Uncle Jess." Maggie tugged on his arm. "How come we can't eat at Miss Sarah's tonight? How come, Uncle Jess?"

"We're eating at the Blue Jay tonight."

"But what about Miss Sarah? Who's she going to eat with?"

"She is—"

Jimmy dropped his licorice on the boardwalk, picked it up and stuck it in his mouth.

"Hold on, there." Jess knelt and pulled it away from him. "It's dirty. You can't eat it if—"

Jimmy let out a scream and grabbed for the candy.

"Wait. Hang on."

Jimmy sobbed harder.

Maggie tugged on Jess's sleeve. "I want to eat at Miss Sarah's!"

"We can't tonight." Jess turned to Jimmy, shouting over his screams. "Listen, it's dirty. You can't eat it with dirt all over it."

Maggie's bottom lip crept out. "Why can't we?"

Good God, that's all he needed, both of them crying. Jess fought off the panic rising in him. People were starting to stare.

"Wait, now, both of you."

"Jess Logan! You old skunk!"

A familiar voice and shuffling feet sounded behind him. Jess looked back over his shoulder, and recognized the Vernon brothers.

Waylon Vernon slapped him on the back. "Where the hell you been hiding, you crazy bastard?"

Deke and Billy Lee, his brothers, laughed uproariously.

"Yeah, Jess," Deke said. "We've been looking all over for you."

Jess turned back to the children, waving to silence them. "Shh. Hush now, just a minute."

Jimmy sniffled. Maggie poked her bottom lip out.

Jess rose, unable to hold back a smile. He and the Vernon brothers had grown up together in Walker, and raised more than their share of trouble along the way.

"How you boys been?"

"Uncle Jess, I want to eat at Miss Sarah's!" Maggie yanked on his sleeve.

Jimmy let out a piercing scream.

"Hellfire...." He bent down. "Look, Maggie, we'll have supper with Miss Sarah tomorrow night."

Her scowl unwound marginally. "Promise?"

"I promise." He'd promise her anything right now. Jess took her paper sack and pulled out the licorice she hadn't bothered with yet. "I'll get you another. Here, Jimmy, eat this one."

Like a pump just gone dry, the boy's tears stopped as he stuck the candy in his mouth.

"You ain't changed a peg, Jess." Billy Lee chucked him on the arm.

"Neither have you boys." Tall, thin towheads, the Vernon brothers looked enough alike to be triplets.

"That's 'cause Waylon is still wearing the same shirt!" Deke elbowed his brother in the stomach and all three of them burst out laughing.

"Deke went and got himself hitched." Waylon shook his head. "That Mabel Ann is one hard woman."

Deke's eyes widened. "Saturday night me and the boys went over to the Green Garter and I got drunk on my ass. And Mabel Ann was madder than a beaver with a toothache when I got home."

"Chased him all the way to Ma's," Billy Lee added.

Waylon rolled his eyes. "And that woman can run."

All three brothers broke out laughing again. Jess couldn't help joining in.

"Your ma doing all right?" Jess asked.

"I reckon." Billy Lee shrugged. "Me and Waylon still live there. Winters are hard, but she's all right."

Jess remembered their ma. She'd let him sleep off a hangover in her barn many times.

Waylon poked his brother in the ribs. "Deke here is the only one who got hitched. That free stuff ain't what it's cracked up to be."

Billy Lee looked down at the children. "Them Cassie's kids? Heard you'd taken them in."

Jess nodded. "I didn't want them living with strangers."

Deke hung his thumbs in his suspenders. "Sure do

miss their pa. Yes sir, that Jed Hayden was one drinking fool.''

"Come on, Jess.'' Waylon nodded across the street. "We're heading over to the Green Garter. Come on and go with us.''

"Damn good idea." Billy Lee grasped Jess's arm and leaned closer. "We're going over to Miss Flora's, too. You remember Miss Flora?''

Jess's pulse quickened. How could he forget Miss Flora's parlor house?

"Got a new girl in from San Francisco.'' Billy Lee slapped his brother's arm. "She put a real hurtin' on Waylon here.''

The brothers laughed again and Waylon nodded anxiously.

Blood surged through Jess's heated veins. Damn, he wanted to go—needed to go.

Jess glanced down at the children, indecision gnawing at his gut. "I've got the kids here.''

"Hell, take them over to Ma's,'' Billy Lee said.

"Yeah,'' Waylon agreed. "Ma will watch them.''

"I don't know....'' Jess pulled on his jaw.

"Come on, Jess, it'll be like old times.''

He looked at his old friends, then at the saloon across the street. "Well...''

A tiny hand pulled on his sleeve.

"Uncle Jess? Jimmy wet his pants.''

Jess gazed down at Jimmy, sticky fingers, a red ring around his mouth and a wet circle on his trousers. For a long moment he just looked at the child, then scrubbed his hands over his face and drew in a big breath.

"I can't."

"Well, okay. Let's go, boys."

The Vernon brothers waved as they crossed the street toward the Green Garter Saloon. Jess watched until they disappeared inside. And stood there for a few moments longer.

"What was Jimmy's bad dream about?"

The afternoon breeze swirled around the hem of Sarah's skirt as she walked Maggie home, listening to the story she was telling.

"I don't know." Maggie pursed her lips. "But Uncle Jess came in and made him feel better. Then Jimmy wet the bed."

"Was your uncle upset?"

"No." Maggie shook her head, sending her braids swaying. "Uncle Jess never gets upset."

Oddly enough, Jess seemed to have the patience of a nun with the children. Sarah had never seen him lose his temper.

At the house they went in through the back door. Delicious cooking aromas filled the air, but it was strangely quiet.

"I wonder if your uncle forgot that I was coming this afternoon?" Sarah crept across the kitchen.

"Uh-uh. He said we could have supper with you tonight before Jimmy and me go to Bible study." Maggie laid her speller on the kitchen table and pointed. "There's Uncle Jess."

In the rocker in the corner sat Jess, his head resting on the back of the chair. Jimmy was on his lap, curled against his shoulder. Both were sound asleep.

A feeling of calmness and contentment came over Sarah, watching them sleep so peacefully. Jimmy looked enviably comfortable snuggled on Jess's wide chest, secure beneath his sturdy arm. For a moment she imagined how it would feel to be in Jimmy's place, safe, secure and loved.

Jess looked just as comfortable, his features relaxed in sleep, his chest rising and falling rhythmically, his eyes closed behind a pair of gold-rimmed spectacles Sarah had never seen before. The vision of Jess wearing those spectacles—and nothing else—sped through her mind like a runaway freight train. Sarah shuddered.

Suddenly feeling guilty for ogling him in his sleep, Sarah decided to wake him. Strange feelings twined inside her as she imagined touching her hand to his shoulder, giving him a little shake, maybe sliding it farther across his chest.

Jess came awake with a start. Sarah jumped back.

He sat up, grabbing the book balanced on his knee just before it slipped onto the floor, and tightening his grip on Jimmy.

"Hi, Uncle Jess." Maggie skipped over and kissed his cheek. She picked up the book. "Which one is this?"

Jess hugged her, then shook his head to get his bearings and caught sight of Sarah. He surged to his feet, holding Jimmy against him.

Sarah felt her cheeks burn. Could he sense what she'd been thinking? "I didn't mean to startle you, I just—"

"It's okay." What a sight to wake to. Jess's chest tightened.

"Maggie told me Jimmy kept you up last night."

Jimmy began to squirm. Jess lowered him to the floor, then stretched, raising his arms upward, rising on his toes, muscles flexing. He scrubbed his hands over his face. "Yeah, he—"

Jess froze as his fingers touched his spectacles. Embarrassed, he pulled them off and tossed them aside. "I, ah, I only need them for reading."

A silly giggle bubbled up in Sarah, bringing a scowl to Jess's face. "I'm not laughing at you—at myself, really. I thought you couldn't read."

"What?" One brow crept upward. "You thought I couldn't read? Did you hear that in town, too?"

"You always have Maggie read recipes, and I know your childhood wasn't the best." She gave him a weak, apologetic smile.

"Uncle Jess reads real good. And he writes all the time." Maggie spread her arms wide. "He can write a hundred, jillion pages."

"Maggie, that's enough."

"They can go all over the whole, whole country."

Jess caught Maggie's shoulders and herded her across the room. "Put your books away. It's time for supper."

"Did you get all the supplies we need?" Sarah's gaze roamed the kitchen.

"Yeah, I got them," he grumbled.

"Complain all you want, but you're baking a pie for the social on Saturday." Sarah grinned at him. "Don't make me get my ruler after you."

They laughed together, then set about making supper. The chicken Jess had put in the oven earlier was nearly roasted. Sarah made cornbread and boiled potatoes while Jess supervised the children setting the table. Maggie and Jimmy ate quickly, anxious to get over to the church for Bible study, but Jess made them sit quietly at the table until everyone was finished.

"Why don't you take them on over? I'll finish up here." Sarah rose and began gathering plates.

He carried the platter and empty bowls to the sideboard. "Okay. I'll be right back. Come on, kids, let's go."

Maggie cheered and hurried out the door ahead of Jess and her brother.

Alone in the kitchen, Sarah recalled the first day she'd visited here and how she'd envied Jess for having such a nice home. Now, the allure of the house went well beyond the comfortable rooms and the sturdy roof. Maggie and Jimmy were wonderful children and her heart ached with the want of babies of her own.

And that made her think of Jess. Strong, solid Jess. So different from Howard. Could marriage to Jess be as different?

Sarah shook her head and scrubbed harder on the sideboard. What was she thinking? She should count her blessings that she had a good job in a town that—

so far—had accepted her. As discreet as she was about coming to Jess's house, there was always a chance someone would see her. But even with that possibility looming over her, Sarah couldn't bear to abandon Jess and the children.

A few minutes later, Jess bounded into the kitchen, rubbing his hands together and grinning.

"Okay, Mrs. Wakefield, teach me how to bake a pie."

Worries of what the town might think of her dissolved at the sight of him.

"Where's the recipe I gave you?"

"Right here." Jess pulled the slip of paper from a dog-eared recipe book, washed his hands and tied on an apron. "What kind are we making?"

"Apple."

"Is that the kind with the lid on it?"

It took her a moment to decipher his description. "Yes. It's called a double crust."

"I like that kind. Where do we start?"

"Get out your breadboard."

"My what?"

"Your breadboard. You have one here somewhere."

"I do?"

Sarah grinned. "All good cooks have a breadboard."

"Well, that's me, all right." Jess started looking through the cupboards. "I guess it looks like a board, huh?"

"Here it is." Sarah located it and laid it on the

sideboard. "Never scrub your breadboard. Just wipe it down when you're finished. That way it will stay seasoned."

"Good. Something I don't have to wash."

"Let's get down to business. We'll start with the crust."

Jess stood behind her, looking over her shoulder as she mixed the flour, salt and water, and cut in the shortening. He'd like to get down to business, all right. But what he had in mind had nothing to do with baking, though it did involve heat. A lot of heat.

He eased closer, watching her hands work the dough, but heard little of her instructions, only the roar of blood rushing through his veins. She smelled so sweet. And even if she was the schoolmarm, she was the prettiest woman he'd ever known. Thinking about her, dreaming about her had nearly made him crazy with want.

Without warning, Sarah backed up a bit. Not much, but since he was standing so close her hip grazed his. Wildfire raced across him, tingling and burning. Though he should have known better, Jess still didn't move away. Somehow, he just couldn't make himself do it.

Sarah did, though, only a step, then turned suddenly as he followed. Her forearm slid across his belt buckle, branding him, causing his simmering desire for her to boil over. Jess shifted. Thank God he had on the apron.

"All right, now. You do the rest," she said.

Jess eyed the dough. He didn't want to stick his

fingers in that mess. He wanted to put them on her. "Can't we make a cake instead?"

"A cake?" Sarah shrugged. "It's pretty hard."

If she only knew. Jess pulled in a deep breath, fighting for control. "A pie is too much work. I'd rather make a cake."

"Do you think you could get it to rise?"

The breath went out of him, weakening his knees. "What?"

"The cake."

"Oh, the cake." Jess rubbed his forehead, want and need consuming him. "That won't be a problem."

"Are you sure?"

His chest swelled. "Positive."

"You have to get the oven very hot."

"I'm known for the amount of heat I can create."

Her big brown eyes fluttered at him innocently. "Really?"

"Really." And he wanted to show her right here, right now. If only she'd let him.

Sarah pursed her lips. Were they still talking about baking? Wary of the deep lines of emotion etched in Jess's face, she turned back to the sideboard.

"I think we'd better stick to the pie."

Jess made himself back up a step. "Yeah, maybe we should."

It was a hellish experience, though. He couldn't take his eyes off her, watching her every movement as she rolled the dough, trimmed the crust, his imagination making his condition worse. It helped a little that she put him to work peeling, slicing and coring the apples.

And he thought he'd actually make it through the whole ordeal until Sarah bent over to put the pie in the oven, just as he stepped forward to help her.

Her round bottom settled against his midsection, nestling him in her soft curves. They both froze. For a stunned second they hung there. Raw desire surged through Jess unchecked. Blood pounded in his veins. He curled his hands into fists, fighting off the overwhelming need to have her, right there on the sideboard. He'd sure as hell have to scrub the breadboard after that.

She moved away, trying to keep her back to him, but Jess saw that her cheeks were pink. She'd felt, even with all those skirts and petticoats. She knew. He thought about apologizing, but figured anything he said would only make her more embarrassed.

"Keep a close watch on the pie. Take it out when it's golden brown." Sarah waved her hand toward the oven. "It needs to cool."

That was for damn sure. Jess shifted uncomfortably. "Thanks."

Sarah hurried toward the door. "Good night."

At the window, Jess watched her cross the small meadow to her little house, then paced fitfully, trying to get her off his mind. At least he wanted to get himself under control. But by the time he'd taken the pie from the oven and gone to get the children at Bible study, neither had happened.

Walking back from the church, Jess couldn't stand it another second. He needed a woman. Now.

"What's wrong, Uncle Jess? Are you mad?" Maggie looked up at him.

About to go mad, but that was all. "No, honey, I'm not mad. But, look, I've got to go into town for a little bit tonight."

Maggie bounced on her toes. "Can Jimmy and I come, too?"

"No, you're staying with—"

Who? He surely couldn't ask the Sullivans to keep them without the whole town finding out about it. There was always the Vernon brothers' ma, but that idea didn't sit well with him.

Jess's gaze settled on the little house across the road with the new porch and the sturdy new roof. Sarah. She'd caused this. She was the reason for his condition. She could watch his children while he did something to alleviate the problem.

A single lantern burned in the kitchen window as Jess and the children rounded the house. The back door opened as Jess reached the bottom step. Sarah walked outside, tucking a stray lock of hair behind her ear.

"Is something wrong?" Her expression was guarded.

"No." Jess held tight to both the children's hands. He gulped in a big breath. "I was wondering if you'd mind watching the kids for a little while?"

She looked him up and down, and that made his condition worse.

"Of course I'll keep them."

Thank God. He'd have ended up sitting in the creek all night if she'd said no.

"I have tomorrow's lesson to plan. When will you be back?"

Jess did a quick calculation. Fifteen minutes to Miss Flora's, fifteen back.

"Thirty-two minutes."

"Fine. Come along, children."

As if the weight of the world had been lifted, Jess dropped a quick kiss on both the children's cheeks. "Be good, now. I won't be gone long."

"Where will you be?"

The question caused his blood to gel in his veins. He looked up at Sarah. "Huh?"

"In case one of the children has an emergency. Where will you be?"

Oh, God. How could he stand here and tell the sweet, refined schoolmarm that he was going to go to the whorehouse and rut with some woman whose face he didn't intend to look at because *she* had made him so randy he could hardly walk upright?

A long, horrid moment dragged by while Jess racked his brain. He could tell her. He could explain it. She'd been married. She knew about such things.

Then she batted her long lashes at him, looking as innocent as a virgin bride. Jess's heart sank.

"Never mind." He turned away.

"Wait, Jess—"

He couldn't answer her, couldn't even bring himself to look at her. God knows what he might do if he got within arm's length of her.

He took both the children's hands and stalked home.

Chapter Ten

How was he going to get through the day looking at all these pies, and not think about Sarah bending over to use his oven?

Jess drew in a heavy breath as he placed his apple pie on the table with the others, forcing himself to stay under control. Many more nights sitting in the creek and he'd have pneumonia for sure.

Around him folks nodded politely as Maggie and Jimmy raced off to play with their friends in the schoolyard. Most everybody in town was there already. He'd wanted to arrive early to keep everyone from staring at him when he walked up, but getting the children dressed and ready had taken longer than he'd anticipated. He'd have to remember to add at least fifteen minutes per child to his schedule from now on.

Jess looked around just as Sarah came down the steps of the schoolhouse carrying a coffeepot. Lordy, she looked pretty today. Usually she wore a dark skirt and simple white blouse, but today she was done up in a pink dress that made her sparkle in the bright afternoon sunlight. Jess started toward her, but stopped when Dwight Rutledge came down the steps after her balancing a tray of coffee cups.

"Good afternoon, Mr. Logan." Sarah favored him with a smile as she approached.

He touched the brim of his hat, pleased she hadn't waited for Dwight to catch up with her.

She placed the coffeepot on the table with the pies and smiled up at him. "Looks like we're having quite a turnout today."

The table was already crowded and more people were arriving every minute. Jess sidled up next to her. "I guess there'll be lots of backsides here today I can kiss."

"Kiss, and kiss often." Sarah rearranged the pies on the table. "I know you're nervous. Try to relax and have a good time."

"You mean, be myself?"

She grinned. "I don't think the town's ready for that quite yet."

Despite himself, Jess laughed with her.

"Everybody will be watching you today. This is your chance to shine."

Jess grinned. "Will I get a gold star?"

"If you're good."

Dwight elbowed his way between them, setting the tray of white cups on the table. He gave Jess a side-long glare and touched Sarah's elbow. "I'll help you with the rest of the things."

Sarah moved away. "Thank you."

A look of smug satisfaction settled over Dwight's face as he followed Sarah back to the schoolhouse.

He could end it all right here, Jess decided. Bust Rutledge square in the face, pack up the kids and move somewhere else. As much as his fist itched to do just that, Jess turned away, determined not to let Rutledge get to him today.

"Why, Mr. Logan, I'm so pleased you're here." Fiona Sullivan placed her pie on the table and smiled up at him.

"Afternoon, ma'am." He drew in a deep whiff. "Everything sure smells good."

She looked over the table. "Looks like we've got a little of everything."

Jess grinned sheepishly. "I brought apple pie. Hope it turned out all right."

Fiona's mouth fell open. "You baked? Why, how nice."

"I had help." He wanted to give Sarah credit for what she'd done, but didn't think it wise.

Fiona looked pleased. "It's wonderful that you baked a pie, just to support this occasion at Maggie's school. Lottie? Lottie, come over here."

Lottie joined them, her husband heading toward the crowd of men gathered under the oaks, her two children scurrying toward the other children.

"Mr. Logan baked a pie."

Lottie's eyebrows shot up. "Really?"

"To tell you the truth, I don't know how you ladies do so much." Jess shook his head slowly. "All that baking and cooking and cleaning is hard work. I can't seem to get it all done. I'd sure appreciate whatever advice you ladies could offer.''

''Well, certainly.'' Fiona smiled broadly. ''Let's go sit down.''

They settled at a nearby table, Jess surrounded by Fiona and Lottie, and several other women who happened by. And all of them were more than anxious to provide helpful information on housekeeping.

Jess shook his head in wonder. ''I didn't realize you ladies did so much. And you make it look so easy.''

All the women smiled and giggled.

''Uncle Jess! My hair!'' Maggie ran up holding her unwinding braid in one hand and the ribbon in the other.

Alma Garrette hurried over. ''Come here, dear, let me help you.''

Maggie pulled away. ''I want Uncle Jess to do it.''

Jess rose and lifted Maggie onto the bench. ''Thanks just the same, Mrs. Garrette.'' He braided her hair and tied it with the ribbon.

Alma put her nose in the air and huffed away.

''Very nicely done.'' Fiona shared a nod of approval with the other women.

''Probably not as good as you ladies could do, but I'm getting better.'' Jess lifted Maggie to the ground.

''Thanks, Uncle Jess.'' She scampered away.

At the refreshment table, Sarah kept her eye on Jess as one woman after another crowded around, and she was pleased that they seemed to be at ease with him. A very good sign. On the other hand, Dwight had been only a half step behind her all day. A very bad sign.

Sarah rounded the table, attempting to outdistance him, but he followed quickly.

"Mr. Rutledge, would you please get the plates from inside the school?"

He gestured to the table. "They're all here."

"No, I'm certain I left a stack in the supply room. Would you get them for me, please?"

"Well, all right. But I'll be right back." He hurried toward the schoolhouse.

"Getting on your nerves?"

Sarah jumped as Kirby joined her. "Is it that obvious?"

"No, not too obvious. But Mother will be disappointed." Kirby nodded toward her mother who sat at the next table. "Don't worry, she'll start looking for another man for you."

Sarah made herself smile. "I'm sure she means well."

"She and Father are leaving on Monday, riding the circuit for a week or so." Kirby grinned. "Father is spreading the word of the Lord. But Mother will be looking for new husband material. Who knows? She may find someone you like."

"I think we should eat now."

As soon as Sarah made the announcement, everyone filed over. Kirby helped serve pie while Fiona poured coffee, then everyone found seats at one or another of the tables. Like the other mothers, Jess helped Maggie and Jimmy with their plates and cups of milk and got them situated on the grass under the trees along with the other children before helping himself. Surrounded in line by the other women, they talked and exchanged recipe tips.

"What kind would you like?" Sarah held her breath as Jess eyed the pies. He was doing so well. But to choose one pie over the other would be a gross insult to the other ladies.

Jess gazed over the table, then at the women around him. "They all look so good. Just give me a slice of each."

The ladies giggled as Sarah heaped pie onto Jess's plate. He caught her eye and gave her a sly wink, and it took all her strength to hide her smile.

Jimmy came over, tears standing in his eyes, cherry pie smeared on his shirt. He tugged on Jess's trousers.

"Looks like you spilled yours, huh?"

Jimmy ground his fists in his eyes.

"Come on, cowboy. Let's eat together." Jess lifted him in one arm and looked back at the women in line. "Maybe one of you ladies can tell me the best way to get out a cherry stain?"

The women looked on, smiling, as Jess sat Jimmy on his lap at the table and shared his pie, a bite for Jimmy, then one for himself.

When everyone else was served, Sarah joined Kirby and her parents at a table with Nate and Alma Garrette. Dwight Rutledge parked himself next to her, much to her dismay.

"You know, I'm getting an entirely different opinion of Mr. Logan," Fiona said as she glanced at him seated at the next table.

Reverend Sullivan shook his head. "Now, Fiona, don't go getting any ideas."

"That's right." Dwight nodded emphatically. "A man with his past can't be trusted."

Alma's head bobbed. "Amen to that."

"People can change, you know." Sarah blurted out the words before she could stop herself.

Alma gave her a disapproving glare. "That remains to be seen."

"The man paid for his crime. Maybe we should find some Christian charity in our hearts." Reverend Sullivan's gaze raked everyone at the table.

Dwight dropped his gaze and shoved a fork full of blueberry pie in his mouth.

"Your house is shaping up real nice, Sarah," Nate said.

She smiled. "I almost wish it would rain again so I can try out the new roof."

"I didn't realize the school board had that kind of money," Alma said.

"It's not the school board," Nate told her. "Jess is doing the repairs."

Alma jumped as if she'd been poked in the ribs. "Jess Logan is fixing up your house? But I—I—"

The stunned look on Alma's face pleased Sarah to no end.

"No, it was Jess's idea," Nate said. "He bought the materials and is doing all of the work himself."

"Really?" Fiona beamed. "I had no idea."

Nate nodded. "That's Jess. Even when we were

kids, if he had a nickel and somebody else needed it, he'd give it away.''

Dwight grunted and he swaggered his shoulders. ''I don't think it's decent or proper at all, a man like him spending so much time at your place.''

Nate's eyes narrowed. ''I tell you what, Rutledge, any time you'd like to head over there yourself and do some of the work, I'm sure Jess would be grateful. Maybe you'd like to pitch in on the cost of the materials, too.''

Dwight's cheeks puffed out and turned red.

''That house belongs to the town,'' Reverend Sullivan said. ''Mr. Logan has saved the taxpayers a pretty penny, I'd say.''

''And it was a very charitable thing to do,'' Fiona added.

Alma pursed her lips. ''I'm inclined to agree with Mr. Rutledge. I'm not sure this is proper.''

''You're all welcome to come by and see the place,'' Sarah said. ''Luke Trenton is helping, and Megan Neville has been by, too. Maggie and Jimmy are always there, of course.''

''Oh….'' Alma turned back to her pie.

Dwight thumped his fist on the table. ''If you ask me, I'd say—''

''Please excuse me. I have things to do.''

Sarah left the table and began clearing dishes from the serving table. Would the town never forget Jess's past? No matter what he did, or how hard he tried, they only saw the worst in him. It made her so angry she could hardly see straight.

Since she'd served, most everyone else was finished and up walking around, talking. Jess eased away from a crowd of ladies and headed her way. From the corner of her eye Sarah saw Alma Garrette watching them, and at that moment, she couldn't care less what that narrow-minded woman thought of her.

"Who lit a match to you?" he asked softly.

Sarah stacked dirty dishes, avoiding his gaze, trying to calm herself. He was trying so hard today, she didn't want to discourage him by repeating what the others had said.

"Nobody worth mentioning."

Jess glanced at the other table. "Sarah, did—"

"More pie?"

Jess grimaced at the near empty pie tin Sarah scooted his way. He splayed his hand across his belly. "I don't want to see another piece of pie as long as I live. Can you have a vegetable social next time?"

"Uncle Jess! Uncle Jess!"

Maggie ran toward him, tears streaming down her face. Jess hurried to her and lifted her into his arms.

"What's wrong, honey? What happened?"

She locked her arms around his neck, sobbing. "Mary Beth said you weren't going to be our uncle anymore. She said you were going to leave, and me and Jimmy would have to go live with somebody else."

Jess's belly twisted into a knot. He pressed her head against his shoulder and patted her back. "Don't worry, honey. Everything is going to be all right."

Maggie sat up and leaned away from him. "Is it true, Uncle Jess? Are you going away?"

Jess gulped down the lump that rose in his throat and threw Sarah a helpless look. Around him, all the townspeople who could take the children away from him watched. "I don't want to go, honey."

Maggie pressed her small hands against her chest. "You can't leave, Uncle Jess. You're half of my heart."

Emotion welled up in Jess, choking off his words.

Sarah stepped up and smoothed Maggie's bangs back. "Your Uncle Jess loves you very much, honey. He wants you to be together forever and ever."

Maggie looked at Jess. "Promise?"

"Oh, honey. There's nothing I want more."

She flung her arms around Jess's neck again and hugged him tight.

"Maggie, why don't you show your uncle how you can swing." Sarah looked up at Jess. "It's her favorite at recess."

She lifted her head and smiled. "Want to see me swing?"

"You bet." Jess set her down and took her hand as they crossed the schoolyard.

Fiona hurried to Sarah's side. "Those children seem quite taken with Mr. Logan."

Sarah smiled, watching Jess's big shoulders as he lifted Maggie into the swing. "He's trying very hard to make a good home for them."

"Hmm." Fiona worked her lips together. "What Mr. Logan needs is some help. Permanent help."

Sarah's breath caught. "You don't mean—"

"Lottie! Emma!" Fiona signaled the ladies and they huddled close. "That young niece of Virginia Conroy. What's her name?"

"Joanna." Lottie nodded. "She's such a dear girl."

"Yes, Joanna. A lovely girl." Emma touched her finger to her chin. "Isn't she down in Laramie visiting her grandmother? She's ailing, I understand."

"Of course Joanna would be there helping," Lottie said. "She's such a delight."

Fiona's eyes widened. "We'll just have to get her up here as soon as possible."

An odd wave of panic engulfed Sarah. "Fiona, I don't think—"

"Joanna will make a perfect wife for Mr. Logan. I must get a letter off before Emory and I leave town."

A sad, sinking feeling overwhelmed Sarah as she watched Fiona hurry away.

"Do I get my gold star?"

Jess stepped into the empty schoolroom, pleased to find Sarah working at her desk. "I was good at the social on Saturday, just like you wanted."

She looked up, happier than she should have been to see him. Fiona and her plan to find Jess a wife had been on her mind since the social.

"Looks like you'll be getting more than a gold star."

"Yeah?" His imagination wandered to a far better reward, but doubted he and Sarah had the same thing in mind.

"Hi, Jess." From the blackboard in the back corner of the room, Luke waved an eraser at him.

"What are you doing staying after school?"

Luke glanced at Sarah. "Let's just say I'm not here to pick up my gold star."

Jess sat down on the edge of Sarah's desk and pushed his hat back on his forehead. Behind her through the window he could see Maggie and Jimmy playing on the swing. "So, what am I getting?"

"I don't want to ruin the surprise."

"Come on now…"

Shouts and sobs burst into the schoolroom. Jess spun around as Sheriff Neville charged through the door dragging Megan by the wrist. A shotgun was clenched in his fist.

"Where the hell is he!"

"Papa, please! Don't!" Tears streaming down her face, Megan pulled against her father.

He brandished the shotgun. "I'll kill that little bastard!"

"Hold on, Sheriff, what's going on?" Jess approached him cautiously.

"Keep away from me, Logan!" His gaze riveted Sarah at her desk. "This is all your fault! What the hell kind of school are you running here!"

She shrank back in her chair. "I don't—"

Sheriff Neville's gaze swept the room and landed on Luke in· the corner. Raw fury contorted his face. "You little bastard!"

"Papa, don't!"

The sheriff pushed Megan away and charged across

the back of the room after Luke. Luke ran the other way toward Jess and Sarah.

"Come here, you little bastard!"

"Papa!" Megan fell against the wall, sobbing hysterically, then hurried toward the front of the room after Luke. "Papa, don't hurt him! Please!"

Luke ran past and Jess stepped in front of Neville, blocking his path in the narrow aisle. "Hold it, Sheriff."

"Get the hell out of my way! I'll kill you, too!"

"Stop! Every one of you stop—this instant!" Sarah shouted, using her most authoritative teacher's voice, freezing Buck Neville in the aisle and Luke near the doorway. A moment dragged by with only Megan's sobs filling the silence.

"Now." Sarah turned to the sheriff. "What is going on?"

His eyes narrowed to slits of fury as he looked across the room. "I'm here to get that little skunk."

Jess's gut told him he already knew the reason. "What did Luke do?"

His face turned a bright red. "Had his way with my daughter. Fixed her—*like that.*"

Sarah gasped. She turned to Megan, who stood sobbing near the doorway. Her first instinct was to take her in her arms and comfort her.

"Calm down, Sheriff." Jess held out both hands. "Killing the boy isn't going to solve anything."

Neville glared at Jess, then drew in a deep breath, calming himself.

Jess breathed a little easier, too. "Put that shotgun down and let's talk this out."

Neville relented and lowered the shotgun, then caught sight of Luke whispering to Megan by the door. "Get the hell away from my daughter!"

Luke jumped back, his face pale. Megan began to cry again.

"You've got every right to be mad, Sheriff. Hell, I'd do the same in your place." Jess suddenly felt very protective of Maggie, imagining himself doing far worse than Sheriff Neville if put in the same circumstances. "Are you sure he's the one? Are you sure Luke's the one who did it?"

Neville glared across the room. "She said he was."

"All right. Let's find out." Jess walked over to Luke. He seemed to have shrunk considerably. "How about it, Luke? Did you do this?"

The boy swallowed hard. A long moment passed while he looked at Megan, sniffing and sobbing. Finally, he squared his shoulders and stepped forward. "Yes, sir. It was me. I did it."

"You little bastard." Neville started toward him.

Sarah stepped in front of him. "There's only one thing to be done now, Sheriff."

He froze and curled his lips back. "Yeah. I guess you're right. Reverend Sullivan will be back next week. That's plenty soon enough."

Luke's eyes widened. "Reverend Sullivan? I—I don't understand."

Jess looked down at him. "You've got to marry her."

He fell back a step. "Marry her?"

"You have to make it right."

"But..." Luke turned to Megan. She burst into tears again.

"I want this kept quiet, understand? I don't want anybody knowing about this until the Reverend gets back." The sheriff stalked across the room. At the doorway he pointed at Sarah. "This is all your fault. You're supposed to be teaching these kids, not letting them run off in the bushes together at recess."

Her cheeks flamed. "I never—"

"Save it for the school board, lady."

Sheriff Neville stalked out of the room, pulling Megan along with him.

The look of sheer contempt the sheriff had given her, and the threat to complain to the school board should have been enough to keep her away, but Sarah couldn't mind her own business this time. Despite the vow she'd made to keep to herself here in Walker, she'd done just the opposite where Jess and his niece and nephew were concerned. She could do no less now.

Glancing over her shoulder, Sarah slipped down the side street and knocked at the small house where Megan Neville lived. She'd just seen the sheriff entering the jailhouse and hoped she'd have a few minutes alone with his daughter.

After a moment, the door opened. Megan looked pale and drawn, her eyes puffy. She glanced up and down the street, then stepped back, waving Sarah inside.

"You shouldn't be here, Mrs. Wakefield."

"You weren't in school today, Megan. I was worried about you."

"My papa…he'll be mad if you're here."

Sarah stopped in the center of the small, neat parlor, hoping she exuded more bravery than she felt. "Let me worry about your father, Megan. I want to know how you're doing."

Megan shrugged and closed the door. "I don't know. All right…I guess."

"Have you been to the doctor?"

"Yes, ma'am." Tears pooled in her eyes.

Sarah's heart went out to her. This should have been such a happy time in her life, preparing to give birth to her first child. Instead, Megan was miserable.

"I can only imagine how you must feel, Megan. But once you and Luke are married, things will settle down."

Big tears rolled down her face. "Oh, Mrs. Wakefield…"

"What is it, Megan?" Sarah draped an arm around her shoulders and pulled her close. "Tell me what's wrong."

She wept, trying to hold in the tears, taking comfort in Sarah's embrace, then stepped away and brushed her hands across her face. "I'll be all right."

"I want you to come back to school tomorrow."

Megan dipped her gaze. "Papa says I'm not fit to be in public, like this."

Anger stiffened Sarah's spine. "Just because you're having a baby doesn't mean your mind has quit working. You're welcome in my classroom, Megan. It will do you good to get out."

"I don't know."

Sarah softened her voice. "No one knows about the baby yet. Come to school tomorrow. I miss you in class."

A tiny smile tugged at Megan's lips. "Really?"

Sarah touched her shoulder. "Anytime you feel like talking, just come by my house."

"Thank you, Mrs. Wakefield."

Sarah gave her a reassuring nod and left, hoping her visit had done some good. She could only imagine how lonely and isolated Megan felt right now, and those were emotions Sarah knew only too well.

At the corner, she ran into Sheriff Neville.

"What are you doing over here?" He pointed a thick finger at her. "You keep away from my daughter. You hear me? You're responsible for this."

"Sheriff, I—"

"I don't know what kind of school you ran back in St. Louis, but I intend to find out. I'm going to get in touch with your old school and find out everything there is to know about you, lady. And I've got my eye on you and Logan, too. You can be sure the whole town is going to learn the truth about you."

Sarah's knees wobbled as she stumbled around the corner and down the boardwalk. Her worst nightmare loomed before her. Sheriff Neville would turn the whole town against her. He'd see to it she lost her job.

God help her, what would she do then?

Chapter Eleven

"New window's put in."

Jess walked through Sarah's back door and hung his hat on the peg by the stove, pleased that he no longer needed to knock. Doing the repairs on her little house had made him feel as much at home here as at his own place, and Sarah accepted his presence as routine now. For some reason, it made Jess feel comfortable and content.

The kitchen was warm and smelled good. Sarah moved efficiently, placing supper on the table, her skirt swishing. Maggie and Jimmy were already seated, waiting patiently. God, he liked it here.

Sarah smoothed a wisp of hair behind her ear. "Supper's ready."

"Come on, Uncle Jess. Me and Jimmy want to get to Bible study." Maggie waved him to the table.

"Have you decided what color paint you want yet?" Jess held the chair for Sarah.

"You've done enough already, Jess." Sarah sat down. "You don't have to paint, too."

"The house needs painting." He took a seat across from her and grinned. "Besides, I figure that if I keep working, you'll keep cooking."

Maggie's head bobbed. "We like eating here. Don't we, Jimmy?"

He nodded and wiggled closer to the table.

They ate supper then sent the children out to play in the yard while they cleaned the kitchen. Jess took up a towel, drying dishes as Sarah passed them to him.

"Something bothering you, Sarah? You've been mighty quiet."

She glanced up quickly. "No."

"If you don't want me and the kids coming over, just say so." Though it wasn't coincidence that Jess did the work on her house only when Sarah was home, he understood she might want time to herself in the evenings.

"No, it's just that—"

Sarah paused with her hands in the basin of soapy water, tempted to confide in him, wishing she could. Ever since Sheriff Neville's threat, all she could think of was having to leave Walker in disgrace, trying to find a job, a home, somewhere else. She didn't want to go. And the man standing beside her was a part of the reason.

Jess edged a little closer. "What is it, Sarah?"

She drew in a deep breath, unable to fight off the need to confide in him any longer. "I went to see Megan today after school."

"How is she doing?"

"As well as can be expected, I suppose." Sarah

swallowed hard. "Sheriff Neville saw me leaving. He blames me for what happened."

"Figures he'd want to blame somebody."

"He threatened to contact my old school in St. Louis."

Jess paused drying a plate. "Something happen back there you don't want him finding out about?"

"No."

The word popped out quickly. Too quickly. She saw the look on Jess's face and turned her head away, afraid to tell him the real reason for her worry. If he knew the sheriff wanted to use her relationship with Jess as a means of firing her, Jess wouldn't stand still for it. And what would that accomplish, except causing him trouble and jeopardizing his chances to keep the children?

"Sarah, is there something you're not telling me?"

She shook her head. "It's just that, well, I don't like being gossiped about."

"Can't blame you for that." Jess shrugged, then looked down at her standing at his elbow. Her face was drawn in tense lines. "There's more, Sarah. What is it?"

She ventured a look at him, temptation to confide in him clamoring through her. She could almost taste the words on her lips, but still, she couldn't bring herself to actually say them.

"Maybe I am responsible," she said. "You were right, after all, about Luke and Megan being more than friends. I don't understand why I didn't see it. I would have kept a closer eye on them if I'd thought something like this might happen.''

"I think you've had other things on your mind lately.'' Jess consoled himself with the hope that maybe he was one of those distracting thoughts.

Sarah shook her head. "It's no excuse. I should have paid more attention to them. My students always come first.''

"Well, you won't hear Maggie complain. She thinks the world of you, Sarah.'' Jess dried the cup she passed him. "She sees you as a lot more than her schoolmarm.''

Sarah's heart tumbled. "Really?''

Jess cleared his throat. "Fact is, we all do.''

How she wished Jess were right, that she could be more. Dare she get any more involved with him than she already was?

Sarah felt the heat of Jess's gaze as he leaned his hip against the cabinet and looked down at her. Something about this man made her heart beat faster, made her want to pour out all her troubles, made her want to take him in her arms and solve all of his problems, too.

Sarah turned back to the pan of dirty dishes, needing to break the tension between them. "Fiona Sullivan has something in mind for you.''

Jess frowned. "Like what?''

She glanced at him. "A wife.''

His brows sprang up. "What are you talking about?''

"Aren't you interested in getting married?''

"I never thought much about it."

"It might be good for you, and for the children." Sarah passed him another plate.

"We're doing all right. Besides, the way I see it finding a wife is like buying underclothes. You've got to pick them out yourself. If the fit isn't exactly right, you're miserable." Jess dried the plate. "What do you think?"

Sarah pressed her lips together to keep from laughing. "I don't think we should discuss my personal garments."

"Okay. What about a husband?"

The cup slipped from her fingers and splashed into the water. "I can't marry again."

"Why not? Didn't you like being married before?"

Every breath of air left the room, leaving a strange heat in its place. Sarah struggled to ignore it and passed Jess the last cup. "It's just that..."

He dried the last cup and wiped his hands on the towel. "Was your husband bad to you?" The thought made him suddenly angry, but he didn't let it show.

She dried her hands and folded the towel neatly. "No. Howard was a good man."

Jess eased closer, backing her into the sideboard. "Did he make you feel like a woman, Sarah?"

Heart pounding, she gripped the edge of the sideboard, her senses reeling. Warmth and desire rolled off Jess in waves, overwhelming her, binding her to him.

He touched his palm to her jaw, gliding his thumb

across her cheek with exquisite softness. "I could make you feel that way, Sarah. If you'd let me."

Short puffs of breath choked off her words. Excitement hummed in her veins.

His mouth closed over hers like a wet, hot vice sealing them together. His tongue slid across her lips, tempting, prodding until she relented. Sarah sighed as he thrust deep inside her, tasting her hungrily, igniting a hunger in her she'd not expected, driving her to match his movements.

He pulled them together, holding her in the curve of his arms. Her breasts gave way to his hard chest, her thighs brushed his, and for a moment—a long, glorious moment—Sarah was lost in the feel, the taste of him. Then fear crept into her thoughts.

Sarah pulled her lips from his, panting. "No, Jess...."

She tasted too sweet to stop. He'd been hungry for her too long. Jess trailed his lips down her cheek into the valley of her throat. He'd promised himself he wouldn't do this again. But he couldn't help himself. He couldn't stop. Not now.

Sarah splayed her hands across his cheeks and pushed him away. Her breasts ached at the distance between them. "Jess, you mustn't."

His heated blood pounded in his veins. Jess struggled to control himself. "Why not, Sarah?"

She leaned away but his arms held her firmly. "I— I shouldn't..."

"Shouldn't what?" His thoughts clouded with desire, Jess tried to make sense of what she was saying. "I don't understand."

"I don't want to hurt you."

"Hurt me? Sarah, what the hell are you talking about?" He released her and stepped back, his desire turning to anger. "It's Rutledge, isn't it?"

Breath went out of her at the sight of his angry face. He didn't understand. And she didn't know how to explain it.

A chill raked him violently. Jess stepped away. So it was Rutledge she wanted after all. Hurt and angry, he grabbed his hat and charged out the back door.

She started after him, but stopped, clutching the doorknob to hold herself in place. He had to go. She had to let him. No matter how much her heart ached.

Sarah closed her eyes and turned away, fighting back tears and wishing to high heaven that she didn't love him so much.

The evening air felt cool against Jess's face as the children dashed off ahead of him toward the church. He kissed them both goodbye as Kirby took them inside. Standing alone in the quiet churchyard, Jess looked at Sarah's little house across the road. For a moment he was tempted to go back there, take her into his arms and drive thoughts of Dwight Rutledge out of her head once and for all. He'd make her forget. He'd make her his.

But then that look on her face popped into his head. Sarah didn't want him.

A hard lump tightened his gut into a knot. Jess headed for town.

At the Green Garter Saloon, Saul looked up from behind the bar. "Jess, what are you doing in here?"

The place was quiet, but at the moment Jess didn't notice. "Give me a whiskey."

Saul poured him a drink and glanced outside. "You best not let anybody see you in here, Jess."

Let the whole damn town see him. He didn't care. "Leave the bottle."

Saul hesitated, then leaned closer. "At least go sit over there in the corner."

Jess tossed back the whiskey. It tasted nasty, burning all the way down. He took the bottle, ambled to the table in the corner and sat with his back to the door.

Half a bottle later, the chair beside him scraped across the floor. Light from the wall lantern reflected off the tin star.

"Nate…you old dog, you." Jess blinked to focus on his friend. "Want a drink?"

Nate glanced at Saul over his shoulder. "I heard you were in here, Jess. What are you doing?"

"Getting drunk." He filled his glass again.

"I can see that." Nate took the shot and drank it down himself. "How come?"

Jess slumped forward on his arms. Everything looked fuzzy. "'Cause of…her."

"Who?"

Jess dragged his palms down his face. "Sarah. She

don't want somebody like me. I don't know what the hell I was thinking.''

Nate slid the bottle just out of Jess's reach. ''You're sweet on her, huh?''

''Oh, God....'' Jess collapsed onto his arms atop the table. ''I want her so bad I can't see straight. But she won't let me touch her.''

''She's a proper woman.''

''Yeah, I know. But I'll bet she lets that Rutledge bastard do what he wants.''

''Naw.'' Nate shook his head. ''Sarah doesn't like him. She told Kirby so—a couple of times.''

''Yeah?'' Jess sat up, a lopsided grin on his face. ''You think I've got a chance?''

''Sure you do. She'd be crazy not to want you.'' Nate glanced over his shoulder again. The saloon was still quiet, but he had to get Jess out of here before anybody saw him. ''Listen, buddy, how about you and me get some air?''

''Nope.'' Jess grabbed the bottle and filled his glass. ''I'm going down to see Rutledge. Tell him once and for all to keep away from Sarah.''

''You are, huh?'' Nate shifted in the chair. ''You can do that tomorrow. You've got to get Maggie and Jimmy at church soon. Bible study is almost over.''

Jess emptied his glass, a few drops of whiskey trickling down his chin. He swiped at it with the back of his hand. ''Nate, I want to keep those kids so much it hurts. Hell, even coming back to Walker feels like home again. I don't want to lose them. I swear, I don't.

I've been behaving myself and being good. And it's not so bad, but…''

Nate leaned closer. "But what?"

Jess shuddered. "But if I don't have me a woman soon, I'm gonna grab the first one I see on the street and—and, and then I'll never get to keep those kids."

Nate nodded. What Jess needed was to get somewhere quiet and sleep it off, a place where nobody in town would see him. He knew the perfect spot.

Nate leaned closer. "Let's you and me go find us some women."

Jess blinked at him. "Yeah?"

"Sure. Like we used to. Come on."

Jess's insides flamed. "You mean, at Miss Flora's?"

"Naw. Too far away." Nate lowered his voice. "I know a place just down the street."

"I don't know…." His mind wasn't working as well as it should, so a minute dragged by before Jess could recall what bothered him about the idea. "Them ol' whores just don't seem the same now. I keep thinking about Sarah."

Nate chucked him in the arm. "Oh, hell, Jess. Just keep your eyes closed."

"Oh. Yeah." A big silly grin spread over his face. "Okay. Let's go."

Nate stood and helped Jess to his feet. He swayed, but Nate caught him under the arm and guided him between the tables and out the back door. Halfway down the alley Jess started to sing.

"Hold it down. You'll scare the women off."

Jess slapped his hand over his mouth and broke out laughing. "Hell, what'll we do then?"

"Shh. Here we are."

Jess touched his finger to his lips. "Shh."

In the back of the darkened building, Nate pushed the door open and urged Jess inside.

"Hell, it's dark in here." Jess's head rolled back and forth. "You sure we're in the right place?"

"I'm sure. This is exactly where you need to be." Nate helped him down a short hallway, then into a small room. "Here. Lay down. I'll go get a woman for you."

Jess felt in the darkness and stretched out on the little bed. "Get me a nice soft one, okay?"

"Okay. You stay here now. It might be a few minutes, but I'll be back."

Nate crept to the hall and waited until he heard Jess's snores. Then he closed the cell door, turned the key in the lock and went into the office to catch up on his paperwork.

Sneaking into the jailhouse at daybreak. Wouldn't that give the town something to gossip about if they saw her?

Clutching the hood of her cloak around her face, Sarah hurried into the jail and shut the door quickly. Across the room Nate looked up from the potbellied stove.

"Coffee?"

She lowered her hood. "No, thanks. Where's the sheriff?"

"Rode out to the Blue Sky Ranch late yesterday. He'll be back around noon."

"How's Jess?"

"Roaring and snorting like a caged bull." Nate walked to his desk. "Kids all right?"

"Both of them were asleep when I talked to Kirby just now. They don't even know Jess was gone. They think it was a treat to spend the night with Kirby. Good thing Emory and Fiona are still gone."

Nate sipped his coffee. "Sorry to bother you so late last night. But I figured Jess would be in a bear of a mood when he woke up this morning, and you'd be the one to calm him down."

"Me?"

Nate grinned. "I have a feeling he'll listen to what you say."

After he'd left her kitchen last night, she wasn't sure she and Jess would ever speak again. "Jess is lucky to have a good friend like you. If he'd been seen in town in his condition, he'd have lost Maggie and Jimmy for sure."

"I can't tell you the number of times Jess took the blame for something I did when we were kids. Kept my pa from taking a switch to me more times than I can count." Nate shook his head. "But I'm the last person he wants to talk to this morning. See if you can get him home quietly before the town wakes up."

Sarah drew in a deep breath. "I'll try."

Nate opened the door that led to the cells and she walked down the narrow hallway. It was dank and dim in here, with rays of early morning sunlight beginning to slant through the barred windows. In the back cell, Jess paced fitfully, mumbling, slamming his fist into his palm.

"Jess?"

He whirled around. Stubbled whiskers covered his jaw, his hair stuck out on one side, his shirttail hung out in the back and his clothes were rumpled. Dark circles shadowed his red, bloodshot eyes.

"Sarah...." He grasped the bars. She was so damn pretty. Even now, feeling like he'd been run over by a freight wagon, he wanted her. But she gave him her teacher's look and that made him feel like the idiot he knew he was.

Jess dipped his gaze. "I guess I really messed things up last night."

"I guess you did."

He licked his dry, pasty lips. Obviously, she wasn't going to make this easy for him. And he deserved that, too.

Jess glanced at her. "Are Maggie and Jimmy all right?"

"Yes. They're both fine, and no one knows about this. Thanks to your good friend Nate."

Jess's temper heated up, sending a new ache reverberating through his already pounding head. Nate—his *good friend*—had tricked him. Promised him a woman. Locked him up in the jail cell. Then wouldn't let him out.

"That bastard is no friend of mine."

Sarah looked him up and down. "Somebody needs a nap."

Yeah, he needed a nap—and a hell of a lot of other things, too. Jess tightened his grip on the cell bars. "Let me out of here, Sarah."

"Not until you calm down enough to walk home and not make a scene."

Jess forced down his anger. If he was going to get out of this cell, he'd have to promise to behave. He could pop Nate in the nose anytime. "I won't cause any trouble. Just get the key from Nate."

She looked as if she doubted it.

"I swear."

He reached through the bars. Sarah backed up, just enough that he couldn't quite touch her. He wiggled his fingers at her. "Sarah, please...."

She stood there, refusing to come closer, and that made him so damn mad that he couldn't see straight. Jess lunged for her and banged his nose against the bars.

"Darnit!" Jess reeled back and grabbed his nose. Blood trickled down. He swiped it with his sleeve and grabbed the cell bars with both hands. "You let Rutledge touch you, don't you! I'll bet you let him do whatever he wants!"

Sarah gasped. "I've never let him lay a hand on me."

Unreasonable anger roiled through Jess. "Is that what killed your husband? Were you so damn cold he froze to death?"

She glared at him through narrow eyes. "Don't you *ever* speak to me again."

Sarah whipped around and stormed away.

"Don't you— Get back here. Sarah!" Jess shook the cell door violently, then kicked the cot over and threw the frame against the wall. Finally, he sank onto the curled-up mattress and plowed his fingers through his hair.

What the hell was the matter with him? Why had he said such things? Why had he treated her that way?

Why had he been so mean to her when he loved her so much?

Heavy footsteps and the rattle of keys caused Jess to look up from the cluttered cell. Nate stood at the door, glaring down at him.

"You stupid idiot."

Jess's fists clenched and he shot to his feet. "I swear to God, Nate, if you don't let me out of here—"

"Just shut up! Why don't you think about somebody else for a change?" Nate pointed toward the street. "You're going to get that woman fired. Fired, disgraced, and run out of town."

Some of the fight drained out of him. "Sarah? What are you talking about?"

"She's risked everything to help you keep those kids."

Jess dragged his sleeve over his nose, soaking up the last of the blood. "She never said anything."

"No, she wouldn't say anything. She knows you've got enough troubles of your own without worrying about her. But think for a minute, Jess. You know what this town is like. If they take it in their head that she's not fit to teach school because she's associating with the likes of you, Sarah will be run out of town quick as a wink.''

''Oh, God....'' Jess clamped both hands over his face and shook his head. ''I never thought of that.''

''Well, maybe you ought to start doing more thinking.'' Nate shoved the key in the lock and swung open the door.

Jess pushed his fingers through his tangled hair. ''I got to go apologize to her.''

''Not looking like that. Go home, sober up and take a bath. Give it a couple of days. She needs time to cool off, too.''

Jess sighed heavily and his shoulders sagged. ''You're right.''

''I know I'm right.'' Nate pushed open the back door leading to the alley. ''Now get out of here, will you? You stink.''

''Thanks, Nate.''

The house of the Lord seemed like as good a place as any to swear off liquor once and for all, so Jess made that silent promise as he walked into church on Sunday morning. It had taken two full days to get over his hangover, neither of them pleasant.

But he felt good today, washed, shaved, scrubbed clean, ready to atone for his sins. In the pew near the front sat Sarah, and he knew he had a lot of forgiveness to ask for today.

''Let's sit with Miss Sarah.'' Maggie pulled him down the aisle by his arm.

"Sure." Good idea. Seated beside him in church, she'd have to sit still for his apology.

Maggie hurried ahead and sat down next to Sarah just as another family filed into the pew from the other end, taking up most of the room. Annoyed, Jess circled to the other side of the church with Jimmy and sat down on the end. He leaned forward. There, eight people away, sat Sarah.

Eight people or not, he wasn't going to let this opportunity pass him by. He glared at her while the congregation filed into the church, filling up the pews. Finally, Sarah glanced at him.

"I'm sorry." Jess mouthed the words at her.

Sarah frowned. *"What?"* She mouthed back at him.

"I'm…sorry."

She understood him that time, because she jerked her chin and put her nose in the air, ignoring him. Annoyed, Jess elbowed the man beside him, whispered and nodded toward Sarah. The man nudged the woman beside him, who poked the man beside her, all the way down the line to Sarah. She looked from face to face until she came to Jess. He opened his mouth, but she turned away. Jess mumbled under his breath.

Deacon Foley took the pulpit and began the morning announcements.

Jess tried again. He spoke quietly to the man, sending a whispered message down the pew to Sarah. This time she refused to even look at him.

Amid the acknowledgments of the ill members of the congregation, Jess dug a paper and nub of pencil from his shirt pocket and scribbled a note. He passed it down, from person to person until it reached Sarah. Jess leaned forward, waiting for her to read his words of apology, to look up and favor him with a smile. Instead, Sarah looked at the paper, threw him a scathing look and ripped it to shreds without reading a word.

Miss Marshall brought the congregation to its feet pounding the usual "Onward, Christian Soldiers" on the piano. Jess grabbed Jimmy's hand and eased down the pew as everyone rose.

"Excuse me…pardon me…oops, sorry ma'am… excuse me."

He reached Sarah, squeezing in front of the elderly woman beside her. "Morning, ma'am." Jess nodded politely and pulled Jimmy alongside him in the tight space.

Jess leaned down to Sarah as she sang along with the congregation. "I've been trying to tell you I'm sorry."

She kept her head forward, ignoring him.

Standing on the other side of her, Maggie leaned around and waved.

"Sarah, please. Would you just give me a minute?"

She kept singing.

Jess pushed his fingers through his hair. "Look, I don't blame you for being mad."

She wouldn't even look at him.

"Dammit, Sarah! I'm sorry!"

The song ended, sending Jess's apology echoing through the church. Heads turned. Eyes bulged. Finally, everyone sat down again. Everyone but Jess.

At the wrong end of the pew, he had no seat to take. Sarah threw him a smug look as she sat down, leaving him the only person still standing, his great height towering conspicuously.

Flustered, Jess pushed past her, picked up Maggie and sat in her spot, pulling both children onto his lap.

At the pulpit Deacon Foley launched into the sermon. Sarah glanced at Jess, squirming uncomfortably beside her. Unable to stop herself, she giggled. He glared at her, then laughed, too.

The service concluded and Jess made his way out of the church holding Maggie and Jimmy's hands. They hurried away to play with their friends, leaving Jess and Sarah alone at the foot of the steps.

"I made a fool of myself in front of the whole church for you. Is that enough to convince you I'm sorry?"

Sarah touched her finger to her lips. "It's a start."

Jess looked down at her. "I'm really sorry, Sarah. I don't know why I said that stuff. I was way out of line, saying those things about your husband and Rutledge."

Somewhere in the foggy recesses of his mind, a voice told him Sarah had no interest in Dwight at all. But, for some reason, he couldn't place the source.

"Forgive me?"

She studied him for a long moment, debating. Finally she sighed heavily. "Yes, I suppose so."

"I'm never doing anything like that again. I swear. It made me realize how close I came to losing Maggie and Jimmy."

Sarah smiled. "Have you and Nate made up?"

Hearing Nate's name made Jess realize that spending time with Sarah in public was just the sort of thing his friend had warned him about. He wanted to stay, talk to Sarah more, but knew he should move along; he'd made a big enough spectacle in church already.

"I've got to go catch up with Maggie and Jimmy." Jess eased away.

Knowing he'd better go home, Jess scanned the churchyard looking for the children, but instead caught sight of Nate hurrying toward the back of the church. Jess followed. Rounding the building he saw Luke flattened on the ground and Zack Gibb standing over him, fists clenched.

Megan ran up and grabbed Zack's arm. "Stop, Zack. Don't hit him again. Please."

Zack glared at Luke on the ground, then at Megan. Nate reached them and pulled Zack away.

Struggling to his feet, Luke wiped the blood from his mouth with the back of his hand. Jess hurried over and steadied him.

"What's going on?"

Wary, Luke watched Zack towering a full head taller than him, held at bay by Nate, Megan at his side. He pulled away from Jess.

"Nothing's going on."

"Do I have to take you two over to the jail to end this?" Nate asked.

Zack glared at Luke, his face twisted with anger. He curled and uncurled his fingers into a fist.

Megan touched his arm. "Please, Zack. Don't."

Finally, Zack turned to Nate. "Won't be no more trouble. Not from me."

"All right. Both of you get on out of here." Nate watched them both until they disappeared in opposite directions. He turned to Megan. "You want me to get your pa?"

"No," she said quickly, and hurried away.

Jess walked over to Nate. "Better keep an eye on those two."

"Uncle Jess!" Maggie raced up, Jimmy on her heels. "Mrs. Myers says me and Jimmy can come to their house for a while. Is it okay, Uncle Jess? Is it?"

"Let me go talk to her." Jess found Lottie standing with Emma Turner.

"Mary Beth got a new doll from her aunt back East and she wanted to show it to Maggie," Lottie explained. "Can she and Jimmy stop by for a while?"

It gave Jess an odd feeling to let the children go somewhere without him, but he agreed. After all, it wouldn't be neighborly otherwise.

"I'll come get them in a little while."

Jess waved goodbye to the children as they left the churchyard with the Myers family, then headed home. Passing Sarah's house he wondered where she was, wishing he could ask her to come over for supper tonight.

As he rounded the corner of his house a man stepped out in front of him. Startled, he reached for his gun, which wasn't there, but the man smiled easily and held up his hands.

"Hold on, there, no need to get all jumpy."

Jess held himself rigid, sizing up the stranger. Tall, slender, with a scraggly beard and soured clothes. "Who are you, and what are you doing sneaking around my place?"

"Your place?" The man's gaze roamed the house and yard. "Well, now, I don't know about it being your place. Where's the kids?"

His eyes narrowed. "You'd better tell me who you are and what it is you want."

The stranger hung his thumbs in his suspenders. "Name's Jed Hayden. I've come to see my kids."

Chapter Twelve

Rain fell in gray sheets, bouncing off the muddy earth, tapping against the roof, making the house seem all the more cozy. Jess put the broom into the cupboard and knelt beside Jimmy, who sat playing with blocks on the floor. Lately, the boy had begun to open up to him. Sarah had been right. Spending more time with him had helped.

Jess sat down on the floor and began stacking the blocks along with Jimmy. "You know, I was thinking about your mama just now. I was thinking how much I miss her."

The boy ignored him, piling the blocks atop each other.

"Your mama loved you a lot, Jimmy. She still loves you. Just because she's an angel in heaven now, doesn't mean she's forgotten you." Jess threaded his fingers through the back of Jimmy's hair. "She's up there watching you all the time."

Jimmy dropped the blocks and looked up at Jess.

"I'm trying real hard to do things just like your

mama did. I'm going to take care of you and make sure nothing hurts you.'' Jess smiled gently at him. ''I love you, Jimmy. Just like your mama did.''

His bottom lip poked out. Jess held out his arms. ''Come here, partner.''

To Jess's surprise, Jimmy didn't pull away as he lifted the child onto his lap and cuddled him against his chest, rocking him slowly. They sat together for a long time, listening to the rain. Finally, Jess rose and settled them into the rocking chair.

''How about a story?''

Jimmy nodded and laid his head against Jess's shoulder.

Jess nearly dozed off in the middle of his own story. He looked down to see that Jimmy was already sleeping, curled against his chest. Jess carried the child to bed, thinking he might have a nap, too, since Maggie wasn't due home from school for a long time yet. Rain made good sleeping weather.

He heard a faint knock at the back door and tensed. In the kitchen he grabbed his Colt from the top shelf of the pantry and peered outside. On the porch, drenched, stood Luke.

He pulled open the door. ''What are you doing out in this weather?''

The dark purple bruise Zack had beaten into Luke's cheek shone against his pale skin. He stood there for a moment looking lost. ''I don't know....''

''Get in here.'' Jess pulled him into the kitchen and over to the cookstove. ''Stand here and warm up.''

Shivering, dripping a puddle on the floor, Luke did

as he was told while Jess put his gun away and got a towel from the linen chest.

"Dry off and get out of those clothes. I'll get a blanket."

Teeth chattering, Luke toweled off and dressed in the long johns and socks Jess brought him. They were a mile too big, but they were dry and warm. Jess wrapped a blanket around him and put coffee on to heat.

Luke pushed his hands through the dangling sleeves and sat down at the table. "Thanks."

"Aren't you supposed to be in school?" Jess spread the wet clothes on a chair in front of the stove to dry.

Huddled inside the blanket, Luke looked small and fragile, with the weight of the world on his shoulders.

"I tried to go, but I just started walking around. I ended up here…somehow."

"You want to tell me what's got you stumbling around in the pouring-down rain?"

Luke glanced up at him. "Megan…"

"I figured." Jess poured two cups of coffee, then got the bottle of brandy he'd found in the back of the cabinet and added a nip to both cups. Weeks ago when he'd found the bottle he'd wondered why Cassie had it; it hadn't taken long before he understood.

Jess sat the cups on the table and took a seat across from Luke. "Have you talked to your pa about this?"

"I'd have to be plumb loco to do that." His shoulders sagged farther. "I got enough trouble without him getting a strap after me."

He couldn't blame the boy for not talking to his

father, under those circumstances. "Okay, so what's on your mind?"

Luke cradled the steaming cup in his palms and took a sip. "I can't marry Megan."

Jess reared back in his chair. "You got to, son."

"No." Luke ran his fingers through his wet hair, panic twisting his features. "He's going to kill me. He's going to get his brother up here and kill me dead."

"Who?"

Luke wrung his hands together. "And—and Megan. She already knows what to do. How am I supposed to marry her if she knows how and I don't?"

"Hold on. What are you talking about? Who's going to kill you?"

Luke sighed impatiently. "Gil Gibb. He'll splatter my guts all over town. He'll do anything Zack tells him."

Jess reached across the table and touched his arm. "Slow down. What have Zack and Gil Gibb got to do with this?"

"If I marry Megan, Zack will have his brother kill me."

"You mean Zack is sweet on her?"

Luke took another sip of coffee, avoiding his gaze. "Yeah."

Jess knew there was more. He wiggled his fingers at him. "Come on. Let's have it."

"Zack's the one that did it. Not me."

"He's the father of Megan's baby?"

Luke covered his face with his palms. "That's why

I can't marry her. I never even done it before. How can I marry her? I'm not sure what I'm supposed to do.''

''You mean you never...''

Color rose in his pale cheeks. ''No.''

''So why did you tell the sheriff it was you?''

His shoulders slumped. ''Megan asked me to. Everybody knows the sheriff's got no use for any of the Gibb family. He'd have run Zack off—or worse—if he knew it was him that did it. Megan asked me to say I was the one to protect Zack. But I never figured on having to marry her.''

''Megan and Zack are in love?''

Luke nodded. ''They've been hiding it from her pa.''

''Well, there's no hiding it now.''

''Megan is afraid to tell her pa. Now, Zack thinks it was me messing with his girl. He's going to have Gil shoot me. Dead. I know he is. Gil's crazy. He don't care who he kills.'' Luke shook his head miserably. ''What am I going to do?''

Jess blew out a heavy breath. This was a mess all right. ''Look, you're just going to have to tell Sheriff Neville the truth.''

Luke's eyes rounded. ''You think I'm going to tell the sheriff his daughter is diddlin' with one of the Gibb clan? He and Gil will end up in a fight over which of them is going to shoot me first!''

The boy had a point. Jess shrugged. ''Megan will have to tell him.''

''She'll never tell him.'' Luke shook his head. ''She

loves Zack a lot. She won't do anything that will get him run out of town—or shot.''

"Somebody's got to undo this mess."

"I was kind of hoping you'd tell him."

Jess lunged forward. "Me?"

"Come on, Jess. Sheriff won't shoot you outright. He might wing you or something, but people in town kind of like you now. He'll listen to you."

He shoved out of the chair and raked his hand through his hair. "I don't know, Luke."

"Please. You got to."

The last thing—the very last thing—he needed was to get involved with somebody else's problems. Especially a problem as big as this one. A problem that involved the sheriff, his pregnant daughter, a gunslinger and the town outcast.

Jess paced across the room and stole a look at Luke. The boy looked absolutely miserable, and scared to death. He didn't doubt for a minute that Zack Gibb would have his brother shoot him. Nor did he question the sheriff's reaction when he found out the truth.

And what about Sarah? She'd been worried sick about what the sheriff might say about her. Though she'd tried to hide it, Jess had seen the fear in her. Maybe he could put a stop to it if he helped.

Jess sighed heavily. He couldn't turn his back on Sarah, or Luke either, for that matter.

"All right. Soon as the rain stops we'll go over and talk to Zack. Once things are straightened out with him, I'll tell the sheriff."

Luke eyes rounded. "You mean it? You'll really do it?"

"Yes. But you're coming with me."

"I'd better tell Megan what's going on."

Jess shook his head. "She doesn't need to know any of this, not in her condition. Wait until it's all settled and Zack can tell her."

Luke heaved a heavy sigh. "Thanks, Jess."

"Don't thank me yet. Let's get through this with nobody getting killed first."

The rain stopped by early afternoon so they headed into town. Jess kept a close eye on Jimmy; beneath his poncho his Colt was strapped to his thigh. The feed and grain store was quiet when they walked inside. Dwight Rutledge was nowhere to be seen, much to Jess's relief.

Zack Gibb walked from the back of the dimly lit store to greet them, then froze when he saw Luke. He charged toward him, his fist drawn back.

"Hold on, now." Jess blocked his path. "We're here to talk. Calm down."

Zack glared at Luke, his black curly hair hanging across his forehead. "I'm gonna get you for what you did."

Luke gulped. "It wasn't me, Zack. I never touched her. Megan made me say it so her pa wouldn't run you off."

Zack squinted at him. "You telling me the truth?"

"It's the truth." Jess stepped back and relaxed his stance. "We're here to make it right."

Zack's mouth sagged open and he looked up at Jess. "Megan's baby is mine? Really mine?"

"That's right."

A big grin spread over his face and his chest puffed out.

"Jess is going to talk to the sheriff and explain everything," Luke said.

Zack relaxed. "Is that true?"

Jess nodded. "But first I've got to hear it from you. Are you going to marry her? Do the right thing?"

The look of a lovesick puppy came over Zack's face. "I love her so much. I wanted to tell her pa a long time ago, but Megan was scared. I've been working hard, saving every cent. I was going to take Megan away, marry her, start over some place where her pa won't make trouble for her."

That settled the issue in Jess's mind. "All right. I'll go talk to Sheriff Neville, try to explain things."

"I'm coming with you," Zack said.

Jess shook his head. "Let me handle it first. I'm sure the sheriff will want to talk to you soon enough."

Zack shuffled his feet, then turned to Luke. "Sorry about the beating."

Luke touched his fingers to his cheek. "You just take good care of Megan."

Zack grinned. "I will."

Jess looked back and forth between the two of them. "This is all settled? No more fighting?"

"No more fighting. Except—" Zack turned to Luke. "Sorry, I already sent for my brother."

* * *

"See? I told you. Didn't I tell you?"

"Yeah. You told me." Jess looked down at Luke at his elbow as they passed the Blue Jay Café. "But he won't let Gil hurt you. You don't have anything to worry about."

Luke shook his head. "Gil Gibb won't like coming all the way to Walker and not getting to kill somebody."

Jess scanned the street ahead of them, keeping an eye on Jimmy, watching out for trouble. "This will all be over soon enough, just—"

Jess froze, his gaze riveted to the other side of the street.

"What's wrong?" Luke followed his line of vision.

"Nothing." Jess swept Jimmy into his arms and passed him to Luke. "Take him over to the jailhouse. Don't let him out of your sight."

"The jail?" Alarmed, Luke held Jimmy against his chest and glanced across the street. "What's going on, Jess?"

"Nothing, I told you. Get over there. *Now.* I'll be there in a while."

Jess watched them disappear around the corner, then he crossed the muddy street to where Jed Hayden lounged in the alley beside the bank. He'd had an ache in his gut since the man had showed up at his house last night claiming to be Maggie and Jimmy's father. Seeing him again only made it worse.

"Thought you were leaving town."

Hayden pulled on his beard. "Right nasty day, wouldn't you say?"

Jess's heart pounded in his chest. Nate had been right when he'd said Hayden might show up. Jess sure as hell didn't want him around the children. He hadn't believed him for a second last night when he'd claimed he had only come to town to pay respects to his dead wife and see the kids. Hayden was here for the same reason he'd always come back before.

"Course I don't expect the rain bothers you too much, living in that nice house that belonged to Cassie, a house that rightfully belongs to me now."

"Is that what you want, Hayden? You want the house?"

He gazed around at the horses and wagons passing by, the few people on the boardwalk. "I saw little Maggie in the schoolyard this morning."

Jess's hands curled into fists and he fought off the overwhelming urge to pummel this man to bits.

"Started to go over and talk to her. Maybe bring her into town for a visit with her pa." Hayden chuckled, a low menacing laugh. "Think she'd like that?"

The need to protect Maggie and Jimmy coiled tight in Jess's belly. "You can do your visiting with me for the time being."

"Yeah, you're right. Be a shame to upset the kids, what with their ma just dying. And, of course, you being new around here, too." Hayden's eyes narrowed. "Heard about the court hearing they had for you over them kids. I'm thinking maybe I ought to go over there and talk to the sheriff, tell him I'm here."

"The sheriff isn't interested in anything you have to say, Hayden. And neither is anybody else in this town."

"I am their pa. I think maybe I owe it to them to take them in." Hayden pulled at his beard. "Course, I don't know how long I could keep them. It'd be a damn shame if I had to ship them off to some orphanage, wouldn't it."

Jess pumped his fists tighter, holding in his anger.

"Or maybe I could send them off to live with some of these fine folks around here. Not likely I'd find somebody who would take them both. Might have to separate them." Hayden's eyes narrowed. "That's what happened to you and Cassie, wasn't it? Got separated, didn't you?"

Raw anger ripped through Jess. That's exactly what had happened to him and Cassie, and Hayden knew it. Jess surged toward Hayden.

The other man backed away and held up his hands. "Now, now, don't go getting yourself all upset. I got business down Laramie way and I might just head on down there, soon as I get a grubstake together."

Jess's stomach soured. He knew what Hayden wanted. The same thing he'd wanted from Cassie every other time he'd come to town.

"Just how much of a stake do you need before you can move on?"

Hayden eyed him and chuckled. "I figured you'd ask."

"Five hundred dollars!"

Sarah clutched her hand to her throat and reeled

against the sideboard. "Five hundred dollars? You can't be serious."

Jess paced across the floor of her small kitchen. "I wish I weren't."

"But that's blackmail." Sarah glanced through the open doorway to the children sitting on her parlor floor, drawing pictures.

"That bastard…" Jess clenched his hands into fists. "He's not laying a hand on those kids. I'm not letting him near them."

"He couldn't care about them. If he did, he'd have been here all these years." Sarah worked her lips together.

"He's been here," Jess said. "Nate told me Hayden had come back to town over the years getting money from Cassie."

"Maybe he really does want the children."

Jess shook his head. "He doesn't want them, Sarah."

"What are you doing to do?"

"I'll figure out something." Jess pulled at his neck. "But that bastard is not getting a dime from me."

"What? You have to pay him, Jess."

"I do that and I'll never be rid of him."

Sarah spread out her arms. "What else can you do? If he goes to the sheriff he'll get the children. Then who knows what he'll do with them? You have to pay him, Jess, you have to."

He whirled to face her. "No. Never."

"Shh." Sarah glanced at the children, then hooked

his arm and walked with him to the other side of the room. His muscles were drawn taut, bulging beneath his shirtsleeve. "If it's the money, I can help. I've got a little put away. It's not much, but you can have every cent of it."

He shrugged and stared out the back door. "It's not the money. I've got money."

Her heart froze in midbeat. Five hundred dollars was the equivalent of nearly two years of her salary—*two years*. And Jess threw the figure around as if it were pocket change. How could anyone have that much money without...

Sarah's blood ran cold. The rumors, the speculation. Jess, a hired assassin. The bank robbery in Fairmont. Could it be true?

He looked down at her as if reading her thoughts. "Go ahead. Ask me how I got it. I know you want to."

She shook her head. "It's none of my business."

He turned to face her. "Wondering, aren't you? Wanting to know if the rumors are true."

The images of Jess she'd stored away in her mind played out before her now. Braiding Maggie's hair, baking the pie, charming the ladies at the social, holding Jimmy on his lap, kissing her with such tenderness. No, she couldn't believe he was an outlaw. Regardless of what anyone said, or how bad things looked, she couldn't believe it.

She looked him square in the eye. "Jess Logan, you are many things, but I don't believe you're a criminal."

A moment passed while he watched her intently, searching her face and finding nothing but sincerity. "You mean that, don't you?"

"Yes. With all my heart."

And that set his own heart to pounding. Sarah Wakefield, the well-bred, refined city woman—the schoolmarm—believed in him. Jess took her hand.

"I've got something to tell you. You'd better sit down."

With some trepidation, Sarah allowed him to lead her to the kitchen table. They sat across from each other, the lantern burning against the gray, overcast day. Jess drummed his fingers on the table, then pulled at his collar and leaned forward on his arms.

"There's something you need to know about me."

Sarah braced herself. "Yes?"

"I'm the Legendary Lawman."

The words didn't even sink in. "What?"

"That's where I got the money. I write those dime novels. Leyton Lawrence, the Legendary Lawman."

Sarah's jaw sagged. "*You?* But—how?"

Jess sat back in the chair. "I told you I went to prison. Believe me, spending a year behind bars gives a man plenty of time to think about which side of the law he wants to be on. After I got out, I kept myself working, stayed out of trouble. Then, some years later I was in a saloon down in Texas when a city fellow came over and said he'd heard I'd done time. He wanted to know about being an outlaw. Said he was writing a book about it."

"He told you how to get started?"

"Not exactly. But it got me to thinking. I didn't want people reading books about outlaws, believing it was some exciting kind of life. So I came up with the idea of the Legendary Lawman and sent it to one of those publishing places back East. They liked it."

"That was the package you got from New York City, wasn't it," Sarah realized. "Why did you keep it a secret?"

"Wasn't anybody's business." Jess rubbed his chin. "I have the money sent to the bank over in Fairmont, close enough that Cassie could get to it anytime she needed it."

Sarah's spine stiffened. "You gave the money to your sister?"

He shrugged. "After that husband of hers ran off, she needed a house, money to raise the kids. Her teaching salary wasn't near enough."

"And you gave her the money? All of it?"

"I didn't need it for anything." Jess sat forward and rested his arms on the table. "I worked, made all I needed for myself."

Sarah's heart swelled. "You did all this? For your sister? And never told anyone?"

"I didn't want anybody to know." He pointed a finger at her. "And I still don't."

"But Jess, everybody in town thinks you're—"

"No."

"If they knew—"

"I said no." Jess surged to his feet and walked to the back door. "Anyway, I've got to deal with Jed Hayden, one way or the other."

Sarah rose and followed him. "Talk to Nate. Maybe he can run him out of town or something."

Jess shook his head. "I don't want the whole town knowing about this. I don't want Maggie and Jimmy around Hayden. He's content to lay low, waiting for the money and that suits me just fine."

"Then what will you do?"

He looked down at her. "I don't know yet. But I need your help."

Hearing those words pleased her. "Of course."

"Watch out for Maggie at school. I don't think Hayden will come around, but I can't chance it. I'll walk her to school and come back for her, but I can't be there all day."

"I'll make her the room monitor and keep her in at recess until this is settled." Sarah touched her hand to her throat. "I'll be glad when this is over."

"I've got some good news," Jess offered. "Looks like you were right about Luke and Megan. Seems that Zack Gibb is responsible for what happened."

"Oh, dear." Sarah shook her head.

"Zack loves her, though. He wants to make it right."

"He seems like a nice young man to me." Sarah shrugged. "Although, I don't think Sheriff Neville will agree."

"Probably not." Jess pulled at his collar. "I promised Luke and Zack I'd break the news to Neville."

"Do you think you should get involved? You're not exactly the sheriff's favorite person." But even as she spoke the words, Sarah knew what his answer would be.

"None of those kids can do it." He grinned. "Besides, knowing the truth will convince Sheriff Neville you had nothing to do with what happened."

Sarah turned away. "And that matters to you?"

"I don't want you to lose your job, Sarah. I know what kind of a chance you've taken just helping me and the kids. I don't want you to—"

She looked back over her shoulder. "You don't want me to—what, Jess?"

He stared at her looking so pretty in the gray afternoon, and drew in a deep breath. "I don't want you to have to leave Walker." There. He'd said it.

Sarah's heart skipped a beat. "I don't want to leave, Jess."

She wanted to live here forever, happy and secure in the little community. Hearing Jess say he wanted the same thrilled her to no end. But she couldn't let him think the reason went any deeper—she couldn't face it herself.

Sarah forced a smile. "After all, I know all the children here at the school already. And I have this newly renovated house, and I've made new friends."

His expression darkened. "Are those the only reasons you want to stay, Sarah?"

No, there was another reason—another big reason. And she wanted to tell him so badly her heart ached. But she couldn't.

Sarah drifted across the kitchen, putting distance between them. She grinned. "The neighbors are nice, too."

Neighbors, hell. Jess reached for his hat and yanked it on. Just what he wanted to be, a nice neighbor.

"I'm going over and talk to Neville. Can the kids stay here a while?"

"Of course. And good—"

The door closed, leaving her alone in the kitchen. Sarah pressed her lips together, fighting the urge to run after him. She'd never experienced such strong feelings for any man before. She sensed Jess felt some of those same things—and it was killing both of them.

Her words had said one thing, but everything about her said something else entirely.

Jess grumbled to himself as he made his way into Walker, contemplating Sarah, as he did much of the time now. The woman was driving him crazy. And not only because he wanted to roll around in bed with her, easing the perpetual ache in his body. Something else was wrong.

The looks she gave him, the way she tilted her head, that special smile she favored him with all told Jess that Sarah had feelings for him. And not just neighborly feelings, as she claimed. Something more. Something deeper. He knew he wasn't wrong.

But she was fighting them. Trying to hide them, pretend they didn't exist. Was it just because she didn't want to lose her job? No, it was more. If he could just figure out what.

And what would he do then? Jess stopped on the

boardwalk in front of the jailhouse. Would he confess that he'd fallen in love with her? Would he pour out his feelings?

Jess pushed open the door and stepped inside the jailhouse. Sheriff Neville sat behind his desk. The lit wall lanterns left the office in dim shadows. Nate was nowhere to be seen.

"What do you want, Logan?" The sheriff growled the words, sparing him no more than a glance as he continued on with his paperwork.

Jess closed the door softly and shook off the claustrophobic feeling this place gave him. "I've got to talk to you, Sheriff."

"Unless you came to say you're leaving town, I'm not interested."

Jess pulled his hat lower on his forehead. "It's about your daughter."

His head came up sharply. "I told you to keep your damn mouth shut about that."

Jess sank into the chair across the desk from him, reminding himself to stay calm. A lot of people were depending on his handling of this situation. "Look, I know this is tough for you."

"The hell, you know. You never tried to have anything decent in your whole life, Logan. I raised my daughter up right so she'd be a good wife, catch herself a good husband." Neville wadded the paper he was writing on and hurled it across the room. "And look what happened. That Trenton boy comes along. And him hardly dry behind the ears. How the hell is he going to look after my daughter? Some snot-nosed schoolboy who can't keep his fly closed.''

''If that's how you feel, Sheriff, I've got some good news for you.''

Neville eyed him suspiciously. ''Yeah?''

''Luke's not the one. The young man responsible happens to love your daughter. He wants to marry her. He's got a job, and he's been saving his money so he can do right by her. Megan was afraid to tell you the truth.''

''Who is it?''

Jess shifted in his chair. ''Zack Gibb.''

''That's a lie!'' Sheriff Neville surged to his feet, knocking over his chair. ''My daughter's got better sense than to get hooked up with the likes of the Gibb clan!''

''Hold on now, Sheriff.'' Jess rose, holding out his palms. ''Just because his family's a little loco, doesn't mean there's anything wrong with Zack.''

Color rose in Neville's face until it was beet red. ''I'll be damned if I'll let my daughter marry one of those Gibbs! I'm sending her away!''

''Wait, Sheriff. You don't mean that.''

''I'll send her to her aunt in Springfield! And when that bastard she's carrying comes along, she'll give it to somebody else! She better never bring it here, if she wants to be a daughter of mine!''

Jess's blood ran cold at the hard, steely look on the sheriff's face. ''That's your daughter, for God's sake—and your grandchild. Think about what you're saying.''

"Get the hell out of my office, Logan!" He pointed toward the door. "I ought to run you out of town— along with Gibb *and* that Trenton boy. Stay out of my business."

Jess walked to the door and opened it. "You're making a mistake."

"The only mistake I made was not running you out of town the minute you got here. But you'll be gone soon enough," Neville snarled at him. "And that schoolmarm you're so friendly with will be leaving, too. I got word back from St. Louis. I know all about what she did there."

Jess felt his anger spark for the first time. "What are you talking about?"

"She'd better start packing now. Because when the school board meets next week, I intend to tell them everything I know about Sarah Wakefield's past."

Chapter Thirteen

"When is Uncle Jess coming home?"

"Pretty soon." Sarah lit the lanterns in her parlor and settled onto the settee again. Both children snuggled closer. "Would you like to hear another story?"

"How come Uncle Jess went away?" Maggie shuffled through the stack of storybooks beside her.

"He had some business to take care of. But don't worry. He'll be home before you know it."

Sarah hoped she was right. Jess had ridden to Fairmont today and she hoped he intended to get the cash from the bank there to pay Jed Hayden. They'd talked about it again and Jess was adamant about not paying, but with the custody hearing drawing closer, there wasn't much choice.

"Uncle Jess is really coming back, isn't he?" Maggie's big brown eyes blinked up at her.

Sarah looped her arms around both children, drawing them closer. Children were smart and very intuitive. Her years of teaching made her realize that Maggie and Jimmy also were aware of her own anxiety, though they had no idea Jed Hayden caused it. She'd wondered a time or two what would happen if Hayden suddenly showed up at her house, demanding to see the children.

"Your uncle loves you both very much. Why, I expect he'll even have a surprise for you two when he gets home." Sarah gave both children a little squeeze. "Now, what shall we read next? Jimmy, you pick this time."

Though the boy still hadn't spoken, he interacted with everyone much more now, communicating with facial expressions, pointing and occasionally stomping his feet. And, finally, he'd stopped wetting his pants. Sarah smiled as Jimmy passed her the same book she'd read to him three times already. Jess had done a good job making the boy feel loved and secure.

Sarah opened the book. "'Once upon a time—'"

Hooves sounded outside, bringing them all up off the settee. The children ran to the window.

"It's Uncle Jess!"

Maggie jumped up and down, then ran into the kitchen, Jimmy right behind. Unable to suppress the relief and joy she felt, Sarah followed. She opened the back door as Jess came up the steps. Looking tired and drawn, he scooped both children into this arms.

"We missed you, Uncle Jess." Maggie threw her arms around his neck and hugged him hard, mashing her face against his. Jimmy laid his head on Jess's shoulder and snuggled close against him.

Sarah forced herself to keep her distance, wanting to run to him as the children had.

Jess kissed both their cheeks and sat them down. "Have you two been good?"

Maggie's smile brightened. "Did you bring us something, Uncle Jess? Did you?"

"Well, let me see here." Jess made a grand show of searching through each pocket and finally bringing out two small bags. "Look what I found. Anybody here like licorice?"

Both children jumped up and down, accepting the candy and giving Jess hugs before they hurried into the parlor. Grinning, Jess watched them plop onto the floor together.

"They missed you."

His gaze settled on Sarah, standing beside the stove. What a welcome sight this woman was. He'd missed her as much as he'd missed the kids today. He wished he could tell her…show her.

Jess shrugged out of his coat and hung it on the peg beside the door. "Sorry to be away so long. Kids all right while I was gone?"

"Fine."

Jess tossed his Stetson on the table. "Any sign of Hayden today?"

"No. I kept an eye out, but didn't see him." Sarah stepped closer. "Jess, I've been thinking about this problem all day and I think you should go to the sheriff."

He held up his hand. "No, Sarah."

"But there must be a law, or something, against what he's trying to do. If Nate gets involved maybe we can send him to prison so he can never get to the children.''

''No.'' Jess paced across the small room. He was tired and hungry and agitated from all the thinking he'd done on the long ride to Fairmont and back today. ''Look, Sarah, I got the money out of the bank today, but I'm not handing it over to Hayden yet.''

''But—''

''I need that money, Sarah. I need it for myself.''

Surprised, she stepped closer. ''Can I ask why?''

Jess blew out a long, slow breath. ''I'm going to buy back the land that belonged to my pa, the place where I was raised. I'm going to start ranching.''

''Ranching?'' Her eyes widened. Could he have any more surprises for her? ''Do you know how to ranch?''

''Yes. While the whole town's been gossiping all these years about what they think I've been doing, I've really been working on ranches, learning the business. That's what I want to do here in Walker.''

A wellspring of emotion bubbled up in Sarah. Not only did he want the children, but he also wanted a home. Just as she wanted.

''Jess, that's wonderful.''

He turned away and paced across the kitchen again. ''Now you know why I'm not giving that money to Hayden.''

''But, Jess, you have to.''

''No, I don't.''

''You can earn it back, eventually.''

"I've waited my whole life for what I want, Sarah, I'm not waiting any more."

"But if you don't pay Hayden, he'll—"

"No!" He turned on her. "I said no!"

Sarah's concern turned to anger in the face of his ill temper. "You're so stubborn! Can't you even consider that I might be right? Or go to Nate for help? Why can't you trust anyone?"

"Trust!" Jess advanced on her. "You're a fine one to be talking about trust!"

Sarah's breath caught. "What is that supposed to mean?"

"You're the one person—the only person—I ever told about my life, Sarah, and what thanks do I get for it? I get to hear about *your* life from Sheriff Neville! I get it thrown in my face like garbage tossed out the back door!"

She gasped and fell back a step. "No...."

Jess's anger escalated, bringing with it the hurt he'd felt since the sheriff had hinted that Sarah had been driven out of St. Louis. "I trusted you. I asked for your help. But could you do the same? Hell, no!"

"What did he tell you?" Sarah bit into her lower lip.

Her face had gone white, driving away some of Jess's anger. He turned away. Maybe he was asking too much of her. "Never mind."

Sarah caught his shoulder. "Tell me what he said. Tell me!"

His anger fired up again. "Look, just forget it—"

"I want to know!"

"Neville wouldn't tell me, exactly! He just hinted at something, trying to—"

"Stop! Stop! Stop!"

A voice, foreign to them both, screamed from the doorway to the parlor. Jess and Sarah turned to see Jimmy standing there, his face drawn in an angry pout.

"Don't talk to my Uncle Jess like that!"

Jimmy ran to Jess and wrapped both arms around his leg. Dumbfounded, Jess and Sarah just stared at him.

His lower lip poked out as he glared up at Sarah. "You better be nice."

Stunned, Sarah said, "Jimmy, you're talking."

Her gaze met Jess's and they both burst into smiles.

Jess kneeled down. "Hey, cowboy, good to hear you've got a voice."

But Jimmy didn't look the least bit happy. He glared angrily up at Sarah. "You're not nice. You're a mule, just like Uncle Jess saided."

Sarah blinked at the child and looked at Jess. "I am?"

Jess held up his hand. "Wait now, Jimmy, don't—"

"And you make ice everywhere. Uncle Jess said so."

"Hold on, cowboy—"

"You're like Jack Frost."

Jess waved his hands frantically. "Jimmy, just a minute—"

"What else did your Uncle Jess say?" Sarah stepped closer.

"You're ornery."

Jess pulled at his collar. "I didn't say that, Sarah, I—"

"Uh-huh." Jimmy nodded his head hard. "You did, Uncle Jess."

"Well, yeah, I might have said it, but—"

"What else, Jimmy?"

The boy's brows drew together. "He saided you smelled good."

"Hellfire...." Jess rose and turned away.

Sarah grinned. "He said that? What else?"

"He saided you're big and round."

"What!"

Jess whirled to face her. "*Soft* and round. I said you were soft and round."

Color rose in her cheeks and her brows arched indignantly. "You said *what?*"

"Oh brother...." Jess plowed his fingers through his hair.

Jimmy folded his arms over his chest. "I don't want you to holler at Uncle Jess no more."

Sarah's heart softened. She knelt down in front of the boy. "I won't holler at your uncle ever again."

"Promise?"

She drew a little *X* over her heart. "I promise."

Jimmy smiled broadly, then threw his arms around her neck for a quick hug and scampered into the parlor.

Grinning, Sarah watched him go as she got to her feet, then looked at Jess across the room. His face was red. "Jack Frost, huh?"

"I didn't mean you were cold, exactly, I, ah..." Jess cleared his throat. "I, ah, just..."

"Just what?"

"I..." Jess flapped his arms against his sides helplessly. "I guess I won't be getting any gold star today, huh?"

"Definitely not today."

"I'm sorry, Sarah." He shrugged lamely and offered a weak smile. "At least he's talking."

"I never realized the child had so much to say."

Jess coughed. "Me either. Look, I'd better go. Maggie, Jimmy! Let's go!"

Jess shrugged into his coat as the children hurried in from the parlor.

"Good night, Miss Sarah." Maggie smiled as she slipped her cloak around her shoulders.

"Good night, honey."

Jimmy gazed around the kitchen as Jess helped him into his coat. "Did you fixted the window, Uncle Jess?"

"Yes, I did. Come on, put your arm in, cowboy."

"So you can't look inside no more?"

Jess stole a quick glance at Sarah and saw her mouth sag open. "Let's go, Jimmy. We've got to get home. Maggie, get your schoolbooks."

Maggie hurried back into the parlor.

"You can't look inside no more, Uncle Jess?"

His whole body ignited at the memory of seeing Sarah through the window dressed in her underthings. "I didn't look inside, Jimmy, I—"

"Uh-huh." The boy nodded his head emphatically.

"Yeah, 'member? When Maggie washded her hair and—"

"Maggie! Let's go!" Jess pushed Jimmy out the door ahead of him and waved impatiently as Maggie hurried toward him.

"'Night, Miss Sarah." Maggie smiled as Jess caught her hand and pulled her out the door.

Sarah stood in the open doorway watching as they clamored down the back steps. Suddenly, Jess turned and bounded onto the porch again. Passion burned in his eyes. He grasped her upper arms and pulled her full against him. Her body ignited at the press of his hard flesh on hers.

"I said them—all those things." Jess breathed the words hot against her lips. "You're stubborn as a mule, Sarah Wakefield, and sometimes you can be cold as ice. But other times—"

He kissed her. Hard, full on the mouth. With no apology and no hesitation. He covered her lips with his, then thrust his tongue inside, branding her with his heat. She groaned softly and he pulled away.

"I swear to God, Sarah, if you were any softer or smelled any better, I'd never be able to walk out this door. It's damn hard enough doing it now."

He turned loose of her abruptly, then stalked away, leaving her breathless on the porch, watching him until he disappeared.

Muffled whispers came down the hallway, but Jess didn't have the heart to tell the children to settle down. After all, how long had it been since Jimmy had actually spoken to his sister, snuggled into their two little beds at night? They'd fall asleep soon enough.

Jess gazed around the kitchen looking at all the things that needed his attention, but couldn't quite find the willpower to get them done. Sarah had sapped all his strength tonight. He'd fought a real battle with himself not to go back over to her place.

A knock sounded on the door and Jess tensed, thinking it was Hayden. He pulled back the window curtain and saw two figures on his back porch. He recognized both immediately.

Jess crossed the room and opened the door. "What are you boys doing out so late?"

"Just got off work, Mr. Logan." Zack Gibb squared his shoulders.

"We wanted to know what happened with the sheriff." Luke slid his fingers in his trouser pockets and hunched his shoulders. "Reverend Sullivan will be back in a few days."

Jess gazed at the two in the pale moonlight, the unlikely bond between them creating a friendship. He stepped outside and closed the door behind him, not wanting the children to overhear. The night air was chilly, but it felt good.

"Wish I had better news, boys." Jess turned to Zack. "Sorry, Zack. Sheriff Neville's pretty mad about everything. He won't give your marriage his blessing. He says he's sending Megan away, making her give up the baby."

Zack whispered a curse.

Jess grasped his shoulder. "Sorry. I wish I could

have done better. I believe you really love Megan and you two ought to be together.''

Zack lifted his gaze. ''I appreciate what you did, Mr. Logan. Nobody else in this town would have helped me. I'm beholden to you from now on.''

''What are you going to do?''

He shook his head and worked his lips together. ''I'm not sure. I need to think on it a spell.''

''If there's anything I can do, let me know.''

''Thanks, Mr. Logan.'' Zack turned to leave, but stopped. ''I meant what I said. I'm beholden to you. I won't forget it.''

Zack left, leaving Luke and Jess alone on the porch.

''Do you think they'll run off together?'' Luke asked.

''I doubt it. Megan's too afraid of her pa, afraid of what he'll do to Zack when he tracks them down.'' Jess shrugged. ''At least you don't have to marry her now.''

''Is her pa really sending her away?''

''Afraid so.''

''That's just not right.''

''It's not over yet. I figure if we give the sheriff a few days to cool off, maybe I can talk to him again.''

''You'd do that?''

He had to. Convincing Sheriff Neville to let Megan marry Zack solved a wagonload of problems, including what the sheriff might say at the school board meeting next week.

''Zack took the news pretty well,'' Luke said.

Jess grinned. "Now you don't have to worry about Gil shooting you."

"He's in town. I saw him today." Luke pulled at his suspenders. "Maybe you ought to worry about him shooting you now."

"Shooting me?"

"Yeah, because you got Megan sent away. Like I told you, Gil won't be too happy about coming all the way to Walker and not getting to shoot somebody."

"I'll take my chances. Better get on home, son. It's late."

"All right. But you watch your back." Luke left Jess alone on the porch.

Slowly he walked down the steps and gazed off at Sarah's house across the meadow. A faint light burned in the kitchen window. Was she up this late eating? Working on her lessons for tomorrow? Thinking about his kiss?

Of all the things that could have been on his mind tonight—the sheriff running him out of town, losing the children at the hearing, Gil Gibb gunning for him, Hayden's blackmail—Sarah was the one thing he couldn't turn loose of. And of all those problems, she was probably the one thing he should let go of. But somehow, he just couldn't.

"Have fun and behave. I'll be here when you get finished."

Jess kissed both the children and handed them over to Kirby on the church steps. Maggie waved and hurried inside.

"Are you coming back, Uncle Jess? Are you?" Jimmy crossed his arms over his chest, refusing to go inside for Bible study.

"Sure, cowboy."

"Promise?"

"Promise."

Kirby smiled at Jess as she took Jimmy's hand. "I heard he was talking again."

"Can we make pictures tonight, Miss Kirby? Can we? I want to make pictures. Uncle Jess lets me make pictures at home. Can we, Miss Kirby? Can we?"

"Certainly, Jimmy." She rolled her eyes at Jess. "He's really talking, isn't he?"

Jess chuckled. "Making up for lost time."

"Nate's inside. Do you want to come in?"

He shook his head. "No, thanks. I'll talk to him another time."

"Bye, Uncle Jess." Jimmy waved as he went into the church with Kirby.

Evening shadows from the disappearing sun stretched across the churchyard as Jess surveyed the area. Hayden had been on his mind all day. He hadn't seen him and he'd expected to. That made him nervous. A bastard like him wasn't likely to up and leave town without getting the money he'd come there for.

Luke came around the corner of the building. "Hey, Jess."

"What are you doing over here?"

"Looking for Megan." He nodded toward the church. "I heard the Toliver gang might be heading this way and her pa is busy over at the jailhouse loading up rifles, just in case. Thought with him tending to sheriffing I might talk to her a while.''

''Who told you about the Toliver gang?'' Jess tensed. His first thought was getting the children home where it was safe, then getting to Sarah.

Luke waved away his worried question. ''Mr. Garrette said Waylon Vernon was talking about it over at the saloon.''

Information that unreliable was no cause for concern, which explained why Nate was in the church making eyes at Kirby and not over at the jail. Jess relaxed. ''I haven't seen Megan, but—''

Jed Hayden appeared at the edge of the churchyard, his outline barely visible in the closing darkness. Jess's back stiffened.

''I've got to go, Luke.''

Luke gazed off at the road. ''Who's that?''

Jess caught his shoulders and urged him toward the church. ''Nothing for you to worry about, Luke. Get inside.''

''Hey, that's the man you saw when we were in town the other day. Who is he?''

Jess grasped his upper arm. ''Get inside, Luke. Watch the kids for me. Don't let them leave until I get back. Understand?''

He gulped hard. ''Yeah, sure, Jess.''

Luke headed up the steps but stopped and turned back in time to see Jess approach the man standing near the road. They talked for a minute. Luke could tell by Jess's stance that it wasn't a friendly conversation. Then they turned and headed toward Jess's house.

A minute passed while Luke debated what to do. Jess had asked him to watch the kids, but Luke figured they'd be safe enough inside the church. Finally, he hurried down the steps and crossed the churchyard, keeping his distance from Jess and the other man. He hid at the corner of the house while Jess went inside and the man waited on the back porch.

Luke studied him in the light from the kitchen window, then gasped and flattened himself against the side of the house. He knew that man. Despite the years that had passed and the beard and battered hat, he recognized him. Jed Hayden. Jess's sister's husband. But he'd run off years ago. What was he doing in Walker now?

Cautiously, Luke peered around the corner and saw Jess hand Hayden a thick envelope. They spoke, but he couldn't understand the words. Hayden opened it and withdrew a handful of money—more money than Luke had ever seen in his life. His eyes bulged in the darkness and he swallowed hard. Finally Hayden left, leaving Jess on the porch by himself.

Luke held his breath as Hayden walked past and disappeared down the road. Unable to hold himself back another second, he bolted to the porch.

"Did you give him money?"

Jess leapt to the ground and advanced on him. "What are you doing sneaking around here? I asked you to watch the kids."

Despite Jess's angry expression, Luke couldn't stop. "That was Jed Hayden, wasn't it?"

"I told you to stay at the church. This is none of your business."

His eyes shone like saucers. "You gave him money, didn't you? How come, Jess?"

"Damnation...." Jess pulled his hat lower on his forehead. "Yeah, I gave him money."

"But why?"

"To get rid of him." He'd hated it. He'd thought long and hard, searching for some other solution. But in the end, he'd done it Sarah's way.

"How come?" Luke frowned. "Why is he here? To see Maggie and Jimmy?"

"No. That's the last thing he wanted."

"You mean...?" A moment passed before realization dawned on Luke. He rubbed his hand over his belly. "He didn't want to see his children? His own children? He wanted money instead?"

Jess heaved a heavy sigh. "That's about the size of it."

Luke shook his head. "I never liked him. Mrs. Hayden kept me after school one time and he came in. I guess he didn't see me because he started yelling at her. He drew back on her, like he wanted to hit her."

Jess's blood ran cold. "He tried to hit my sister?"

"He didn't, though. He saw me standing in the corner." Luke turned and gazed off down the darkened road where Hayden had disappeared. "Wasn't too long after that he left town. I heard she'd run him off with the shotgun, but I don't know for sure."

Anger rumbled in Jess's gut. He thought about going after Hayden, taking care of the problem once and for all. But he held himself back.

"He's leaving town."

Luke looked up at him. "What's he going to do when the money you gave him runs out? He'll come back again. Don't you think?"

"Yes, I do, Luke." He was sure of it. "But right now I can't do anything but pay him. I've got the whole town breathing down my neck. That judge will be back here any day trying to take the kids away from me. I can't have any trouble."

Luke nodded. "I guess you're right. But—"

"But what?"

"But isn't there something I can do to help? I mean, if it hadn't been for you I'd have had to marry Megan. You're the only one in town who tried to do anything."

Jess patted his shoulder. "I appreciate the offer, Luke, but it's all right."

"Well, okay. I'm going over to church and see Megan."

Watching Luke disappear around the corner of the house, Jess was suddenly overwhelmed with loneliness. The ranch he'd planned to start was in question now. The children could be lost to him any day, when Judge Flinn rode in and decided his future. He'd spent too much time alone already in his life. He didn't want to face another day by himself.

Jess's gaze strayed to the little house across the meadow. Sarah. His heart suddenly ached for her. She had become as important to him as the children, or the ranch he'd dreamed about. He didn't want to lose any of them.

Jess pounded his fist into his open palm. He wasn't going to lose them. Sarah included. If he only knew whether she wanted him or not. The taste of her kisses, the feel of her body coming willingly against his told him that yes, she did want him. But her words, they said something entirely different.

The thought tickled a spot in his memory reminding him of something Sarah had told him once. She'd said that people often talk without using words. Maybe she'd been trying to tell him all along. Maybe he just wasn't listening the right way.

Well, damned if he'd stand around one more minute trying to solve this riddle on his own. Jess headed across the meadow toward Sarah's house. He'd get to the bottom of this. And he wasn't leaving until she told him everything he wanted to hear.

Everything.

Chapter Fourteen

Sharp banging against her back door brought Sarah straight up in bed. She tossed her book on the bedside table and grabbed her wrapper. Someone coming to call this late at night could only mean trouble.

In the kitchen she pushed her hair back over her shoulder and lifted the curtain. A figure paced her small porch. Even in the darkness she recognized Jess.

Sarah opened the door. "What's wrong?"

The breath went out of him at the sight of her silky hair hanging loose around her shoulders and her wrapper cinched tight around her waist. Jess gulped hard, forcing himself to gaze at her face and no lower.

"I didn't mean to wake you. I didn't think you'd be in bed so early."

She gestured behind her. "I was reading."

"Oh." Jess pulled on his collar, the fire and determination he'd felt in demanding answers from her disappearing with each wobble of his knees.

"Is something wrong? Are the children all right?"

"They're with Kirby at the church for Bible study.

Everything's fine, except...'' He pulled his Stetson lower on his forehead. "Hayden came by the house tonight."

"Oh, dear." She stepped back from the door. "Come inside."

The kitchen smelled good, like fresh baked bread, cinnamon and Sarah. It smelled like home.

Jess took matches from the shelf beside the cookstove and lit the lantern on the table, as familiar with this kitchen as his own. He dropped into a chair.

"What happened?" Sarah asked.

Jess hung his hat on the back of the chair beside him, his eyes straining to see Sarah standing beside the sideboard, just out of the circle of lantern light.

"I paid him."

She walked closer, her fingers closing around the chair across from him, and heaved a sigh of relief. "Is he gone?"

Jess nodded. "For now."

"At least the children are safe."

Jess rose from the chair and pulled in a deep breath. "We need to talk."

She fell back a step, clutching her wrapper tighter against her throat. "It's late, Jess, and—"

"It's late all right, Sarah. Too late for me to come to call, too late for me to pretend anymore."

She inched toward the doorway. "I—I don't understand."

"Yes you do." He followed her across the room and caught her arm. "You've been running since the day I laid eyes on you. I thought you were running from me, Sarah, but you're not. And it's not that you're worried about getting fired. It's something else.''

She turned her head away. "No, you're wrong.''

"You've been trying to tell me, but I wasn't listening.'' Jess urged her closer and touched his palm to her cheek. "I'm listening now, Sarah.''

The intensity of his gaze burned into her, bound her to him in the dim kitchen. The feel of his big hand against her flesh scored her skin. Emotion rose to close off her throat.

"Sarah, I never felt about a woman the way I feel about you. Can't you give me a chance? Can't you trust me?''

Forcing down her runaway feelings, Sarah pulled away from him. He followed, not letting her go far, but without his touch soft and warm against her, she could think better.

"It's not a matter of trust, Jess.''

"I know you're worried about what the town will think of you, Sarah. And I don't blame you.'' He slid his fingers into his hip pockets, fighting the urge to take her in his arms. "But can't you see that people are going to talk, no matter what happens? You have to follow your heart, Sarah. You can't let other people decide your life for you.''

Sarah chanced a look at him. "I know it was hard for you to come back to Walker, knowing what you'd face.''

"Damn right it was hard. I almost didn't make it.''

Jess softened his voice. "I wouldn't have made it, Sarah, if it hadn't been for you."

Sarah turned away again. "You don't understand, Jess. It's not just the talk about you, it's—"

"It's what? Tell me, Sarah. What is it?" Jess studied her in the dim light. "Something happened back in St. Louis, didn't it. Neville hinted around about something, but he wouldn't tell me what it was."

Sarah shook her head quickly. "No, Jess, don't—"

"Something happened that you don't want the sheriff to find out about. Something that you think the school board will fire you over, if they take it in their heads you're spending too much time with me, too."

"I don't want to talk about this."

"Does it have to do with your husband?" her persisted. "Neville told me something happened after he died."

A little whimper escaped from her lips and she pressed her hand over her mouth quickly. "He found out…?"

Jess strained to control his patience. "Found out what, Sarah? What happened?"

She shook her head frantically. "Don't ask, Jess. Please don't."

Now he had to know. "Did his kin say you stole their inheritance?"

"No—"

"Did you dance on his grave?"

"No!"

Jess grabbed her arm, holding her against the wall. "Did they claim you married him for his money?"

"No!"

"Darnit, Sarah, what did you do?"

"I killed him…I think."

Breath went out of Jess in a single huff. He loosened his grip on her arm. "You what?"

Sarah straightened, her emotions boiling over. "I—I did something wrong."

"I don't believe it." He shook his head. "What happened?"

Some of the fire went out of her. She eased away. "I don't know."

"Did you shoot him? Hit him on the head with the chamber pot? Drive the horses over him? What?"

She stopped beside the table, keeping her back to him. Waves of humiliation crashed over her bringing with them all the horrible memories.

Jess stepped closer and laid his hand softly on her shoulder. "Did he hurt you, Sarah?"

"No." She looked back at him. "No, he never hurt me. We weren't married long enough for anything like that to happen."

"How long were you married?"

She turned her head away again. "About eight…"

"Months?"

"No."

"Weeks?"

"Hours."

"Hours?" Jess stepped around in front of her. "You were only married to him for eight hours?"

She looked up at him. "I didn't mean to do anything wrong."

"What did you do?"

"I don't know!" Sarah flung out both hands.

Jess rubbed his hand across his chin. "Where, exactly, were you when he died?"

Color rose in her cheeks and she winced. "It was our wedding night. We were…in bed."

His brows bobbed upward. "You mean you and he were…"

"Yes." Sarah plastered her palms against her cheeks. "Oh, Jess, it was horrible. One minute we were…you know, and the next, Howard just fell over. Right there. In bed."

Jess blew out a heavy breath and raked his fingers through his hair. "Just like that, huh?"

"The whole thing was a horrid nightmare." Sarah pressed her fingers to her forehead. "My mother died when I was young so my father raised me. He was a schoolteacher, too. We had a wonderful life together. But when he got sick and knew he didn't have much time left, he didn't want me to be alone."

"So he found Howard for you to marry?"

"He was a friend of Father's. A dear, sweet man. I'd known him since I was a child. I didn't object to the marriage, even though he was considerably older than me, because I liked him well enough and I didn't want to be alone." Sarah wrung her hands together. "I had no idea my behavior would…"

Jess shook his head. "Sarah, I think you've got this all wrong. He was an old man. His heart probably just gave out."

"No." She shook her head frantically. "I did something wrong. My behavior was too—wanton."

Jess's insides flamed, fighting off the images and his reaction to them.

She dipped her gaze. "That's why I couldn't let you kiss me. I didn't want anything bad to happen to you."

"What if I tell you it's a chance I'm willing to take?" Jess stepped closer.

She backed up. "No. I can't have another death on my conscience. We can never be more than... friends."

Jess closed his hands around her upper arms. "Don't you want to get married one day, Sarah? Have kids? A family of your own?"

"Oh, yes, more than you could know. But, Jess, I can't take that chance. You don't know how awful it was after Howard died. People gossiping and talking. Pointing at me on the street. Whispering behind my back. And the men—they wouldn't leave me alone. They flocked around me. They had some sort of bet going to see which of them could live through an evening with me. They made the most suggestive comments—even offered me money. It was horrible."

"That's why you took this job here in Walker."

She nodded. "I had to get away from there. I couldn't stand it any longer."

"It took a lot of guts to come all the way out here by yourself and start over again."

"I didn't think anyone here would find out."

"Sheriff Neville did. And I'm to blame."

Sarah sighed heavily. "It's not your fault. It's my fault for being so...lustful."

Jess slid his arms around her and drew her closer. "You're a special woman. I care about you."

Sarah braced her arms against his chest, but he held her tight. "Don't talk that way, Jess. Can't you understand, it just makes it harder for me?"

"You've made me half crazy since the first time I saw you, Sarah. I can't just walk away."

"Don't say that." She splayed her hands across his chest.

"I want to make you mine, Sarah. I want to show you how I feel."

"No!" She curled her fingers into the front of his shirt. "You can't! You'll die if you do."

Jess touched his fingers to her hair. "No, Sarah. I'll die if I don't."

He eased her closer and lowered his head until his lips brushed against her cheek, fluttering kisses on her soft skin.

She squirmed. "Jess..."

"Shh." He whispered against her ear. "You like me, don't you Sarah?"

"Well, yes."

He trailed his lips down her throat. "You're not afraid of me, are you?"

"No." She looked up at him. "You're a very special man, Jess. I'm not afraid of you, only of what might happen to you."

Tightening his grip on her, he pulled her full against

him. He felt the tension in her. "You won't kill me, Sarah."

"We can't be sure."

"Yes, we can." Jess sank his hand into the thick hair at her nape, massaging her neck. "There's a way to put an end to this once and for all."

She wanted to pull away. She knew she should. But the feel of his hand on her skin, his body full against her robbed her strength and her thoughts.

"I'll make you forget, Sarah." He brushed kisses across her cheek. "I'll make you forget what happened in St. Louis."

His warmth and strength overwhelmed her. "I—I don't know...."

Jess lifted his head, gazing at her in the dim light. "I trusted you with my kids, Sarah. I trusted you with my life. Can't you trust me? Just a little?"

Emotion swelled her heart. "I want to, Jess, but—"

"That's all I wanted to hear."

He covered her lips with his, smothering her words, kissing her gently. His own body reacted quickly, filling him with urgency. He'd wanted her for so long, he'd thought of nothing but this moment. Yet he had to go slowly, had to savor it, had to make it wonderful for Sarah.

Jess deepened their kiss, plying and coaxing her with his lips, his tongue. He slid his hand down her spine, marveling at her delicate build beneath her wrapper and gown, her thighs, her breasts melting into him.

He lifted his head, his breath hot against her. "Oh, God, Sarah, you're sweet. So sweet."

Hungrily, he kissed her again and groaned deep in his throat. She moaned softly and relaxed in his arms, parting her lips for him.

Desire, hot and raw, surged through him. He felt it building in her, too, as she pressed herself tighter against him. He wanted her. Now.

His hand slid lower on her spine, pressing her closer. She shifted, settling herself intimately against him. Jess closed his palm over her breast and she gasped, but didn't pull away. Instead she arched forward, urging him on.

He couldn't wait another second. Jess lifted her into his arms and carried her to her bedroom. She clung to him, her arms tight around his neck.

Jess stopped in the middle of the room. Even with all the repairs he'd done around the house he'd never been in her bedroom before. A lantern burned low on the bedside table, illuminating the brass bed with its pink daisy coverlet and eyelet linens. The covers were turned back, the pillows slightly rumpled. It looked delicate and refined, yet homey and comfortable. It looked like Sarah.

He set her down, kissing her hungrily, as his fingers feverishly worked the tiny buttons on her wrapper until they gave way one by one. He pulled the sash apart and slid his hands inside. His palms covered her hips. A groan rumbled in his chest at the exquisite feel of her feminine curves. He slid his hands lower, cupping her soft, round bottom, lifting her to him. Hot blood pulsed in him as he slid one hand up to cup her breast. Even through her nightgown, she filled his palm. His thumb caressed the peak and it tightened beneath his touch.

All conscious thought left Sarah, leaving behind swirling feelings and emotions. The incredible heat and power of his body overwhelmed her. His touch blocked out everything. Except for her desire to touch, as well.

Awkwardly, Sarah pulled open the buttons of his shirt and pushed it back. He helped, yanking the sleeves over his hands and tossing it aside. She splayed her fingers across his chest. Heat penetrated the fabric of his long johns. She tore open the buttons and he shrugged out of them, leaving his bare chest.

Hard, molded muscles covered with crispy hair. She'd never seen a man's chest before. At least, none like Jess's. Sarah pressed her hands against him, marveling at the feel. He sucked in a quick, hot breath as her fingers found the tiny coppery disks buried there. They tightened at her touch.

He kissed her again, blindly, madly and urged her onto the bed. Jess pulled off his boots and socks and turned the lantern lower before shucking off his trousers and long johns and stretching out beside her. She came against him willingly, kissing him with a passion he'd not expected. He throbbed for her, for relief, and fought to control himself.

Sarah locked her arm around his neck, lost in the feel of his kiss, while her other hand explored his hard angles, the strength of his arms, the width of his shoulders. His skin burned her fingers.

Frantically, Jess unbuttoned the tiny pearls at the top of her nightgown, then lifted the hem and laid his hand against her leg. He groaned and covered her mouth with his. She was all silky softness, as he knew she'd be. Higher he moved, over the curve of her hip to the tight flesh of her belly, then lower to the curls at the center of her thighs.

They both gasped. He broke off their kiss only long enough to pull the nightgown over her head and send it flying. Pale light from the lantern cast her in a pink hue. God, she was beautiful, her dark hair spread out on the white pillow, her skin glowing. An ache, deep and primal, surged through him. He wanted to wait. He wanted to savor this moment. He didn't want to rush her. The demands of his body were strong, as he'd never experienced before.

Sarah looped her arms around his neck and slid her thigh along his. Desire pounded in him, and he was lost.

Rising above her, Jess settled between her thighs, touching himself against her intimately. She was hot, like liquid silk, and it took all the control he had not to drive himself inside her. Instead he locked his lips to hers, kissing away the passion he couldn't otherwise express yet. She kissed him back, curling her hands around his neck, threading her fingers into his hair. He pressed deeper inside her.

Then everything stopped.

She was tight. Small and tight and ungiving. Jess

lifted his head and saw the grimace on her face. Oh God, she was still a virgin.

He nearly filled her right then, overcome by the realization that no man had touched her before. Jess curled his fists into the pillow, his heart pounding in his chest.

Sarah opened her eyes and her arms fell loosely on the bed. She had no idea how to interpret the look on his face.

"Howard and I didn't get quite this far."

"I figured that out already."

"I'm sorry."

"Oh, Sarah, don't be."

Jess clamped his mouth over hers, driving away her thoughts with his demanding kisses. Slowly, carefully, he eased himself deeper within her, making a place for himself. Finally, she moved with him, rhythmically lifting her hips to meet his.

A strange urgency stole her breath, left her panting, lost in the feeling. His movements mesmerized her. Desire built inside her, rising steadily. Hotter and hotter it flamed. Faster and faster it grew until it burst inside her. Sarah grabbed a handful of his hair and called his name as great waves of pleasure broke within her. Over and over again they pulsed, leaving her sated.

Blood pounding in his veins, Jess strained to hold back as Sarah writhed beneath him, each second both ecstasy and torture. Finally, when she stilled, when he knew for certain, when he couldn't hold himself back another second, Jess drove himself into her. He filled her on the first thrust, emptying into her everything he'd held inside for so long. Overwhelmed, he collapsed onto the pillow beside her.

A delightful warmth she'd never known enveloped Sarah as she opened her eyes. Jess lay beside her, his arms around her, his legs entwined with hers. But his eyes were closed, and he lay still, so still it frightened her.

Panic struck. Oh dear, had she done it again?

"Jess!"

"What!" He shot straight up in the bed, nearly dumping her on the floor. "What? What's wrong?"

Sarah pulled the sheet up over her. "I thought you were dead."

"Oh, that." Jess snuggled into the pillow again and pulled her against him. She had nearly killed him, but he certainly couldn't tell her. At the moment he actually felt a little envy for ol' Howard. What a way to meet your Maker.

Sarah bit down on her lip. "Are you all right?"

"Believe me, honey, I haven't felt this good in a long, long time."

"Nothing hurts, does it?"

He took her hand and gently kissed her palm, then splayed it against his chest. "Feel that?"

Beneath her fingers, his heart thumped sure and strong. Sarah frowned. "It's beating awfully fast."

"It's supposed to."

"Oh."

He pulled her onto his shoulder and wrapped both

arms around her. He wanted to hold her and never let her go. They lay together, lost in the contentment of the moment.

Sarah looked up at him. "I'm glad you didn't die."

He laughed. "Me, too."

"Do you think this was just a fluke? I mean, you don't think that next time you might die, do you?"

"Sarah, stop worrying." He planted a wet kiss on her forehead. "I'm strong and well."

She gazed at him for a long moment. "You really are, aren't you?"

He nodded somberly. "Yes, Sarah, I am."

Contented, she lay against him strumming her fingers along his arms. So strong. Muscles so hard. Then she touched the scar and stopped.

"Nate said you got this the night of the fire, when you were a child."

He planted a kiss against her temple. "Cut it on the glass sailing out the window. Good thing it was snowing. I might have broken something, otherwise."

"It must be hard for you to see the scar every day and be reminded of what happened."

Jess shrugged. "Not really. I got this scar because my pa loved me enough to toss me out the window. He loved my family enough to stay inside and try to save them. Nothing wrong with being reminded of that."

Sarah traced her finger along the thin scar. "You have a lot of love inside you, Jess. That's where you learned it. Lucky for Maggie and Jimmy."

"Oh, shoot. The kids." Jess pushed himself up on

one elbow. "I hate this, but I've got to leave. They'll be done at Bible study by now."

"I'll come with you."

"No." Jess ran his hand over her hair. "Stay here. I want to remember you like this."

She watched him dress. First, his lean naked body standing among the delicate lace of her room. His fingers buttoning his long johns, pulling on socks, fastening his belt buckle. Big arms sliding into his shirt. Manly tasks she'd never seen before.

For a fleeting moment she considered what she'd just done. Given herself to a man who wasn't her husband. A man who'd promised nothing, hadn't even said he loved her. But in her heart, Sarah couldn't find fault with what had happened. Nor was she sorry for it.

"I guess you'll be needing this." He found her nightgown on the floor and sat down on the edge of the bed. He put it on her, closed the buttons and lifted her silky hair over her shoulders.

A long moment passed while they gazed at each other. She wanted to ask him to stay. By the look on his face, she knew he wanted the same. But they both knew it couldn't be.

"Go get the children. They'll be scared if you're not there." Sarah planted her hands on his shoulders and eased him away. She nodded toward the bedside table. "Besides, I'm in the middle of a good book I want to finish."

He glanced at the book that lay open on the table

and grinned. "You're reading about the Legendary Lawman?"

"I bought it at the mercantile." She picked up the book. "Now, run along. I want to see what secrets of Jess Logan are hidden in these pages."

Jess swiped his hand over his face and rose. "It's just a made-up story. Remember that."

"Good night, Jess." She turned her attention to the book.

He walked to the door and looked back. Bless her, for making this easy.

Sarah forced her eyes on the written words, not needing to see to know when Jess left the room. It felt cold and empty without him. She snuggled the quilt closer and made herself read, not wanting to think too much. But a short while later when she heard her back door open again, she wasn't surprised to see Jess walk into her bedroom.

Sarah looked past him. "Where are the children?"

"I got them in bed," Jess said. "Nate's staying with them."

"He is?" She put the book aside. "You didn't tell him you were coming here, did you?"

"No," he said quickly. "Nothing like that."

He eased onto the edge of the bed, watching her intently. She was so pretty and he wanted her so badly. He hadn't gotten her out of his mind since he'd left. But still, despite their earlier lovemaking and his desire to roll around in bed with her all night, he couldn't rush her.

Sarah leaned back against the pillows. "How long can Nate keep the children?"

"I told him I'd be back around dawn."

"Dawn?" Sarah grinned. "And what did you plan to do until dawn?"

His insides flamed. "I wanted to be here with you, just in case you needed more proof that you wouldn't really kill me if we made love again."

"You're willing to sacrifice yourself?"

"As often as you want."

Sarah dipped her lashes. "Would it be all right if we did it again?"

"Oh, yeah." Jess drew in a big breath. "But just so you'll know, you don't ever have to ask."

"But how will I know if you want to?"

"I always want to."

She waved her hand toward his lap. "How will I know if you're...ready?"

"I'm always ready."

She grinned. "Is that so?"

"Yep." Jess gestured at the book that lay on the bedside table. "I don't want to brag, but I'm sort of a legend myself."

Sarah pursed her lips, intrigued by the playful look on his face. "Really?"

"Not as a lawman." He leaned closer.

Sarah's breath caught as his lips fluttered against her neck. "If not a lawman, then what?"

"Let me show you."

Jess pulled off his clothes in a frenzy while Sarah slid out of her nightgown. He was ready for her at once. She welcomed him into her bed. They spent a long frantic moment kissing, touching, feeling before Sarah parted her thighs and Jess filled her again. Coupled, their bodies moved as one, climbing upward, rising together to a fever pitch until great tremors broke over them, leaving them spent in each other's arms.

"Are you certain it's all right if this keeps happening?"

"Oh, Sarah...." Jess collapsed on the pillow, panting heavily. They'd made love sometime during the middle of the night, and now as the first gray streaks of dawn filled her room, she'd only crooked her finger at him and they'd gone at it again. At this rate, she really might kill him.

Sarah snuggled closer, the glow of their lovemaking warming her. "You get your gold star now."

Jess chuckled. He'd sure as hell earned it.

"I'd better get ready for school." Sarah sat up, holding the sheet against her.

"I've got to go, too." Jess forced himself out of bed and stretched, his body achy. He gathered his clothes. "I'll heat up some water so you can bathe."

She grinned and dipped her lashes. "Thank you."

How could she look so innocent after what they'd shared? God help him, he wanted her again. But he made himself leave, hating every step he took that led him away from her. She'd been more than he'd expected, more than he'd even dreamed of. Open, giving, quickly aroused and as anxious as he. Quite a surprise, for a dignified schoolmarm.

She came into the kitchen just as he poured the last bucket of water into the big washtub she kept in the pantry. He'd fired up the cookstove, warming the room, and put coffee on. None of which seemed the least important as he stood looking at her, tousled hair loose around her shoulders, the front of her wrapper crossed but not fastened.

Jess drew in a deep breath. "You're making it pretty hard to leave."

"I suppose I should say I'm sorry, but I'm not." Sarah took a step closer. "Not the least bit sorry."

Jess grasped her upper arms. "I'll meet you after school today."

Would he want to talk of the future? Their future together? Sarah shoved those thoughts aside. She'd been his for one night. What they'd shared had been special. Maybe she shouldn't hope for more.

They kissed and Jess took his hat from the peg beside the door and left. She watched him go, remembering how she'd come to Walker looking for a place to call home. She'd thought living alone, keeping to herself would make her happy. She'd thought that kind of life would make her content.

Sarah pressed her palm against the cold glass pane. Now, it would never be enough.

At his own house, Jess bounded up the back steps and into the kitchen. A pot of coffee bubbled on the stove and Nate sat at the table having a cup.

"Did the kids give you any trouble?" Jess asked as he closed the door behind him.

Nate shook his head. "Slept all night. They didn't even know you were gone."

"Thanks, partner. I owe you one." Jess dropped his hat on the table and poured himself a cup of coffee.

Nate rose from the chair and squared his shoulders. "So, how were things over at Miss Flora's?"

He looked at him over the rim of his cup. "Fine."

"I didn't know Flora had moved her parlor house." Nate hung his thumbs in his gunbelt, glaring at him. "I didn't know she'd taken up residence just down the road at the schoolmarm's house."

Jess gulped and put down his cup. "Were you spying on me?"

"Hell, I was just watching you leave last night, thinking about the good turn I was doing for my friend, giving him a night off to have himself a tumble or two. Then I see you go inside Sarah Wakefield's place. I don't mind keeping your kids so you can go rut with one of them whores, Jess, but I don't like being a party to you having your way with a respectable schoolmarm."

"It's not like that, Nate."

Nate's eyes narrowed. "Are you saying you weren't with her all night? Hell, I can tell by the grin on your face what you've been doing."

Jess swiped his hand across his mouth, holding his memories in check before his body reacted and gave Nate further proof of his accusations.

"Look, Nate, let me explain." Jess pulled at his neck. "I think…I think maybe I'm in love with her."

His brows shot up. "With Sarah? Did you tell her?"

"No. Not yet."

"Why not?"

Jess shrugged. "I don't know. Afraid, I guess."

"I know how that feels." Nate nodded. "People in town are going to have a lot to say about this."

"I'd rather keep it to myself for a while."

"Can't say as I blame you." Nate relaxed his stance. "Anyway, Sarah's a fine woman. You could do a lot worse."

"So could you. You're a fool to leave Kirby stewing, taking a chance she'll get away."

Nate grunted and waved away his comment. He opened the back door and gazed around the kitchen. "You've got this place looking real good, Jess. Hell, maybe I'll just marry you."

"Get out of here before you get me started cursing again." Jess grinned at his friend and followed him outside. "Think about what I said. Kirby's a fine woman. You're darn lucky she's given a scruffy old dog like you a second look."

Nate stopped at the bottom of the steps and pointed a finger at him. "And don't make me have to whip your butt for ruining Sarah's reputation."

"That will be the day." Jess waved as Nate headed toward town.

Jess got Maggie and Jimmy up and gave them their breakfast, the morning going smoothly. When he arrived at school Sarah stood beside the steps, watching over the children playing in the yard. His heart tumbled at the sight of her.

A faint blush colored her cheeks when she saw him. "Good morning," she whispered.

Instinctively, he touched her arm, but she bobbed her brows toward the children and Jess moved a discreet distance away.

A low heat that had simmered in him for weeks suddenly burst into full flame. He didn't like standing apart from her. He didn't want to worry about what people would say. He wanted to hold her and he didn't care who saw him. He wanted to show her off to the world.

"Will you have supper with me in town tonight, Sarah?"

She glanced across the schoolyard at Lottie Myers, who was heading their way. "I have to start school now, Jess."

A little ache throbbed in his chest. He shouldn't have asked her so suddenly. It was too soon. Having supper with him in front of the whole town was a lot to ask of her.

Jess pulled his hat lower on his forehead. "I'll be waiting here when school's out."

Sarah smiled, a special intimate smile that swelled his heart inside his chest. He stood beside the steps until she disappeared into the school, then he and Jimmy headed back toward home.

"Uncle Jess, can we go fishing today? Can we? Can we, Uncle Jess?"

Jess grinned down at the boy. "How about if—"

"Jess! Jess!"

Luke raced up the road, his face red, his breath gone.

Jess grabbed his shoulder. "What's wrong?"

"You've got to come, Jess. You've got to get into town. The Toliver gang just robbed the bank." Luke pressed his hand to his chest, sucking in great gulps of air. "They shot Nate. You've got to come, Jess. He's shot real bad."

Chapter Fifteen

The dozen horses tethered to the hitching post outside the jailhouse tossed their heads and pranced fitfully. Faces peeked out from the shops and businesses along Main Street, but few patrons ventured outside. The early morning gray cast the town in somber shadows, matching the mood of the people.

Jess dismounted and tied his stallion to the railing in front of the Blue Jay Café. He swung Jimmy down and strode inside. A numb silence hung in the empty room. Kirby stood near the kitchen entrance clutching a handkerchief in her fist. Alma Garrette was beside her.

"Kirby, what happened?"

She ran into Jess's arms, her face chalky, her eyes brimming with tears. "I'm so glad you came, Jess."

He cradled her against his shoulder. "How is he?"

She sniffed and lifted her head. "He looks bad, Jess. The doctor is with him now."

Jess squeezed her shoulders. "Nate's strong as an ox. He'll pull through."

The door to the adjoining kitchen opened and Dr. Burns walked through, sleeves rolled back on his long, skinny arms. He eyed them and pulled on his white chin whiskers.

"I won't lie to you. It could go either way."

Kirby gasped and fresh tears rolled down her cheeks.

Alma pressed her hand to Kirby's back. "There, there, dear."

Jess tightened his hold on her. "I sent Luke for your ma and pa. They'll be here any minute." He knew the reverend and his wife had gotten back to town just last night.

"Nate's strong," Dr. Burns offered. "I've seen men shot up worse than this and pull through."

"Can I see him, doc?" Jess asked.

He shook his head. "Won't do any good. He's unconscious."

Kirby whimpered and laid her head on Jess's shoulder.

He drew in a deep breath and set her away from him. He turned to Alma. "Take care of her, Mrs. Garrette."

Alma gasped. "Where are you going?"

"Watch out for Jimmy, too, will you?"

"Yes, but—"

"Jess, no." Kirby grabbed his arm, her eyes wide with a new fear. "No, please, don't do this."

He eased her hand away from him. "I've got to, Kirby."

Alma dug her knuckles into her lips and glanced at the gun on Jess's hip. "The posse…"

Jess knelt in front of Jimmy. He looked him up and down and ran his fingers through the boy's dark hair.

"I'm going out for a while, Jimmy. You stay with Mrs. Garrette and be good. Okay?"

Jimmy shook his head frantically. "No, don't go, Uncle Jess."

Jess smiled gently. "Don't worry."

He crushed the child against his chest in a big hug, then rose and looked at the women.

"I'll be back."

Jess strode out of the café.

Men crowded the boardwalk outside the sheriff's office, their faces drawn in grim lines as they checked the rifles Dwight Rutledge handed out. In the middle of the gathering stood Buck Neville, deputizing the bunch.

Rory Garrette left the crowd of men looking on, those too old or too sick to join the posse, and hobbled over to Jess.

"Who'd a thought it? Who'd a figured them Tolivers would hit us?" He squinted up at Jess. "You riding out?"

Jess nodded as he stepped up on the boardwalk. "You bet I am, Mr. Garrette."

"Damn, boy, I knew you would." He leaned closer. "You watch yourself, though, you hear? Town's just beginning to like you."

Jess scanned the crowd and spotted Luke among the

men. He motioned him over and leaned down to whisper in his ear. "Go find Zack and get him over here. Right now."

Luke's eyes widened. "What for?"

"Just get him. And hurry. Tell him to bring a gun and a horse."

Luke took off down the street.

"Listen up, now!" Sheriff Neville clutched a Winchester in his fist, looking at the men gathered around him. "These Tolivers mean business. And so do I. They shot my deputy and Mr. Purcell when he opened the bank this morning, then barely missed Leo Turner. And that's saying nothing of the property damage they caused and the money they got away with. So I don't want any man riding with me that's not willing to shoot to kill."

Neville glared at the men. They straightened and returned his gaze. They were ready.

"I'm not leaving the town unprotected. Rutledge will stay behind and keep an eye on things." Sheriff Neville looked out over his men. "I'm sure I hit a couple of them Tolivers when they hightailed it out of town after the robbery. They won't be riding very fast. We should catch them pretty quick. Anybody got any questions?"

Zack and Luke weaved through the crowd. Jess pulled Zack aside.

"Did your brother have anything to do with the bank robbery?"

"Gil?" Zack shook his head. "Naw, not Gil."

"You sure?"

"Yesterday was Gil's birthday. He's drunk on his butt out at Ma's place. I saw him there just this morning before I came to work. He's out cold."

"All right, men, let's mount up!" Buck Neville pushed through the crowd toward his horse but stopped when he saw Jess. "What are you doing here, Logan?"

Jess rested his hand on his Colt. "I'm riding after the Toliver gang."

Neville snorted and pushed past him. "No thanks. I've got no want to get shot in the back today."

Anger roiled through Jess. Damn that sheriff, too stubborn to accept the help the town needed.

Jess went after him. "Look, Neville, this has nothing to do with you and me."

The men crowded around turned and stared.

"My friend's been shot," Jess said. "My town's in trouble. I'm not standing around and doing nothing."

The sheriff's eyes narrowed. "Look, Logan, I told you—"

"What's it going to hurt to let him go?" Rory Garrette said. "Ol' Jess is good with a gun—probably gooder than any man in town."

Leo Turner nodded. "Yeah, Sheriff. We need every man we can get."

A grumble of agreement rose from the men.

Sheriff Neville looked at the faces of the townspeople, then glared at Jess one final time. "Mount up."

Rory slapped Jess on the back. "That's the way, boy. You show 'em."

Jess found Zack in the crowd. He nodded toward the gunbelt he wore. "Do you know how to use that?"

"Yeah, sure, but—"

"You're riding with the posse."

His eyes rounded. "Me? But—"

"Here's your chance, Zack. Show Neville what you're made of."

Understanding of Jess's intentions dawned on Zack. He squared his shoulders and made his way through the men to the sheriff. "I want to ride with you."

Neville swung around, looking Zack up and down for a long moment. His lip curled back in a sneer. "All right. Let's head out."

Jess climbed onto his stallion. A knot coiled tight in his stomach as the posse mounted up. He hoped he hadn't done the wrong thing. He hoped Zack wouldn't be the one shot in the back today.

Sarah hurried down the deserted streets, pulling Maggie along behind her. The silence that hung over the town caused her heart to pound faster, worsening the sense of dread that had plagued her since mid-morning.

Halfway through morning classes parents had shown up at school bringing the news of the bank robbery and taking their children home. Sarah dismissed class, pairing up older children with the little ones to see them home safely. She'd gone to Jess's house to take Maggie home and found the place empty. A new wave of fear had washed over her.

"Is Uncle Jess here?" Maggie asked as she hurried along beside Sarah. "Where's Jimmy?"

"I'm sure they're both here in town. At the Blue Jay, probably, seeing about Nate." Sarah gulped down the lump in her throat. She hoped for the child's sake she sounded convincing and her voice didn't betray the unfounded fear that squeezed her like a vice.

The bell over the door at the Blue Jay Café jingled as Sarah and Maggie went inside. Sarah's gaze swept the crowd of people gathered there. Alma Garrette, the Reverend and his wife, Kirby and Dwight Rutledge. Jimmy sat on his knees at the back table eating cake.

Jess. Sarah's heart pounded in her chest. Where was Jess?

Kirby hurried across the room, her arms outstretched. "Oh, Sarah, I'm glad you came." Tears pooled in her eyes again.

Sarah clasped her hands. "I heard about Nate. How is he?"

Kirby sniffed. "The doctor is staying with him. It's too soon to tell for sure."

"We're all praying for him," Reverend Sullivan said.

Sarah gazed around the room again. "Where's Jess? Have you seen him?"

A troubled look passed over all their faces. Sarah's chest tightened into a hard knot.

Dwight Rutledge stepped away from the group of people and drew in a deep breath. "He's with the posse."

Breath left Sarah in a sickly wheeze. Her knees

trembled. She'd known. Since Lottie Myers had told her about the robbery at school this morning, she'd known. Jess wouldn't stand by and do nothing, though she wished to God he would have.

Kirby cupped her elbow. "You'd better sit down, Sarah."

She slumped into a chair, pressing her hand to her forehead.

"You seem mighty upset." Alma pressed her lips tightly together, her brow drawn in a disapproving wrinkle. "Maybe a bit more upset than is proper."

Sarah felt the gazes of everyone in the room boring into her. Anger, a welcome diversion from the fear, swept through her.

"Miss Sarah?" Maggie pulled at her sleeve. "Where's Uncle Jess? How come he's not here?"

She forced aside her feelings, her concern now for the children.

"Your uncle is out for a while, Maggie." Sarah made herself smile. "But he'll be back."

"You promise?"

A new pain stabbed her heart. She wanted to promise—more than anything she wished she could. But Jess was in grave danger, as were all the men with the posse. Sarah wouldn't make a promise she couldn't keep.

"Let's go over here with your brother." Sarah took Maggie's little hand.

"But, Miss Sarah—"

"Jimmy is having cake. You can have some, too."

Kirby brought a slice of cake from the kitchen and

placed it on the table as Sarah settled Maggie into a chair; Kirby seemed almost grateful for something to do.

Everyone else could do nothing but wait. Wait for a change in Nate's condition. Wait for the posse to return…if it returned.

Moments later, the front door opened and Megan hurried inside, Luke close behind. Tears welled in her eyes. Sarah went to her.

"Mrs. Wakefield…" Megan hiccupped, trying to hold back her feelings.

Sarah slid her arm around the girl's shoulders. "I know you're worried, Megan, but your father is a very capable lawman. He won't—"

"No, no." She sniffed and shook her head. "Zack went with them. He's gone with the posse."

"Zack?" Sarah closed her eyes, feeling the girl's worry matching her own. "Jess is gone, too."

They clasped each other's hands, their mutual worry binding them together.

"Why did he have to go?" Tears spilled down Megan's cheeks.

Sarah shook her head. She wished she could find some words of comfort, something to say that would ease her worry, but couldn't. Not while those same feelings consumed her.

Megan gulped. "Men are so stupid."

"Yes, they are." And she honestly meant it.

Alma Garrette tossed her head. "I doubt your father would approve of your concern for that Gibb boy."

"Alma, this is hardly the time," Fiona said.

Alma drew herself up tighter. "I think it is the time. What would Sheriff Neville say if we stood by and did nothing? Why, he's out risking his life and here's his daughter concerned for that Zack Gibb."

A tingle of anger jolted Sarah's stomach. "A great many of our men are out risking their lives, Mrs. Garrette. They all deserve our concern."

Alma's eyes narrowed. "Meaning Jess Logan?"

"Now, ladies, please," Reverend Sullivan said. "This will do us no good."

"It's plain as day what's happened." Alma spat the words at Sarah. "Don't think people haven't seen what's going on. That Jess Logan has been nothing but trouble in this town. Trouble when he was a boy, and trouble since he's returned. Everybody knows you've been spending time with him, Sarah—too much time. And now people are starting to talk about you, too."

Sarah gasped. Heat flooded her cheeks.

"Your reputation is in question, Sarah. You'd better be more careful about who you're seen with." Alma's chin rose a notch. "Just don't be surprised if this matter comes up at the next meeting of the school board. And it's all Jess Logan's fault."

Anger rose in Sarah like an erupting volcano. She couldn't abide another cross word about Jess. She clenched her fists at her sides.

"Does everything that happens in this town get blamed on Jess?"

Everyone looked at her with stunned expressions.

"You've done nothing but belittle him ever since

he returned to Walker! You've searched high and low to find fault with everything he does! And why? Because of the way he acted years ago when he was nothing but a child. A child who'd lost his home and his family. And because of the silly gossip that's circulated about him since he left Walker. But that's all it is—gossip. There's not a hint of truth to it. And if you'd bothered to get to know him, you'd realize that was true.

"Everyone still sees Jess as he was when he left Walker. But I didn't know him then. All I know of Jess is what I see now. And what I see now is a generous, kind and caring man who took a very big chance in coming back to Walker, knowing how you'd all react. And he did it just so his niece and nephew would have a family."

Sarah glared at Alma. "If it puts my reputation in jeopardy to associate with Jess Logan, then that's a risk I'm glad to take."

Sarah whipped around and walked to the front window, staring out at the street. She'd never been so angry in her life. She could feel the uncomfortable silence in the room. But she didn't care. And she wasn't sorry for what she'd said. She only wished she'd had nerve enough to say it a long time ago.

A hand touched her shoulder. She turned and saw Kirby beside her. Kirby smiled, draining away Sarah's anger. Grateful, Sarah managed a weak smile.

The afternoon dragged by slowly. Dr. Burns stayed with Nate, coming into the restaurant periodically to report changes in his condition; he was improving.

Kirby spent time at his bedside, too. Fiona made coffee and warmed up food, but no one ate. Maggie and Jimmy played silently in the corner. Alma kept to herself. Occasionally folks stopped by to check on Nate. There was no word on the posse.

Sarah paced at the front window, keeping watch on the street. Few people were out today. From the corner of her eye she saw Dwight beside her.

"Why don't you come sit down?" He touched his hand to her elbow.

To her surprise she saw concern in his expression, concern and compassion. Sarah eased her arm away and pressed her cheek against the cold glass. "No, I'm fine."

"Don't worry, Sarah. Jess knows what he's doing."

Though she knew he was right, Dwight's words brought her no comfort. She thought of Nate lying in the back room, Kirby and the doctor keeping vigil. The last thing this town needed was another hero.

Footsteps pounded on the boardwalk and the door burst open. Luke ran inside.

"They're back! Posse's back! They're riding in now!"

"Heavenly Father…" Reverend Sullivan began to pray.

Sarah rushed for the door, but Dwight caught her arm, holding her back.

"Wait, Sarah. Let me go see."

Her heart thumped in her chest as she gazed up at Dwight. She read the meaning on his face. Let him go first, see who'd come back alive.

No, she couldn't wait. She needed to know now. Jess had to be all right. He just had to. Sarah jerked free and ran outside.

"Wait, Sarah!" Fiona ran after her.

Seconds ticked off as she stood rooted to the boardwalk, the doctor, Megan, Dwight and the Sullivans crowded around her, watching the men ride back into town. Behind the sheriff, three horses carried bodies wrapped in blankets draped across the saddles.

Frantic, Sarah searched the faces of the men as they drew nearer. Where was he? Where was Jess?

Finally, he rode into view.

"Jess!" Sarah ran to him, pushing her way through the men and horses as they dismounted in front of the jail. In the center of the crowd, Jess swung down from his horse.

Emotions roiled through her. Sarah drew back her fist and whacked him on the chest.

"You scared me to death! I thought you were dead!"

Jess opened his arms to her. She burst out crying.

He pulled her against him and buried his face in the valley of her neck, holding her, rocking her while she sobbed into his shirt. Finally, she looked up at him.

"Why, Jess? Why did you take that chance? Why did you go without telling me?"

"I had to go, Sarah." He wiped her cheeks with his finger, catching the final tear that rolled down. "I just had to."

Rory Garrette forced his way into the crowd of men. "Well, what happened? Did you git them Tolivers?"

"Sure did." Sherman Myers gestured toward the blanket-draped horses, then slapped Jess on the back. "Jess here got two of them."

"Hot damn...." Rory hobbled away.

"Good having you with us, Jess," Leo Turner said.

Several other men echoed those words, then moved on to find their loved ones.

Jess tightened his grip on Sarah. "Are the kids okay?"

"They're fine."

"And Nate?"

"So far, he's holding on. It's not as bad as the doctor thought."

He looked deep into her eyes. "How about you?"

"I was so frightened, Jess, so worried. Don't ever do that again. Promise me you won't."

He shook his head. "I can't promise, Sarah. If the town needs me I've got to do my part. Can you understand?"

Sarah gazed into his strong, determined face and understood completely. She slid her arm around his waist. "The children want to see you."

On the boardwalk outside the Blue Jay, Sarah saw Alma Garrette in deep conversation with Emma Turner and Lottie Myers. She knew they were talking about her.

The words she'd so defiantly flung at Alma only hours earlier rang in her ears. She'd defended Jess to the town's biggest gossip, Jess's worst critic. What she'd said would be told, and retold. She could be sent packing when the school board met next week.

Sarah's spine stiffened. She didn't care. The comfort of Jess's arm around her, his nearness, overwhelmed all feelings of regret. Besides, she'd told the truth. She'd said what should have been said weeks ago.

The men of the posse moved along, offering a quiet word to Jess and Sarah. Sheriff Neville glared at them both for a long moment, then turned to leave.

"Sonofa—" Neville stopped. On the boardwalk in front of the jailhouse, Zack and Megan embraced. Tenderly, Zack held her, mumbling softly as tears slid down her cheeks.

"They're in love, Sheriff," Sarah said gently.

He glared at her, then at Jess. "You ought to worry about your own problems, Logan. I got a telegram from Judge Flinn. He's on his way to Walker."

Chapter Sixteen

The clang of the school bell faded into the clear morning air as Jess hurried across the yard with the children.

"We're late, Uncle Jess," Maggie said. "Will Miss Sarah be mad?"

He grinned down at her. "I'll take care of Miss Sarah."

"Swing!" Jimmy took off like a shot toward the tree at the edge of the schoolyard.

Jess let him go and walked up the stairs and into the school with Maggie. The children were all seated in their desks. At the front of the class stood Sarah.

She looked all prim and proper in her dark skirt and simple blouse, her hair pulled back in a neat bun. Despite the sharp intake of her breath and slight coloring of her cheeks when she saw him, Sarah was the picture of a respectable schoolmarm.

But Jess knew what lay just beneath the surface, and the recollection caused his insides to quiver. Passion. And not just the kind that had led to the demise of her husband. She was a hell of a woman, no doubt about it.

But Sarah's feelings ran much deeper. He'd found out just how deep last night when he'd talked to Kirby and learned how Sarah had defended him in the café yesterday.

Pleased to see that his presence in her classroom flustered her a bit, Jess waited by the door while Sarah gave the students an assignment. Silently, they went outside together.

"I just wanted to tell you I'm sorry for having Maggie late to school," Jess said as they walked down the stairs.

She detected a subtle tug of his lips. "Are you really?"

"Well...no." Jess glanced at the empty schoolyard. He grinned at her. "I knew if I came late I'd get you to myself for a few minutes."

Sarah couldn't help smiling. "Honestly, Jess..."

He studied the soft, early morning sunlight on her cheeks, the wisps of dark hair that curled around her face, and the grin disappeared from his lips.

"Kirby told me what you said at the restaurant yesterday. She told me how you stood up to Alma Garrette." Now, his chest ached as it had last evening when he'd seen Kirby at Nate's bedside. No one had ever spoken up for him before, and certainly no one in Walker.

Sarah stood a little straighter. "I told the truth, Jess. Something that should have been said long ago."

"Thank you, Sarah."

She touched his arm. "Maybe it will help with the judge this afternoon."

Jess gazed at Jimmy playing in the swing, then turned to the schoolhouse where Maggie sat at her desk. He drew in a deep breath.

"Putting them to bed last night I kept thinking it might be the last time. This morning getting their breakfasts and walking them over here, I thought the same." Jess dragged his hand over his face. "Sarah, what if the judge—"

"Don't think such things." She felt the pain radiating from him, felt it seep inside her with the same intensity. "Think good thoughts and hope for the best. That's all you can do."

He pulled on his neck. "I guess."

Hoofs thudded on the dirt road then brushed the grass of the schoolyard. Sheriff Neville swung down from his horse in front of Jess and Sarah.

He eyed them with disdain. "Figured I'd find you here, Logan."

Jess moved in front of Sarah, shielding her. "What do you want, Neville?"

"I want to know where you were last night." The sheriff's eyes narrowed. "You might think you proved something yesterday riding with the posse, but to me you'll never be nothing but trouble. A man was shot and killed outside of town last night. I want to know where you were."

"A man killed?" Sarah gasped softly. "Who was it?"

"Jed Hayden."

Jess and Sarah exchanged a look, but neither spoke.

Sheriff Neville's gaze riveted Jess. "Your sister's husband. What do you know about it?"

Anger ribboned through Jess, but he held his temper in check. "I was at the Blue Jay seeing about Nate. Kirby was there, too, and so were the Sullivans. Lots of folks came by. Except for you, Sheriff."

"What about after that?" Neville jerked his chin toward Sarah. "Is she vouching for the rest of the evening?"

"You bastard...." Jess surged toward the sheriff, fists clenched.

"No, Jess, don't." Sarah grabbed his arm, pushing herself in front of him. "Don't. Please. Just keep away from him."

Jaw set, Jess glared at the sheriff, but backed off.

"That's some good advice. Keep away from me." Sheriff Neville climbed onto his horse again. "And that goes for my daughter, too, Logan."

A new, deeper anger wound through Jess. Within hours he faced the very real possibility of having his children taken from him. His whole body ached at the prospect. And here the sheriff stood, purposely driving his only daughter away.

"You stupid sonofabitch! You don't deserve Megan! She doesn't need your permission to marry Zack, and he doesn't need your approval. But they're both trying to do the right thing." Jess pointed his finger at the sheriff. "You're going to lose her. And you're going to end up a lonely, bitter old man. You'd better think about that.''

Sheriff Neville whirled his horse around and rode away.

Jess paced the empty courtroom. The hearing would start soon, but he'd gotten here early wanting time to think. The townspeople would testify again, surely, and those not testifying would come just to witness the spectacle. He had to be ready with what to say when he confronted the judge.

But Jess couldn't think—at least about the hearing, anyway. He paced, his thoughts lost in years gone by. Images, feelings, desires that had simmered in the back of his mind now took over all rational thought.

''Jess?''

He wheeled around. Sarah stood only a few feet away. He hadn't even heard her open the door of the small courtroom, or walk inside.

''Sarah…''

She hurried to him and he locked his arms around her.

''I'm so glad you came,'' he said.

''Fiona took over the class for me. I wanted to be here with you.'' Sarah touched her fingers to his face. ''You mustn't worry so. You've done a good job with the children, Jess. Anyone can see that.''

''No, that's not what's wrong—well, that's not *all* that's wrong.'' He tightened his grip on her and looked deep into her eyes. ''Sarah, I've been such a fool. When I left Walker years ago I was a hotheaded kid. I thought I'd find what I was looking for out in the world somewhere, but I didn't.''

"What are you saying, Jess?"

"I could have left Walker again. I could have said to hell with this custody hearing and taken Maggie and Jimmy and gone someplace else where nobody knew me. But I didn't want to, Sarah. Walker is their home. It's my home, too."

Jess shook his head fiercely. "No matter what that judge says today, I'm not leaving here. This town, this place, these people are what I was looking for all along. Walker is my home. I don't want to be alone anymore. I want to build a life here…a life with you, Sarah."

She gasped. "Me?"

"I want you to marry me."

Tears swelled her eyes. "Marry you?"

"I'm sorry to just blurt it out like that, Sarah. But I love you. I love you like I've never loved anything in my life." Jess cradled her against his chest. "Will you marry me? Please?"

"Yes!" Sarah flung back her head and sniffed. "Yes, I'll marry you."

A big smile stretched across his face. "Yeah? You mean it?"

"Yes, I mean it. I love you, Jess, and I'll marry you."

He clasped her arms. "I'm buying back my pa's place, Sarah, just like I told you. I'm starting my own ranch. I want it to be our home. And—and if the judge takes Maggie and Jimmy away, well, that doesn't mean I'm not their uncle anymore. I can still watch over them. I'm staying here in Walker, Sarah."

Jess covered her lips with his, sealing his words with all the love his heart felt. She came against him, kissing him back with equal intensity.

"Enough of that dang foolishness, you two."

Jess jerked his head up to see Rory Garrette stumping into the courtroom with his cane. Jess's stomach bottomed out. Crowded in the doorway and along the back wall were most of the townspeople, watching and listening.

He didn't know how long they'd stood there, or how much they'd heard. No one spoke. Silently, they filled the empty seats in the courtroom.

The side door opened and Judge Flinn strode into the room, adjusting his spectacles and carrying sheafs of paper.

"All right, let's come to order." The judge sat down and rapped his gavel.

Jess eased his grip on Sarah. A long moment passed while they gazed at each other.

"Everything will be all right," she whispered. "I love you."

He smiled, a silly lovesick smile, oblivious to the many gazes that bored into him as Sarah took a seat with the other townspeople.

"Quiet down!" Judge Flinn pounded his gavel again, then pointed it at Jess. "Logan, sit down. Sheriff? Let's get this thing over with."

Jess eased into a chair and looked out over the courtroom. They were all here again, same as at the first hearing. Reverend Sullivan, the Turners, Alma Garrette, Lottie Myers and her husband, even Mrs.

McDougal, along with most everybody else in town. But this time Jess felt no anger toward them. His gaze settled on Sarah and his heart lurched.

Sheriff Neville made his way to the front of the crowded courtroom.

"I can't say that anything has changed since the last time you were here, Your Honor. Logan has done nothing to prove himself any better than before."

Judge Flinn peered over the top of his spectacles. "Is that right?"

A knot of emotion rose in Jess's throat. He squeezed his eyes shut.

"That's right." Sheriff Neville hung his thumbs in his gunbelt. "I see no reason he ought to have those children."

A murmur went through the courtroom.

"Suits me fine." Judge Flinn picked up his pencil. "You know somebody who will take them?"

"Yes, I do. A good Christian family out near the Blue Sky Ranch will take them in."

"Well, that settles it." Judge Flinn raised his gavel. "It is the judgement of this court that—"

"Your Honor? Excuse me, Your Honor?"

He frowned over his spectacles. "You want to say something, miss?"

Sarah rose from her seat, her knees trembling, her palms dampening. "I disagree with the sheriff, Your Honor. I believe a great deal has changed since the first hearing."

Judge Flinn squinted at her. "You're the school-teacher, aren't you?"

Sheriff Neville waved both arms. "Don't listen to her, Your Honor. She's got no business here, and no business showing her face in town, after what she's done."

A gasp rippled through the room.

"Quiet in the court!" The judge banged his gavel. Murmurs persisted, growing from whispers into shouts.

Leo Turner shot to his feet. "Jess has caused no problems in town. He rode with the posse."

"Yeah, he brought down two of the Tolivers," Saul called out.

"He brings the children to Sunday services, and Bible study, too," Reverend Sullivan said. "He even fixed up the schoolteacher's home out of his own pocket."

Kirby sprang from her chair in the back row. "Judge, you can't take those children from Jess. They love each other!"

A chorus of agreeing voices rose from the courtroom, shouting, pointing and waving toward Jess. Judge Flinn threw the sheriff a sour look, then pounded his gavel again.

"Order! Order in the court!"

As the noise waned and the townspeople took their seats again, Alma Garrette stood, arms folded, lips pursed.

"Judge, may I speak?"

A hush fell over the courtroom. Jess felt the color drain from his face. He looked at Sarah and saw his fear mirrored in her expression.

Sheriff Neville pointed to Alma. "You ought to listen to her, Judge. Mrs. Garrette is an important woman in town."

"All right, ma'am, let's hear what's on your mind."

She drew in a big breath and looked around the room. "Well, Your Honor, I think we all felt the same when Jess Logan first got to Walker, worried sick about what would happen to those children, given his past and all."

Alma glanced down at Sarah seated nearby. "It's been brought to my attention that Jess Logan is a changed man. He's been a good citizen in our town, and a good father to those children. If they're separated, it would be a crime. And I think everyone in town agrees with me."

A cheer went up from the courtroom.

Sheriff Neville waved his arms wildly. "Your Honor, you don't—"

"I've heard enough!"

Silence fell over the crowd as everyone turned to face the judge.

"I'm awarding custody to Jess Logan. Case dismissed!" Judge Flinn banged his gavel against his desk.

Jess hurried toward Sarah. She took his hand, but that wasn't enough for him. Jess pulled her against him and kissed her full on the mouth, right there in front of the whole town. A cheer went up as everyone made their way toward the front of the room.

Rory grinned and slapped his back. "I knowed it would turn out for the good. I just knowed it."

"Congratulations, Jess." Reverend Sullivan pumped his hand. "The Lord has smiled on those children today."

"Thanks, Reverend." Jess tightened his grip on Sarah's arm and gazed down at her. "He's smiled on me, too."

"Couldn't help overhearing. You two are getting married, huh?" the Reverend asked.

Jess gaze Sarah a little squeeze. "I say we do it this afternoon."

She swatted him playfully. "I'm having a proper wedding. I want the whole town there."

"I'm going straight to the schoolhouse to give Fiona the news. She'll be tickled pink."

The crowd gathered around them parted as Nate approached, leaning heavily on a cane, one arm in a sling. At his side, Kirby helped steady him. "Congratulations, Jess."

"What are you doing up and around already? Did the doctor say you could be here?" Jess asked.

"Of course he's not supposed to be up yet." Kirby smiled. "But if he wasn't this hardheaded, he might not have pulled through."

"Hell with that doctor." Nate winced and shifted uncomfortably. "I had to be here for you, Jess. I had to speak up in case things didn't go your way."

"I appreciate it, Nate. But you're not looking so good. Maybe you ought to listen to Kirby."

Nate grinned. "I guess I ought to get used to it. I'll be hearing it for the rest of my life."

Kirby smiled proudly. "We're getting married."

Sarah gasped and hugged her. "How wonderful! I'm so happy for you."

"Something about nearly dying that makes a man take stock of his life." Nate leaned closer to Jess and whispered, "Truth is, I'm kind of liking this."

Jess chuckled. "You dog."

Nate laughed, then winced again. Kirby latched onto his arm protectively.

Alma pushed her considerable girth into the crowd of people and eyed both Jess and Sarah sharply.

"Now listen here, Jess Logan, if you need any help with those children, you'd better tell me. That's what neighbors are for, you know."

"Yes, ma'am, Mrs. Garrette. Thank you."

Alma threw a look at Sarah. "It's about time he asked you to marry him. You two are perfect for each other. And anybody who disagrees will have me to answer to."

Alma jerked her chin and flounced away.

Jess slid his arm around Sarah's waist as other townspeople came forward. Apparently everyone had heard Jess's marriage proposal, as well as the other things he'd said, and were anxious to congratulate them on the custody hearing and the upcoming wedding.

From across the room, Mrs. McDougal drifted toward them, her mouth set, her nose in the air. She caught Jess's eye.

Sarah clasped his arm, feeling him tense at the sight of his nosy neighbor. "Now, Jess, be nice," she whispered.

Jess smiled. "Afternoon, Mrs. McDougal."

She didn't speak, didn't utter one sound, but gave him a brisk nod and kept walking.

"Hey, Jess! Mrs. Wakefield!" Luke bounced over to them. "I'm sure glad you get to keep Maggie and Jimmy."

"Me, too," Jess said. "Thanks."

"I heard you two are getting married." Luke blushed. "Glad it's you and not me."

"How is Megan doing? Have you seen her since yesterday?" Sarah asked.

Luke opened his mouth to speak but clamped it shut when Sheriff Neville approached.

"I want you to know, Logan, that this hearing doesn't change anything as far as I'm concerned," the sheriff said. "I want you to know, too, that what you said has got nothing to do with why I changed my mind about my daughter and that Gibb boy."

"You've given them your blessing?" Jess asked.

"I'd heard he'd been working hard, saving up his money to take care of her proper, but I had no idea he'd saved over five hundred dollars."

Sarah gasped. "Five hundred dollars?"

Luke coughed. "I've got to go."

Jess dropped his hand on Luke's shoulder. "Five hundred dollars, huh? That's a pretty good nest egg."

The sheriff shrugged. "Besides, if Zack doesn't marry her, what decent man would, after word of this thing gets out?"

"You're doing the right thing, Sheriff," Sarah said. "They'll be very happy together."

He grumbled and walked away.

Jess curled his fist into Luke's shirtsleeve and leaned down. "Start talking, boy."

Luke lifted his shoulders. "I—I don't know what you mean."

"I'm talking about that money."

Luke shook his head. "I—I don't know nothing about what goes on between Zack and his brother."

"Gil is involved in this?" Jess released his hold on the boy. His eyes narrowed. "Did you tell those two about Hayden wanting money from me?"

Luke winced. "I might have mentioned it. Maybe."

"Where's Zack?"

A long moment dragged by while Luke squirmed under Jess's harsh glare. "He's outside. The sheriff told him to be here today so he could talk to him."

"Tell him to get in here."

"Is something wrong?" Sarah asked as Luke hurried through the crowded courtroom.

"No, nothing's wrong."

Dwight Rutledge stepped up next to them. "I want to extend my congratulations to you two."

Sarah smiled. "Thank you, Dwight."

"I hope you'll be very happy together. Well, I've got to run now. I'm having supper at the Sullivans' tonight." Dwight looked past them. "Reverend Sullivan, wait up! What's that young woman's name? The sweet, kind one? Joanna? Was her name Joanna?"

Sarah watched him go. "It didn't take long for Dwight to find another woman."

Jess grunted. "I had a few words with him."

"No, Jess, you didn't."

"Damn right I did."

Zack stepped into the doorway of the courtroom and walked over to Jess.

"I need to talk with you, Mr. Logan."

"Excuse us a minute, will you Sarah?" Jess went with him to a quiet corner of the room. "What do you know about Jed Hayden getting shot?"

Zack shrugged. "The man was a bastard. He deserved to die."

"Did you have something to do with it? Did your brother?"

"Gil's got his own idea of how justice ought to work."

Jess shook his head. "You can't..."

Zack looked Jess square in the eye. "You're the only person in this whole town who raised a finger to help me, Mr. Logan, the only person. I told you I wouldn't forget what you did."

"Did you tell Gil—"

"I'd appreciate it if you wouldn't ask me nothing else, Mr. Logan. Gil rode out of town this morning. He left some money with me."

"Five hundred dollars?"

Zack nodded. "It was a fair amount. I know you gave about that much to Hayden, so I figured I'd offer it to you, seeing as how you helped me and Megan."

Jess studied the young man, the grim set of his jaw. Better to leave things as they were, he decided. Asking too many questions would serve no purpose.

"I tell you what, Zack. You keep that money. You and Megan are going to need it a lot more than I am."

"Thank you, Mr. Logan." Zack headed for the door.

Jess caught his shoulder. "We're even now, Zack. I don't want you doing any more favors for me. Understand?"

"Yes, sir. Whatever you say."

Most of the townspeople had left the courtroom. Jess went over to where Sarah waited with Kirby and Nate.

"I want you two to have supper with us tonight," Kirby said.

Jess glanced down at Sarah, who nodded. "Sounds good. I'll pick up the kids from school and we'll come on over."

"Fine. Let's go." Kirby grasped Nate's arm as they slowly made their way outside.

Jess leaned down, speaking softly to Sarah. "You know, school won't be out for a while yet. Is there anything you'd like to do?"

She looked up at him. "What did you have in mind?"

"Going by your place."

"Jess!"

He tightened his grip on her. "You're not mad at me for thinking that, are you?"

"No." Her cheeks pinkened. "I wish I'd thought of it first."

Jess chuckled. What a woman. She really *might* kill him one day.

Arm in arm they strolled down the boardwalk. Shoppers hurried past, and horses and carriages filled the busy street.

Sarah sighed contentedly. "I guess neither of us have anything to fear about our pasts now."

"No, I guess not. Our reputations are pretty safe. Of course—"

Jess stopped suddenly, looped his arms around Sarah's waist and pulled her tight against him.

She looked around at the heads turning. "Jess, please, it's broad daylight. People are staring."

"That's my plan." He grinned and snuggled her closer. "I say we need to make a new reputation for ourselves."

Despite herself, Sarah smiled up at him. "And what did you have in mind?"

Jess nibbled little kisses across her cheek. "I say we become known as the most loving couple in Walker, Wyoming. How about it?"

Sarah sighed at the heat of his lips on her face. "I say earning that reputation will be heavenly."

* * * * *

Looking For More Romance?

Visit Romance.net

MEN at WORK

All work and no play?
Not these men!

January 1999
SOMETHING WORTH KEEPING by Kathleen Eagle
He worked with iron and steel, and was as wild as the mustangs that were his passion. She was a high-class horse trainer from the East. Was her gentle touch enough to tame his unruly heart?

MEN of STEEL

February 1999
HANDSOME DEVIL by Joan Hohl
His roguish good looks and intelligence drew women like magnets, but Luke Branson was having too much fun to marry again. Then Selena McInnes strolled before him and turned his life upside down!

TALL, DARK AND SMART $E=MC$

March 1999
STARK LIGHTNING by Elaine Barbieri
The boss's daughter was ornery, stubborn and off-limits for cowboy Branch Walker! But Valentine was also nearly impossible to resist. Could they negotiate a truce...or a surrender?

MEN OF THE WEST

Available at your favorite retail outlet!

MEN AT WORK™

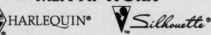

HARLEQUIN®   Silhouette®

Sexy, desirable and...a daddy?

THE

AUSTRALIANS

Stories of romance Australian-style, guaranteed to fulfill that sense of adventure!

This February 1999 look for
Baby Down Under
by **Ann Charlton**

Riley Templeton was a hotshot Queensland lawyer with a reputation for ruthlessness and a weakness for curvaceous blondes. Alexandra Page was everything that Riley *wasn't* looking for in a woman, but when she finds a baby on her doorstep that leads her to the dashing lawyer, he begins to see the virtues of brunettes—and babies!

The Wonder from Down Under: where spirited women win the hearts of Australia's most independent men!

Available February 1999
at your favorite retail outlet.

HARLEQUIN®
Makes any time special ™

Turn up the heat this March with

Mallory Rush

L O V E
P L A Y

From the author of the sexiest Harlequin® book ever...

Whitney Smith was the classic good girl. But now the Fates had conspired against her and for once in her life she was going to live....

Desperately falling in love, Whitney learned about passion and fire, not caring if she stepped too close to the flames...until Eric wanted one thing Whitney couldn't give him—forever!

Look for *Love Play* this February 1999, available at your favorite retail outlet!

HARLEQUIN®
Makes any time special ™

COMING NEXT MONTH FROM

HARLEQUIN HISTORICALS